R A C H E L
L E E

"A suspenseful, edge-of-the-seat read."
—*Publishers Weekly* on *Before I Sleep*

"Rachel Lee deserves much acclaim for her exciting tales
of romantic suspense."
—*Midwest Book Review*

WITHDRAWN
FROM THE RECORDS OF THE
MID-CONTINENT PUBLIC LIBRARY

"Lee crafts a heartrending saga...."
—*Publishers Weekly* on *Snow in September*

F
Lee, Rachel.
Shadows of myth

3/05

MID-CONTINENT PUBLIC LIBRARY
Oak Grove Branch
2320 S. Braodway Street
Oak Grove, MO 64075

OG

RACHEL LEE

SHADOWS of MYTH

LUNA™

www.LUNA-Books.com

If you purchased this book without a cover you should be aware that this book is stolen property. It was reported as "unsold and destroyed" to the publisher, and neither the author nor the publisher has received any payment for this "stripped book."

MID-CONTINENT PUBLIC LIBRARY
Oak Grove Branch
2320 S. Braodway Street
Oak Grove, MO 64075
OG

LUNA™

First edition January 2005

SHADOWS OF MYTH

ISBN 0-373-80212-9

Copyright © 2005 by Rachel Lee

All rights reserved. Except for use in any review, the reproduction or utilization of this work in whole or in part in any form by any electronic, mechanical or other means, now known or hereafter invented, including xerography, photocopying and recording, or in any information storage or retrieval system, is forbidden without the written permission of the editorial office, Worldwide Library, 233 Broadway, New York, NY 10279 U.S.A.

All characters in this book have no existence outside the imagination of the author and have no relation whatsoever to anyone bearing the same name or names. They are not even distantly inspired by any individual known or unknown to the author, and all incidents are pure invention.

This edition published by arrangement with Harlequin Books S.A.

® and TM are trademarks of Harlequin Books S.A., used under license. Trademarks indicated with ® are registered in the United States Patent and Trademark Office, the Canadian Trade Marks Office and in other countries.

www.LUNA-Books.com

Printed in U.S.A.

To Aaron, for whom the first seeds of this tale were planted. Thank you, son, for waiting so long for the tree to mature.

ADASEN BASIN

1

She awoke to the smell of blood, the sound of running water and the icy bite of the wind on her back. For a long moment, that was all she could be certain of, as if her brain had to learn all over again what it meant to be conscious. Then, in the instant when disorientation gave way to awareness, terror slammed into her gut like a falling tree. She fought to breathe, even to open her eyes and see.

She wished she hadn't.

The scent of blood spilled from the cooling, inert form upon which she lay. His throat had been slashed from ear to ear, the flesh parted in an obscene smile, still glistening in the brilliant moonlight. His eyes were fixed forever in a terror-filled gaze.

Bile rose in her throat, and she rolled off the body, pushing at it, pushing at the air around it, as if she might somehow banish the event, erase it from her mind, never to have happened. But it was not to be, for as she rolled backward, she tumbled upon another body.

The boy was small, not yet seven to judge by his features. Deep brown eyes seemed focused vaguely beyond her head. His abdomen had been laid open in an ugly, razor-smooth diagonal gash from just beneath his left nipple nearly to his right hip. Tiny, dirty hands clutched a small walking stick over his belly, a terrified, confused, tormented child's futile attempt to both hold his innards within him and protect himself from further blows. To judge by the savagery that must have followed—for surely that sort of mutilation could not have been done until he stopped fighting—he had succeeded in neither aim.

Her eyes rose to take in the rest of the scene around her. A river gurgled black with blood, stinking of it, over rocks worn smooth by the water's patient, insistent, inexorable caress. She looked upstream for the source of the blood in the water. She didn't have to look far. For at least a hundred paces, the bodies of men, women and horses sprawled along the bank like so much litter, as if haphazardly thrown over the side by a passing ship, their last agonies visible in every vivid, stomach-wrenching detail.

She fought the dizzying wave of nausea and lost. As she spat the last of it into the river, she realized she was naked and covered in blood. A new panic tore through her as her hands roamed over her body, feeling for wounds. There were none immediately apparent, so she made her way upstream, methodically checking each body in a manner and for reasons she could not fathom, until she reached the head of the column and clear water.

The water stole her breath away, so cold it nearly burned her skin. Gritting her teeth, she steeled herself to the pain and washed the gore from her body, then checked again for wounds in the pale light of the moon. Nothing so much as a scratch. She stepped out of the river, and the wind bit anew, sending her into an uncontrollable shiver.

At this temperature, I'll freeze to death in less than an hour, she thought, then wondered why she would know such a thing with such utter certainty. With that wonderment came the most terrifying shock of all. She had no idea who she was, or where, or how she'd gotten to this place.

Nor was there time to find out.

The whimpered moan sent a chill down her spine. She looked around, wondering if it might have been the wind, but then it came again, the sound full of pain and fear. Every rational thought told her to hide, and yet she was drawn to the moan like a moth to a flame, working her way back down the column, pausing every few steps to listen until the sound repeated.

It was a girl, perhaps the same age as the boy she'd seen earlier, perhaps even his twin. The girl's lips, thin and almost white, quivered as she gasped for breath. She knelt beside the girl, feeling for a pulse in the bloody mess that was a throat, and finding it fluttery and weak. The girl's eyes seemed to search the darkness before finding her.

"Oon-tie," the girl moaned. "Oon-tie."

She had no idea what the word meant, but the message was clear enough: *help me.* Her fingertips probed the wound at the girl's throat. Somehow the killers had missed the artery, although the slash had opened several smaller blood vessels. It was a superficial wound. Fear, cold and shock had done the rest. The girl must have lain still, clinging to her dying mother, feigning death until the attackers had grown bored with their blood sport and melted away into the darkness.

"Shhhh," she whispered, trying to find a reassuring calm that would quiet the girl. "Don't talk. Let me try to help you."

It was then that she noticed her fingertips were burning. She decided it was the cold.

"I'll be right back," she said, rising to look for something to wrap around herself and the girl.

"Ooooon-tieeee," the girl moaned as she moved away.

The sound tore at her heart, but discipline and a training she did not remember took control. If she didn't find a way to keep them both warm, nothing else would matter. They would simply die here, in the dark, in the cold, vainly clinging to each other for a warmth neither could give.

She picked through the slashed bundles that lay on the ground, finding nothing but sacks of wheat and rice. Surely one of the bundles ought to hold a blanket or spare clothes. But there were none to be found. Shuddering at the thought, she combed through the column again, finding the body of a woman roughly her own size. She closed her eyes as she undressed the woman, whispering a nearly silent *I'm sorry,* fighting back revulsion as she pulled the damp wool garment around her, knowing that the dampness was blood.

Still, wool dried from the inside out——yet another fact she wondered how she would know——and she knew she would warm up soon. She ran back to the girl.

"Hah-gee," the girl whispered. "Oon-tie."

"Yes," she said, nodding her head. "Oon-tie. I'll help you. Oon-tie."

She pulled the girl inside the cloak with her and tied the sash, sharing her body heat with the pale, cold girl. Tucking the girl's legs around her hips, she rose and once again searched the column for anything she could use for a bandage. Finally realizing that a torn strip of sackcloth was the best she would find, she did her best to wrap it around the girl's throat while keeping the girl inside her cloak. It wasn't a proper field dressing——where had that phrase come from?——but it would have to do.

"Oon-tie," she whispered in the girl's ear as she bound the wound. "Oon-tie."

It was then that she realized her fingers were still burning, even though she'd grown warmer. This wasn't the burn of cold-numbed nerves. It was as if she had dipped her hands into a bag of ants, and the burning itch was spreading up to her palms.

"Oon-tie," she whispered again, carrying the girl with her to the river, where she knelt and plunged her hands into the icy water, then scrubbed them against each other.

The water soothed the burning enough that she could focus on what to do next: move away from this place. She had no idea if the killers would return, but the bodies themselves would soon draw natural scavengers. She didn't want to be there when the vultures arrived, didn't want this girl to watch them peck at the flesh of people she had known and loved.

In the darkness, she picked out a hard, stony road that ran alongside the river. She went upstream, for the simple reason that at least this way they would have access to clean water. After a few minutes, the river widened again, and the sound of water over rocks faded into the darkness. The road bent closer to the river, and a neat stack of thick, smooth logs seemed to materialize out of the night.

A portage, she thought. *Perfect place for an ambush. And why do I know this? Who* am *I?*

She let her mind wander over that question for a few minutes but could find no answer. Her back ached with the weight of carrying the girl, and she needed to rest. In the distance, a tree line beckoned. At least she would have cover. She could make it that far. Then they could rest.

But the tree line hovered just out of reach. Her depth perception had been skewed by the flat light of the moon, the crystalline nighttime air and the fact that she was climbing a slow, steady slope. Her breathing grew labored, but she pressed on, the girl shivering in her arms.

The girl ought to be warming up, too, she thought. Yet the girl's breaths came in ragged rasps. The girl's legs slid off her waist again and again, as if they were increasingly weighted with stones. Each time, the girl seemed to struggle harder to pull her thin legs back up. She was losing the battle for life.

The woman didn't let herself think about that. The tree line. The tree line. It became a mantra, the whispered words keeping a rhythm to her stride as she forced herself on into the night.

Finally she could make out distinct trees, some kind of pine, tall and straight, wreathed in bunches of needles that looked as fluffy as a squirrel's tail.

Just a few more steps, she told herself. *You can do this. You've done it before.* She had no idea where, or when. But she had done it— and more.

The girl went into spasms just as they reached the trees. The woman lowered herself to the ground, pulling the heavy wool even tighter around them, but the warmth did nothing to stem the spasms.

"Ooh-ooh-oon-tie," the girl gasped.

"I'm trying" the woman answered. "I'm trying to help you, honey. *Oon-tie. Oon-tie.*"

She felt for a pulse again. It was weaker than before, tiny flutters fighting a rising black wave. The girl's skin was clammy, her breath shallow. She laid the girl on the ground, in a pile of needles, and turned the girl's face to her.

"Keep fighting," she said, hoping her tone of voice would convey what the words could not. "Don't give up. Don't you quit on me."

But the girl's eyes grew cloudy, her breath more ragged, until finally she let out a tiny gasp.

"Teh-sah."

Then she was still.

The woman lifted the girl and clutched her inside her cloak, sobbing in the darkness, vainly crying out to any god who might listen in this strange place, "Noooooooooo."

Sara Deepwell hefted a barrel of ale from the stack and lowered it into a V-shaped cart, then rolled it out of the alchouse and in through the back door of the Deepwell Inn. Despite the cold of the morning, with mist still drifting in off the Adasen River and across the Commons, she wiped a sheen of perspiration from her forehead with a sleeve.

"That's four barrels," she said.

Her father, Bandylegs, looked up at the icy-blue sky and nodded. "I'm sure that will be plenty. Let's get the stew going."

"Yes, sir," Sara said, suppressing a small sigh.

She could remember when four barrels of ale wouldn't have lasted through half an evening at harvest festival. This year, it would probably be more than enough.

She went into the kitchen, dipped her fingertips in a basin and flicked the water onto the skillet atop the stove. The water danced and popped. Satisfied, she speared a huge mutton roast on a metal fork and pressed it onto the skillet, taking in the scent of searing meat, turning it every few minutes until it was nicely browned. The roast went into the boiling water in a cast-iron cauldron, along with the onion, garlic and herbs she had minced before dawn. Later she would add the potatoes, carrots and other vegetables. For now, though, she had other chores.

Always other chores, she thought sadly. The inn was too much work for her father alone, and she had been helping him for what seemed like forever. In truth, it had been six years. Six years to the day since she'd heard her mother's laugh, since she'd heard her mother's songs in the public room, since she'd seen her mother's smile, since she'd tasted her mother's fish chowder, since she'd felt her mother's hand pushing at her shoulder to wake her in the morning. Six years, and it could have been yesterday.

It had been a morning just like this one, clear and cold, misty, with a north wind. Sara had been fourteen then, more worried about meeting her friends at the market and giggling as they watched the young men work the dock, pushing carts laden with sacks of wheat off the river barges, or carts laden with wool and furs onto them to be taken downriver. They would watch the men's muscles ripple as they labored and try to guess which of them would be best at quelling the urges that fluttered in fourteen-year-old girls' bellies. Not that Sara or any of her friends would have considered actually doing anything about those urges. The watching and the whispering, the giggling and the dreaming, were enough.

Sara had been planning exactly such an adventure that morning as she'd spread feed in the trough for the goat, drawn water from the well that gave the family and the inn its name, and picked an apron full of fresh tomatoes from their small garden. She'd gone into the pantry to put up the tomatoes and come out just in time to see her mother at the door, waving.

"I'm off to the market for flour," her mother had said, the distinctive musical lilt in her voice as clear to Sara today as it had been six years ago this morning.

And then she was gone.

By midmorning, her father had grown anxious, and together they'd walked across the commons to the waterfront, first to the miller, then to the fish market, then to every other shop along the row, from the wool and fur drying sheds to the ice house. No one had seen her.

Together with a growing band of friends, they'd searched the commons, shooing sheep from their paths as they walked, then fanned out into the town as word spread before them. Townsfolk had checked back gardens, sheds, the stables, the waterfront again, the commons again. They'd expanded the search outside the wall, as farmers walked their fields and trappers looked for tracks in the dense pine forest that swaddled the rugged hills around town like a green blanket.

It was as if she had vanished into thin air.

A pall of gloom had hung over the harvest festival that year, as it did again this year. Winter had come too soon, with bitter night-time cold borne on the wind that whistled through the Desa Pass and down on Whitewater like an angry avalanche, turning leaves black and crops to mush. The farmers had taken to their fields early, and the townsfolk to their gardens. With autumn only just begun, they'd done what they could, but it was not enough. Not nearly enough. Just last night, in the public room, she'd heard a man say he'd lost nearly half his crop. The other men had nodded agreement. It would be a lean winter.

Sara pulled her cloak tighter around herself and went upstairs to clean the few unoccupied rooms. The cold had forced the trappers down from the mountains early, for not even the hardiest soul dared risk being stranded in these mountains, where temperatures could plunge from mild to deadly in the space of an hour. There would be few white wolf pelts to sell downriver.

At least there would be ale. Her father had put up extra barrels over the past three years, when the fields had been lush with hops, barley and malt. He would trade more this year, he'd told the men in the public room last night. Deepwell ale was a prized commodity downriver. It would make up for the lost pelts and bring in enough grain from the valley for the town to make it through the winter. They would get by, he'd reassured them. Whitewater folk always got by.

But the barge caravans had grown sparse as the summer wore on, and the big harvest barges were three weeks late. There would be no fish chowder and fry bread at this year's festival. Only mutton stew. And four barrels of ale.

Sara tried to shake off the sense of doom that seemed to stalk her like a hungry mountain lion. Her father had spoken reassuring words in the public room, but in their private quarters, his face was dark. Sara could almost read the troubled thoughts as they flickered across his face. And last night, again, she'd heard his quiet sobs through the wall.

He had, no doubt, once again taken out the white wool cloak and white lambskin boots he'd bought that same day six years ago, intending to give them to his wife six years ago this morning. She'd thought of suggesting he should sell them but could never bring herself to do it. For they were more than mere memorabilia. They were the tangible hope that someday, by some miracle, the light would walk back into his life.

There should be children, Sara thought. Children bouncing in the courtyard, helping her mother to hang the dried stalks of barley and string the seeds and pinecones that would dangle from the trees. Children scurrying around the commons, chasing sheep and splitting the morning air with high-pitched peals of laughter. Children in the public room, sitting on their heels, eyes wide, breathless, hands clasped tight, as the old men's voices rose and fell in the cadence of old poems, their words rich with the tension of the hunt or the din of battle.

There should be children underfoot, Sara thought, returning to the kitchen where her father sat, looking out the window at the women crossing the commons on their way to market, their bodies hunched and leaning into the north wind. There should be joy instead of this grim, quiet determination that folk in Whitewater adopted to steel themselves for hard times and winter storms. There should be hearty laughter, and hearty fish chowder with just a splash of mead added to make it sparkle on the tongue and glow in the belly.

Instead, there was only the unceasing moan of the wind. And mutton stew.

"There's evil coming," her father almost whispered, his gaze still focused out the window. "Evil and blood."

Yes, Sara thought. *Evil and blood.*

And more loss.

2

The woman slid deeper into the bushes as the blue-black forms padded silently through the morning mist. Strange men, tall and slender, with long, sinewy muscles that rippled like the flanks of a horse. Their nostrils flared as they sniffed the breeze, dark eyes seeming to search every shadow, their broad, curved swords at the ready. The two men stopped. The one on the right flicked his tongue over his lips as if tasting the forest. An almost inaudible series of grunts emerged from deep in his throat. Then silence again, save for the breathy whisper of the breeze moving through pine branches.

She silently cursed herself. She had heard the rhythmic *clip clop* of horses' hooves on the road long before she had seen anyone and slipped off into the underbrush. But she had gone to the river side of the road, leaving herself upwind. It was a stupid mistake, born of exhaustion and sorrow and thoughts of the dead girl she still held to her breast. But the reasons didn't matter. If they scented her, she would still be just as dead.

She scooted backward a few more feet, into the deep shade of a low-spreading pine, almost burrowing into the pillow of dry needles that lay beneath it, feeling the sap stick to her skin. Her eyes remained focused on the two men, their skin so dark it glimmered an iridescent blue in the shadows, as she gingerly reached around for anything she could use as a weapon. The man on the right sniffed again, then lowered his sword. She realized she'd been holding her breath, and tried to let it out slowly and silently.

It was then that she felt the sharp prickle against the back of her neck.

"Ee-esh mah lah-rain."

Like the girl's words last night, these words flowed like water. But the man's tone of voice left no doubt. This was no plea. It was a command. Hoping she guessed the meaning correctly, she extended her arms beside her, spreading her fingers to show that her hands were empty, all the while kicking herself mentally for being so intent on the two men on the road that she'd missed the one who had apparently circled behind her through the woods. A beginner's mistake. The kind that got people killed.

"I mean no harm," she said. Then, remembering, she added, "Oon-tie."

"Rah-so-fah-meh lay-esh?" the man asked.

Or so she thought, assuming that the rising tone at the end of the sentence indicated a question.

"Oon-tie," she repeated. "Oon-tie."

"Foe-doo-key," he said, and she saw two pairs of unshod, blue-black feet approach through the underbrush, stopping just beyond her reach.

She drew a breath, rich with the scent of pine, and let it out slowly. "Oon. Tie."

The pressure of a boot in her side told her the man wanted her to roll over. She did so, slowly, wrapping her arms protectively around the girl, even knowing the act was futile. "Oon-tie."

The man was tall, over six feet, with piercing gray eyes that almost glowed beneath the black-green cowl that nearly hid his face. Unlike his companions, his skin held the darkening of weather, the tan of many suns, but nothing of the deepness of night.

The prickle had traced around her neck as she rolled, and now she saw the sword, as long as her leg and broad as her hand, curving upward to a menacing point that rested against the pulse in her neck. The rest of his cloak was as black as the cowl, the barest hint of deep green in its folds, making him almost invisible in the darkness of the forest. Even if she'd been looking for him, she might well have missed him. The boot on her shoulder was soft leather, snug to the foot and muscled calf. One gloved hand held the sword, while the other rested by his side, the barest twitch in the last two fingers the only indication that the man sensed danger.

"Ay-oon-tie?"

She started to nod, then remembered the sword and held her head still. "Oon-tie."

The man casually used his sword to nudge her arm from her chest, then open her cloak. His eyes seemed to bore into the girl's body.

"I found her last night," the woman explained, hearing the plea and pain in her voice. "She shouldn't have died. I treated for her shock, and the wound was superficial. She shouldn't have died. I didn't kill her."

The two blue-black men seemed confused by her words, and they exchanged almost inaudible grunts with the black-cloaked man whose sword rested on her collarbone. The men's body language said the cloaked man was the leader. Finally the cloaked man lowered his sword and extended a gloved hand. Inviting her to get up, or so she hoped.

She reached for the hand, and he grasped her wrist. His grip could have snapped the bones in her hand like so many dried twigs, but he hefted her to her feet, then sheathed his sword, as if neither she nor the sword weighed an ounce. He reached for the child.

"No!" she said, half turning away.

He paused for a moment, then lifted the cowl from his head to reveal hard, care-worn features beneath raven-black hair. The faintest hint of a smile creased his cold eyes.

"Leh-oon rah-tie," he said softly, in a voice that seemed to echo within him before making its way out into the world. He reached for the child again. "Leh-oon."

Conflicting emotions warred within her. His tone, his face and his gesture seemed to convey "Please," as if he were offering to help the girl. But she knew the girl was beyond help. And this was a man who, mere moments before, had held a sword to her throat. And the girl was...hers.

Apparently seeing her hesitation, he repeated the word, more softly this time. "Leh-oon."

Reluctantly she let him lift the girl from her arms. He took her gently, supporting her head with one hand, and seemed to study her for a moment. His eyes flicked up to her, cold and hard.

"Trey-sah."

The woman shook her head. "I don't understand."

"Trey-sah," he said again, motioning toward the girl with his head. "Tah-ill loh trey-sah."

She compressed her lips, studying his eyes. Then it clicked, and she slowly nodded. "Yes. She's dead. Trey-sah. Last night."

The man nodded, and for an instant sorrow softened his icy-gray eyes. He handed the girl back to her, then pointed back down the road. "Yah-see. Roh-eem trey-sah."

"Yes. They're all dead. I..." It struck her that even if she had known his language, she could not have explained what had happened last night. She stopped and simply angled her head toward the road. "Yes. Trey-sah. This girl wasn't. She no trey-sah. I tried to help her, but I couldn't. She died last night, in my arms."

The taller of the two black men, behind her to her left, muttered quietly. The cloaked man looked at him, then at her, and nodded. "Pah-roh. Ee-esh."

Slender black fingers closed around her upper arms, gently but insistently. Whoever these men were, they were taking her with them. There was little point and less hope in fighting. Helpless to argue, she let them take her, her heart full of dread.

Young Tom Downey should have been asleep. He'd been up most of the night, opening the gate for the trappers who straggled in by ones and twos, not wanting to spend another night out on the ground in a fur sleep sack when they could walk a few more miles and have a pint of ale, a hot meal and a comfortable bed at the Deepwell Inn. By all rights he should have been exhausted and snug in his bed, catching up on his rest so he could enjoy the festival tonight.

But then there was Sara. He'd promised to help her set up tables and torches in the inn's courtyard, not so much because she wanted or needed his help—she came from big-boned, Whitewater stock and was strong as most men—but because it was a good excuse to spend a day with her. The opportunity to look into her deep blue eyes, to see the broad smile break out on her oval face, to hear the flowing music in her idle humming. Faced with that, well, sleep came in at a far-distant second place.

The sun was well past high, and they had almost finished hanging the lanterns and decorations that crisscrossed the courtyard. Next they would build the firepit and, while the flames burned down, begin to carry out the long serving tables and stack the pewter flagons, bowls and spoons. By the time they had finished those tasks, the coals should be ready for them to heft the soup cauldron and bring it out from the kitchen. Another two or three hours.

Another two or three hours of Sara's almost sole attention, a rare treat indeed. She was usually too busy taking care of patrons at the inn for him to get more than a few words in edgewise, and that only when he wasn't busy with his mother's garden, or minding the gate for his father. In truth, he lived for a day like this.

"A bit tighter," Sara said, as he pulled the last line of lanterns over a tree limb. "There. Perfect."

He tied off the line and looked up at their work. Gaily painted pinecones and lanterns formed a canopy over the courtyard. Tonight, with the fires lit and the stars winking overhead, the place would seem almost magical.

"Looks great," Young Tom said. "It will be beautiful tonight." Then, after a momentary pause, he added, "And I can't wait for your mutton stew."

She nodded, her features darkened by a passing thought. "I just hope people will come."

Yes, they'd lost some crops this year to the cold. Yes, the trap lines were lean, and the river trout had moved downstream to warmer waters earlier than usual. But this was still the harvest festival, a last chance to celebrate the warmth of summer and growing things before ice crusted the river, and the fields and trees and gardens and roofs donned a white blanket of snow. And Young Tom was determined to enjoy it, if for no other reason than that it was one of the few times of the year when he felt any sense of wonder, of adventure.

After dinner, while the children scattered across the commons and around the town in search of the harvest lamb, while mothers clucked and *tsked* at their charges and gossiped about their husbands, the men would gather in the public room and swap stories. For the townsfolk, the tales were largely embellishments of mundane activities. For in Whitewater, and especially at harvest festival, it was unmannerly to simply state that one's tomatoes had grown well this summer.

Instead the tilling and seeding, the watering, weeding, nurturing and, finally, picking, became an epic, often comic, battle of man against nature, where the storyteller was both conquering hero and court jester. He would be spurred on by the interjections and objections of those listening, until the tale dissolved in gales of laughter. Sometimes the stories would loop back to others told in past years—Young Tom's first attempt to milk a goat was by now the stuff of legend, first told by his father and repeated countless times since, to his endless embarrassment—and the whole became the living history of Whitewater, high points and low, to be carried on in the years to come.

But as amusing as those tales could be, for Young Tom the highlight of the evening would come when a trapper or, better yet, a trader would take his place by the roaring fire. Eyes alight with excitement and tongue loosened by Bandylegs' ale, he would talk of strange lands and faraway cities. There were stories of noblemen and guild masters, of fortunes won and lost on a hand of tiles, of street thieves skulking in alleys, of merchant sailors and pirates.

And always, always, of the shimmering white streets of Bozandar, where anything that one could want—and much that one ought not to have—could be bought and sold in the markets and streets and on the docks.

It was these stories that held Young Tom rapt. Stories of places that didn't smell like sheep and drying pelts, places where a man could make his mark on the larger world. Places Young Tom would never see.

He would never see them, quite simply, because he could never imagine taking himself away from Sara. Sure, he dreamed of carving his life on the stone of the world, preserved forever for all to see. But the truth was that he was a simple Whitewater lad, madly in love with a simple Whitewater lass. Someday, if the gods could instill courage in him, he would find the words to tell her that. He would ask her to marry him. She would say yes. And he would spend the rest of his days here, with her. With not a single regret for the places he did not see and the things he did not do.

"You are dreaming again, Young Tom Downey," Sara said, looking over at him with that playful smile that almost dared him to disagree or, worse, tell her of his dreams.

He stammered for the right words and instead resigned himself to a clumsy nod. After a moment, he added, "I'll just get another stack of bowls," as if by focusing on the task at hand he could slow the beat of his heart or will the quiver from his hands.

She laughed. Oh, her laugh!

"You just do that," she said with a wink. "And I'll just be for setting out what you've already brought."

She doubtless knew, of course. His mother said a blind man could see the way he looked at her. His friends had long since given up on teasing him about it. She knew, and that made it all the harder. In his mind, she loved him, too, and had imagined a thousand ways he might finally speak his heart, imagined words that soared like an eagle to its mountain eyrie or sparkled like the morning dew. There was simply no way he could ever match the words she had imagined, and thus whatever he said would surely be a disappointment.

That daunting prospect held him back, knotted his tongue and kept the dream of holding her at bay, forever just one act of courage away.

Archer had heard that a mother can identify her own baby's cry in a room full of crying babies. He was sure he could tell his horse from Ratha's or Giri's simply by the roll of its gait and the way its flanks felt between his legs. All of that seemed very ordinary and believable. And none of it explained what he felt as he held the woman against him.

They'd spent the day riding higher into the hills and deeper into the forest, farther from the butchered remains of the caravan they'd come upon that morning. He'd chosen this course not because he sought to avoid the band that had ambushed the traders, but simply because he didn't want to confront them while saddled with this strange woman and the dead child she refused to relinquish. She needed shelter. And he would need all his limbs and attention free when that confrontation happened. The nearest shelter was the town of Whitewater, another few hours' ride upstream. So there they would go, and there he would leave her, before coming back to deal with the bandits.

The woman had slept for most of the day. Whatever had happened last night, however she had escaped unharmed from the carnage, she was exhausted. Somehow, even in sleep, she kept her arms around the girl. What she could not do while sleeping was keep herself in the saddle.

So he kept an arm around her, steadying her, as he and his companions rode along in a silence broken only rarely and briefly. The occasional whispered warning was all that passed between them. And that left Archer alone with his thoughts, which was becoming a distinctly uncomfortable state of affairs.

If he were not so certain they were being followed and likely overheard, and if he were not concerned about keeping their purpose from their followers, they might have engaged in the kind of traveling banter that usually passed among them. Ratha in particular had a biting sense of humor that, coupled with his Anari gift of observation, might have had them alternately groaning and guffawing all day. But today there was no such relief. Today there was only the sound of their horses' hooves, the occasional rustle of underbrush despite their pursuers' stealth, and the woman's slow, even breathing.

And the feel of her in his arms.

There was no reason this woman should feel familiar. Her language was certainly not one he'd ever heard before, though at least they'd been able to work out a minimal shared vocabulary by which to exchange the most basic information: *stop, hungry, thirsty, cold* and the like. She was attractive enough that he was sure he would have remembered meeting her. And he was sure he hadn't.

Still, from the moment he'd looped an arm around her and pulled her against him in the saddle, he'd felt it. And that feeling grew stronger when he saw the mark of a white rose on her ankle, etched into the skin. As if his body remembered something his mind would not. It was not the sort of thought he enjoyed. He'd spent year upon year layering on a sense of who and what he was, as an Esegi hunter might use sticks and dried leaves to cover the void of a tiger pit. In fact, there was a sleeping tiger in his mental pit, and he had no desire to rouse it. His sense of self was probably no more authentic than the cover of that trap, but at least it had grown to be a bit more stable. He could walk on it. He could live on it. As long as none of the connecting tendrils was disturbed.

The mere act of holding this woman against him was disturbing those tendrils, and the specter of the tiger beneath hovered in the back of his mind like the sound of his pursuers, not yet ready to expose itself, waiting for the most opportune moment to spring free of the trap. He had no desire to face that again. For that reason, if for no other, he had to get this woman to shelter, to be rid of her and the disturbing, half-formed memories her presence evoked.

In truth, there wasn't much that frightened him. He had stared down an angry bear protecting her cubs and walked away without so much as a scratch. He had hunted sawtooth boar in the dense underbrush of the Aktakna hills, where a moment's inattention could leave a flowing gash in an arm or leg or belly. He had faced down petty thieves in the alleys of Sedestano, young men with more courage than sense who thought quick reflexes and a sharp dagger were an adequate substitute for actual fighting experience. He had slain the slaver who had intended to auction off Ratha and Giri, and parted a swath through the mob of angry men who saw no evil in buying and selling human beings.

He'd faced whatever dangers the world had thrown his way with an almost eerie calm that unsettled friend and foe alike. But this woman—and that tiger—scared him.

The sun was sinking behind the distant mountains as they finally emerged from the forest into the now barren fields that surrounded Whitewater. As they crested a knoll, he could see a faint glow over the wall, in the heart of the town, and the sound of clapping and singing made its way on the wind.

"Their harvest festival," Giri said, his voice barely audible. "I'd forgotten."

"Not much to celebrate," Ratha answered, looking at the freeze-blackened fields.

Archer pondered that for a moment. "We celebrate what we can. That's all life offers us."

And we try to forget the rest, he thought.

He debated whether to rouse the woman and decided against it. There would be plenty of time to rouse her after they passed through the gate, when he could offer her a hot meal at Bandylegs' inn. In the meantime, he would let her sleep.

And try not to think of the fog-shrouded memories.

The gatekeeper, Jem Downey, was not at the harvest festival. Oh, no. Not for him the revelry, food and storytelling, not that there would be much to miss this year. But as the gatekeeper, one whose son was stapled to the innkeeper's daughter's petticoats, Jem had no choice but to stay at his post.

At least until the sun had been set a while longer. With these cold days and nights, there might be other trappers and travelers seeking shelter, and Jem wasn't one to let them freeze outside the city walls, much as he might grumble about missing all the fun.

Nor could he leave the gate open, as had been the custom during festivals in years past, to welcome any who might care to join the carousing. Not this year. Not with the rumors of fell things in the woods, of terrible events in the cities to the south.

This year a man couldn't feel safe except behind the sealed stone walls of the town.

Not that Jem was unduly worried. He'd seen too many years not to have learned that rumors were usually far worse than fact.

So he sat in the kitchen with his wife, Bridey, sipping the lentil soup she had flavored with a piece of hamhock from a neighbor's smokehouse. Everyone in town gave something to the gatekeeper from time to time. It was his pay. And this winter it might make him either the most fortunate man in town or the least. There was no way to predict how people's hearts would face a rugged winter that boded to be the worst in memory.

But even that Jem didn't truly fear, because he knew that come the worst, there would always be a meal for him at the Whitewater Inn. Bandylegs always managed to pull something out of his hat and was always ready to feed the Downeys.

The lentil soup was good and filling, though Bridey had made little enough of it, trying to save both hamhock and lentils for another supper.

Satisfied, Jem took out his pipe and indulged the pleasure of filling it just so with what little leaf he still had from the south. He couldn't often indulge, but tonight, being a festival and all, he decided he could afford just this one bowlful.

He lit it with a taper from the fire—wood at least was plentiful—and told Bridey to leave the washing up and go join the festival. "You've worked hard enough today, my dear," he told her fondly. "I'll do the cleaning up."

She smiled almost like the girl she had once been and gave him a kiss that brought a blush to his cheeks.

"You be coming along soon," she told him.

"Aye. Soon as I'm sure there are no other poor souls out this night."

As his wife departed the tower, Jem heard the keening of the wind. Aye, it was going to be a bad night. The outdoor festivities were probably already moving into the warmth of the inn's public rooms. Not everyone could fit there, of course, but most of those with wee ones would be looking for their own beds soon, anyway.

Puffing on his pipe, he poured hot water from the kettle that always hung near the fire into the wooden pan, and washed the dinner bowls and spoons. There was still soup left in the big pot that hung to one side of the fire, and he decided to leave it where it was. 'Twas a cold night, and he might be wanting that bit of victual before he crawled into his bed.

He was just puffing the last of his pipe when the gate bell rang, a tinny but loud clang that was supposed to wake him even when he was soundly asleep.

Muttering just because he felt like muttering, he stomped across the room and pulled his thickest cloak off the peg. Wrapping it tightly around himself, he went down the circular stone stairway until he reached the tower's exterior door. There he picked up a lantern that was never allowed to go out and stepped out into the night's bitter cold.

The bell clanged insistently once again. Jem shook his head. Could he help it that he was no longer a boy who could run up and down the stairs? He was lucky he could still swing the gates open.

He opened the port in the gate and peered out.

Three mounted men, faces invisible beneath hoods pulled low. One of the men held what appeared to be a dead woman in front of him.

"What business?" he demanded gruffly, already thinking he might let these strangers freeze out there. He didn't like the look of this at all.

"Open the gate, Jem Downey," said a familiar voice. "This woman is hurt and needs attention."

Jem peered out again, and as the nearest horse sidled, he recognized the cloaked figure. "Why, Master Archer!" he exclaimed. "'Tis a long time since you darkened this gate."

"Too long, Jem. Are you going to let us in?"

Of course he was going to let Master Archer in. There was always a gold or silver coin in it for Jem, and the man had caused nary a whisker of trouble any of the times he had passed through town.

He quickly closed the porthole, then threw his back into lifting the heavy wood beam that barred the gate. He might have arthritis in every joint, did Jem, but he still had the strength in his back and arms.

The bar moved backward, out of the way, and Jem pushed open one side of the gate.

As the three riders started to enter single file, Master Archer, still concealed within his cloak, tossed Jem a gold piece.

"Mark me, Jem Downey," Archer said. "There are fell things abroad. Do not open this gate again tonight. Not for anyone."

"No, sir." Jem bobbed his head. "Not for anyone."

Then he stood, gold piece in hand, watching the three ride down the cobbled street toward the inn and the harvest celebration.

"Fell things, hmm?" he murmured to himself. When Master Archer said it, Jem believed it. All of a sudden he realized he was still standing outside the wall with one side of the gate open.

Unexpected fear speared him, and he looked quickly around. Snow was falling lightly, but the barren fields were empty as far as he could see.

Still… He hurried to close and bar the gate. As he locked it, an eddy of wind washed around him, chilling him to the bone.

Maybe he wouldn't go to the harvest festival at all. Someone ought to keep a weather eye out.

The public room at the inn was crowded to the point that no person could stand or sit without being pressed tight against another. Good fellowship prevailed, however, so none minded the continual jostling.

Nanue Manoison, the most recent and probably last of the traders to come up the Whitewater River this year, held the attention of everyone in the room. One of the butter-colored people of the west, Nanue came every year to buy Bill Bentback's scrimshaw, and wheat from the harvest for the more crowded western climes. This year he would get scrimshaw, but no wheat.

He held the entire room rapt as he spoke of his trip east and the strangenesses he had beheld. Strangeness that ensured he would not be back this year, even if the weather took a turn for the better.

"It was like nothing I had ever seen," he was telling the crowd. "My captain wanted to turn us around, he became so afraid. But I reminded him that we were five stout men and had little to fear on the river."

Heads nodded around the room. Leaf smoke hung in the air.

"But," Nanue said. "But. I tell you, my friends, it is not just the early winter. The farther we came down the pass, the eerier became the riverbank. First the deer disappeared. Never have I sailed a day on that river without seeing at least one or two deer come to drink or watch us from the shore. Then I realized that we barely heard any birdsong. None. All of you know that even in deepest winter there are birds.

"I know not where they have flown or why. But if the birds have gone, some evil is afoot, you mark my words. Some true evil. The last three days of our journey, I saw nothing living at all. And every league of the way, I felt we were being watched."

The room became hushed. Then there was a mumbling, and finally a voice called out, "I felt it, too, Nanue Manoison. In my fields these past two weeks, trying to save what I could. It was as if I was being watched from the woods."

"Aye," others said, nodding.

"And the fish are gone," someone else said. "We can fish even through the ice in winter, but there are no fish. It's as if the river is poisoned."

Someone else harrumphed. "Now don't you be saying such things, Tyne. We drink the water safe enough. If 'twere poisoned, we'd be as gone as the fish."

"It's just an early winter," said a grizzled voice from the farthest side of the room. "Early winter. Me granddad spoke of such in his time. It happened, he said, the year that Earth's Root blew smoke to the sky for months, and ash rained from the heaven for many days. Maybe 'tis Earth's Root again."

Tom, who was standing as near Sara as he could, listened with wide-open ears. Just then, the front door of the inn flew open.

Startled, Tom turned and saw a cloaked man entering with a bundled woman in his arms. Behind him came two even taller men, faces invisible within their hoods.

"Why, Master Archer," said Bandylegs, hurrying to greet the newcomers. "Oh my, what trouble have we here?"

"The woman is ill," said Master Archer. "The child with her is dead. We need your best rooms, Master Deepwell. One for the woman, and one for my friends and myself."

"Well, don't you know, it's as if I've been saving them for you,"

Bandylegs said, heading for the stairway. "Two rooms with a parlor between. It's dear, though, Master Archer."

"I'm not worried about that."

"Fine then, fine," said Bandylegs hurrying up the stairs with the men behind him. "Sara?"

"Aye, Dad?"

"Hot water and towels. This poor ill woman will be needing some warmth."

"Aye, Dad."

"I'll help you," Tom said quickly, his heart thundering. Master Archer, the mysterious visitor of years past. Perhaps he would get a chance this time to ply him with questions about his travels. This was clearly an adventure of some kind, too, and Tom had no intention of being cut out of it.

Sara nodded her permission, and Tom followed her to the kitchen.

Nanue Manoison tried vainly to recapture the attention of his audience, but he failed. It was as if, with the arrival of the strangers, worry had crept in, as well. People exchanged uneasy glances, and a pall seemed to settle over the room.

Little by little, the local residents drifted away, leaving the public room occupied only by trappers and traders.

Outside, the cheerful decorations blew dismally in the breath of the icy wind, and the last of the party lanterns flickered out.

Sara Deepwell had some knowledge of tending the sick. Over her short years, she'd been called upon many times to help when someone was injured or ill, most likely because her mother had been a healer and Sara had learned at her side. Many of the skills remained, and there was little in a sickroom that could shock her or cause her fear.

But as she entered the room of the mysterious woman, what she saw *did* shock her. Her dad had lit the fire, and by its light she could see that the woman's ragged wrap was stained with blood. And she could see the pallor of the child clutched in her arms, a child who was plainly dead, who had a bandage around her throat.

"Great Theriel," she murmured. Behind her, she heard Tom stumble slightly beneath his burden of a cauldron of hot water.

"Just set it over here by the fire, Tom," she said briskly, as if there were nothing of note occurring.

Tom complied, then at her gesture left the room.

Slowly, Sara approached the bed. The child was already frozen, as cold as the ice upon the winter river. But the woman, who still breathed shallowly, was hardly much warmer.

Bending, Sara tried to take the dead child from the woman's arms. At once her eyes flew open, eyes the color of a midsummer's morn, and a sound of protest escaped her.

"Let me," Sara said gently, almost crooning. "Let me. I'll take care of her. I promise I'll take care of her."

Some kind of understanding seemed to creep into those blue eyes, and the woman's hold on the child relaxed.

Gently Sara picked up the corpse, and just as gently carried it from the room. A small, thin child, no older that seven. Gods have mercy on them all, when someone would kill a child of this age.

Outside, she passed the body to a nervous Tom. "She will need a coffin, Tom. See to it."

He looked as if he might be ill, but he stiffened and nodded.

"And treat the child as gently as if she were your own. Her mother would want it that way. Get one of the women to clean her up and dress her."

Again Tom nodded, then headed for the stairs.

Back in the strange woman's room, Sara found her patient had lapsed into some kind of fevered dream, muttering words and sounds that made no sense. She threw a few more logs on the fire, knowing her patient would need every bit of heat she could get.

Then, tenderly, with care and concern, Sara undressed the woman and washed her with towels dipped in hot water, chafing her skin as she did so to bring back the blood.

When she was done, her patient looked rosier and healthier. All the dried blood was gone, and the rags had been tossed upon the fire.

Gently Sara drew the blankets up to the woman's chin and took her hand. "You're going to be all right," she crooned. "Everything will be fine, you'll see."

But she wasn't sure she believed her own words. With dread in her heart, Sara Deepwell went downstairs to make sure the child was being properly tended.

In the public room, all attention had fixed on Archer—or Master Blackcloak, as some called him. His two companions had disappeared into their room, unknown and unknowable, but Archer had joined the small group of men still remaining around the fire. He ordered a tankard of Bandylegs' finest and put his booted feet up on a bench.

"A caravan was attacked," he said in answer to the questions. "Slaughtered, every man, woman and child. The only survivor I found is the woman I brought in."

"Who would do such a thing?" Nanue marveled. Traders and caravans were rarely attacked, for while they carried much wealth, they also traveled heavily guarded by stout men. It had been a very long time, a time almost out of memory, since anyone could recall such a thing.

"And to kill everyone," muttered Tyne, who was seated across the room. "Thieves need only to steal a packhorse or wagon. They don't need to kill everyone."

"These weren't thieves," said Archer.

A collective gasp rose. "How can you know that?" Nanue demanded.

"Because all their goods still lay there. Bags of rice and wheat and dried meats. All of it lying there, cast about thither and yon, much ruined by blood and gore."

The silence that filled the room was now profound, broken only by the pop and crackle from the fireplace. The chill night wind seemed to creep into the room, even as it moaned around the corners of the inn. It was as if the fire had ceased to cast light and warmth.

"Tomorrow," Archer said, his voice heavy with something that sent chills along the spines of the perceptive, "I will return to the caravan. I will seek for some sign of the attackers, and for some sign of where they went after. I welcome any who care to join me."

"Join you?" asked Red Boatman, stiffening on his bench. "Why should we want to tangle with such things?"

"Because you might be able to recover some wheat, meat and rice. Unless I mistake what I saw in your fields, you'll have some use for it before this winter is done."

A few *ayes* rippled around the room.

"But to steal from the dead..." Tyne sounded troubled.

"They have no more use for it," Archer replied. "'Twere better if it saved the children of Whitewater."

A stirring in the room, then silence. A log in the fire popped loudly.

Archer put his feet to the floor and leaned forward, scanning every face in the room. "Mark me, there is evil afoot. Evil beyond any seen in your memory. Look to your larders and look to your weapons. For none will remain untouched."

Then he rose and strode from the room, his cloak swirling about him, opening just enough to reveal an intricately worked leather scabbard and the pommel of a sword. It seemed a ruby winked in the firelight.

No one moved until his footsteps died away.

"Who *is* he?" Nanue asked. "Should you trust him?"

"Aye," said Bandylegs, who'd been listening from behind the bar. "I'd trust him with my life, I would. None know anything about him, but he's been passing through these many years, and never a bit of trouble come with him."

"Trouble has come with him this time," Tyne responded darkly. "Much trouble indeed."

Bandylegs shook his head. "Next you'll be telling me he brought the winter. Enough, Tyne. The man is right. If there's food up there we can use, we need to get it for our families. Beyond that, I plan to stay safe behind these walls until spring."

A murmur of agreement answered him. It seemed the matter was settled. Once again tankards needed filling, and life settled back into it comfortable course.

If Evil were afoot, it wasn't afoot in Whitewater.

Yet.

4

Firelight flickered over the dark wooden walls of the room. Sara lay on the settle, curled into a ball beneath a blanket, watching her charge sleep. The woman's color had become more natural now, and her breathing had finally settled into an easy, regular rhythm.

She thought she ought to sleep herself, now that it appeared the woman was going to be fine. But it was already approaching dawn, almost time to get up and rekindle the cook fires for baking bread. Almost time to go roll, knead and punch the dough, and set it to rise for breakfast.

But not yet. For now she could lie on this settle and watch the light of the flames dance on the walls like creatures out of myth. The cold wind keened noisily, and the curtains over the windows stirred a little but kept the draft out. Those curtains had been made and mended by generations of Deepwell women, including her mother. She imagined that if she closed her eyes and touched the fabric she might be able to sense all the hands that had touched them and tended them.

She sighed lightly and closed her eyes. She was so weary, far too weary for someone of her years. She was only twenty, but already life had become an endless grind of sameness. She loved her father, yes, and loved the inn, but the sameness of it all was not suited to someone so young. Then there was Tom. Sometimes he made her heart smile. Sometimes she looked at him and saw her future laid out in an endless progression of days all the same.

She shook her head sternly, trying to brush away the thought. Such as she were not made for great adventures. She was made to run the inn in her father's stead, and provide ale and food and shelter to all who needed it, to someday bear children of her own and raise them to the same solid life.

The faint, sparkling dreams that sometimes tried to take hold of her were just that: dreams. She was blessed with a good life, and she knew she should be grateful for it.

There was a light knock at the door. Rising, she cast aside the blanket and crept to the door to answer it.

Her father stood outside, and in his arms he held a familiar white bundle topped by boots of the finest, softest white leather.

"She'll be needing something to wear," he said gruffly.

Sara looked at her father's burden, her eyes suddenly stinging. "But, Dad..."

"She'll not be coming back, lass," he said. "Six years... Nay, she'll not be coming back. Better this should be worn by someone who has nothing than waste away in a chest."

She accepted the bundle from him reluctantly. It felt as if she were giving up her last hope. Her heart squeezed, and her eyes burnt.

"It's all right, Sara," he said gruffly, his eyes reddened. "It came to me in the night. That woman…she should have these. I love you, girl."

"I love you, too, Dad."

"Sleep late," he said. "I can manage the bread, and Mistress Lawd is going to help me. You worked hard yesterday. Get some rest."

Mistress Lawd? Sara watched her father walk toward the stairway and wondered if the Widow Lawd had done something no other woman had done in six years: catch her father's eye.

It would do him good, she thought as she reentered the room and closed the heavy plank door behind her. He needed someone besides his daughter in his life.

But inside her, something was cracking wide-open with a new kind of grief, as she recognized the final farewell to her missing mother.

The woman on the bed was sitting up, awake, blanket pulled to her chin. Her eyes were wide and fearful.

Sara at once hurried to her, smiling, setting the clothes down on the bed.

"Good morning," she said cheerfully. "'Tis good to see you awake. I reckon you must be hungry."

The woman managed an uncertain smile and said, "Water?"

"Of course." Sara hurried to the ewer and poured water into a cup, bringing it to her.

The woman accepted it with a murmur that Sara couldn't understand. A different language, perhaps?

She touched her chest as the woman looked at her. "Sara," she said.

The woman nodded, then hesitated. Suddenly her eyes widened with astonishment, and she touched her own breast. "Tess," she replied, her tone hushed.

"Hello, Tess." Sara kept her voice bright and her smile cheerful.

"Hello, Sara," the woman replied, her syllables a tad uncertain.

"Now don't you worry about a thing," Sara said, patting Tess's shoulder. "I'll bring you some broth, and while I get it, you get dressed."

There was only more confusion on the woman's face, so Sara carefully unfolded the bundle, displaying the fine leather pants and the finest wool over-tunic, which would reach the floor and was slit for riding up front and back. The belt, hand-embroidered with gold thread. The boots soft as butter.

She pointed to the clothes and then to Tess. "For you. Clothes."

Comprehension dawned on Tess's face.

Miming, Sara said, "I'll get you something to eat."

"Food?"

"Aye, food."

Tess nodded and smiled.

Sara hurried out, wondering what in the world they were to do with the woman if she didn't speak their language. It might be months before they learned anything about her.

The kitchen fires were already roaring, and Mistress Lawd and her father were up to their elbows in flour. Tess scooped some of the stew from yesterday's pot and found a slice of day-old bread.

"She's awake and hungry," she told her dad. "And her name is Tess."

"Good news," he agreed. "Take the food up to her, then get yourself into your own bed, child. You haven't slept a wink, I wager."

Tess was dressed when Sara returned, and the girl caught her breath as she saw the woman standing by the window, the curtains drawn back. Beautiful, she thought. So beautiful. It was as if the clothes had been made for her. They certainly had not been made for Sara, who had inherited her father's sturdy build rather than her mother's willowy slenderness.

But on Tess the clothes seemed to become something more, and Sara felt an urge to call the woman *my lady.*

But it was a sorrowful face Tess turned toward her, blue eyes haunted by loss, by sights better not seen. She moved her arms as if cradling a child and made a questioning sound.

She wanted the dead child. Perhaps her own child. Probably her own child.

Sara carried the stew and bread to the small table in the corner and set them down. "Eat first," she said, once again miming. "Then I'll take you to your child."

As if she understood, Tess obediently sat and began to eat.

Sara sat with her, chattering as if to stem the pain to come. "You don't understand me at all, do you?" she said. "I don't understand you, either. Pity of it is, it'll probably take you weeks or months to say the simplest things."

Tess astonished her by answering. "I learn."

Then Tess herself looked amazed, as if surprised that she had spoken the words.

"Maybe," Sara said, "you just forgot how to speak, because of the terrible things that happened."

"Terrible," Tess agreed, nodding, her blue eyes shadowing. "Terrible."

She bowed her head for a few moments, then resumed eating as if she understood that she must fuel herself regardless.

After breakfast, Sara took Tess downstairs to the room where the child was laid out. Tess approached slowly, noting that someone had garbed the girl in a green dress that covered the wound at her throat, and had washed her and brushed her hair to a golden sheen. She lay within a rough-hewn coffin of planks set upon two sawhorses.

"I'm sorry, Tess," Sara said behind her. "It must be so hard to lose your child."

It was as if the skill of language was returning to her with each passing moment, for Tess realized she could understand Sara. But the words were barely filling in the black void that was her memory, a memory that began when she woke among the slaughtered caravan.

She looked at the girl lying so still, feeling a sense of pity, and a deeper sense of failure that she had been unable to save her. She felt loss and sorrow for a life snuffed out too soon, but one thing she knew for certain.

"Not my child," she said quietly. "I found her."

"Oh," said Sara, stepping up beside her. "How sad."

"Yes."

Tess reached out and touched the cold little body, and felt again the wrenching sense that she had failed this child.

"She'll be buried this morning," Sara said. "It can't wait any longer."

"No. Thank you."

After a few more moments, Tess turned from the little coffin.

"Come," said Sara. "I'll take you to your parlor. It's right next to your room. Then I'll bring you some tea and cakes. And then," she added, with a smile. "I'm going to get some sleep."

"Thank you for caring for me."

"I was glad to do it."

Alone in the parlor with tea and cakes and absolutely no idea who she was, where she was going or what she would do next, Tess sat by the window and watched the darkness slowly fade from the sky.

The mind was a singularly empty thing when one had no memory. The only images that would come to her were of the horror she had found upon awakening amidst the carnage of the caravan, of her struggle to save the little girl and herself, of the riders who had rescued her. And of them she had only snatches of memory, because exhaustion had taken her so deeply.

Exhaustion or shock.

At least language seemed to be coming back to her, albeit slowly, words that belonged to this time and place, to judge by her brief talk with Sara, and words that came from elsewhere.

Those other words were doubtless a clue to her origins, but so far no one had seemed to recognize them except herself.

And even now they seemed to be growing dimmer in her mind, fading bit by bit as they were replaced by new words, words that were growing increasingly familiar.

She must have suffered a severe blow to her head. Somehow she had jangled her brains, and perhaps for the last few days she had been babbling nonsense that only seemed to make sense.

She counseled herself to patience, for if her memory of words was returning, surely her memory of other things would return, as well?

But before the instant when she'd awoken amidst the caravan, there was only a huge darkness in her mind, as if everything had been erased.

As if nothing had ever been there. As if she had been born only three days before.

Panic rose within her, and she had to force herself with steady calm to regain her self-control. What was she going to do? Run out into the frigid night until she collapsed and froze to death in the snow?

No, she could only wait.

Turning from the window to survey the lantern-lit room around her, she spied a mirror. It wasn't a very good mirror, although how she knew that she couldn't be certain. Hesitantly she rose and walked over to it, wondering what she would do if she didn't recognize herself.

Closing her eyes at the last moment, she took the last step and faced the mirror. Then, by exerting every bit of her will, she opened her eyes and looked.

A surge of relief passed through her. She recognized the face as her own. Blue eyes, small nose, delicate mouth and oval chin. Yes, that was her, although she couldn't have said why she thought her hair was longer. Much longer. But at least she hadn't forgotten her own face.

And the clothes… Taking a few steps back, she looked at the beautiful white garments that had been given to her and felt somehow that she was used to different attire. Perhaps something plainer and more simple? Something less expensive and beautiful?

Finally she could look no more. The only answer the mirror gave her was that she hadn't forgotten her own face.

She didn't know what she would have done if a stranger had looked back at her from the glass.

Spreading her hands before her, she recognized them, as well. Including a small scar between her thumb and forefinger, though she had no idea how she had come by it.

But at least not everything had been stolen from her.

Feeling a little better, telling herself that soon all her memory would come back, she returned to the table by the window and poured a cup of tea.

Everything would work out somehow. She had to believe that.

There was a creak from behind her, and she turned quickly to see the stranger who had rescued her, the tall man with the gray eyes.

"My lady," he said, his eyes sweeping over her.

She wanted to argue with him that she was nobody's lady, but the words stayed frozen in her throat.

This morning his cloak was gone, revealing garments of leather and wool. His black hair fell to his shoulders, thick and shiny. He was not armed, so his leathern tunic fell straight around his hips. His boots, unlike hers, were heavy and thickly soled.

Finally it dawned on her that he was staying on the threshold because he didn't want to frighten her. With effort, she found the words.

"Please. Come have tea and cakes."

A faint smile softened his austere features. "You have remembered how to speak."

"A little."

He nodded, apparently finding this to be a good thing, and joined her at the table, pouring himself a cup of tea, then reached for one of the thick sweet cakes.

"I'm sorry about your child."

She shook her head slightly. "Not mine. I found her."

He nodded. "I'm still very sorry. I could tell how much you wanted to save her. Can you remember anything of the attack?"

Her throat tightened up as she thought of the child, of finding her in all that gore and blood, of the unimaginable carnage that was her first memory of life. "I remember nothing before I woke up afterward," she said finally, her voice thick with unshed tears. She turned her face toward the window, seeking signs of a brightening day, hoping for anything that might alleviate the darkness that surrounded her and filled her.

Right now she didn't even have a foundation on which to stand. Nothing but emptiness behind her. She wasn't even sure how old she was.

"Nothing?" he said finally. "You don't remember *anything?*"

"Nothing," she repeated. Let him think she spoke of the savage attack. She wasn't ready to admit to anyone at all just how vulnerable she felt, how vulnerable she *was,* knowing nothing at all of her past.

He drained his tea, swallowed the last of the cake and said, "I'm going below. Today we'll ride back there and see what we can learn. If you remember anything to tell us before we go…."

She compressed her lips and nodded. He strode from the room as if he were master of all the world. If that man had ever known a moment's fear, she couldn't imagine it.

Which made him that much less approachable to a woman who right now could feel nothing else.

The funeral was a sad little affair at midmorning. Several men had dug the grave in the cemetery outside the town walls, then volunteered to carry the pitifully small coffin. Tess walked right behind it, Sara holding her arm. Behind them came Archer and his two companions, their hoods drawn low over their features.

Bandylegs Deepwell said a few words about the gods welcoming such an innocent in the hereafter; then the clods of earth began to fall on the wood with a hollow sound.

The bitter wind cut through all clothing, even through the heavy green cloak Sara had given Tess to wear over her new garments. Then the few turned back into the town, heading toward the inn. Tess was hardly aware of the tears that trailed down her cheeks until Sara reached out to wipe them away, murmuring, "They'll freeze on your face, they will."

At the inn, however, when Tess saw Archer and his companions bringing forth their horses, something steeled within her.

"Take me with you," she said to Archer.

"'Tis cold, milady," he replied, scratching behind one of his black horse's ears. "You'll slow us down."

"I might. But I might also remember something if I see it again."

He hesitated, gray eyes meeting blue. "Very well," he said finally.

Other men were joining them now with packhorses, to save what they might of the meal, rice and dried meats of the caravan. Among them was Tom, looking at once bold and frightened as he bade farewell to Sara. Sara for her part looked torn between a longing to go and fear for Tom. It was so plain to everyone that more than one villager drew near Sara to promise they would keep an eye on young Tom.

To Tess's vast relief, mounting the gray gelding that was offered to her came easily, and the saddle, while feeling somewhat strange in its shape, still felt familiar. At least she knew how to ride.

The horse's movements beneath her gave her a sense of near victory. *Yes, I have a past! I have done this before.*

At that moment she realized she how desperate she was for the familiar. Any little thing would do.

Drawing up the hood of the green cloak, her hands fitted into fur-lined gloves Sara found for her, Tess struck out with the party, filled with both dread and hope.

Giri, one of Archer's two Anari companions, rode at his side. "The woman," he said.

"What about her?"

"Are you sure she should be trusted?"

Archer looked into his friend's dark face. "Why should she not be? Have you forgotten how we found her?"

"Have you forgotten that she was the only one to survive the attack?"

"No, I haven't. But I also remember how we found her hiding and terrified. Calm your suspicious Anari mind. Besides, I'm offering her no trust. But perhaps we can learn something from her."

Giri fell silent and resumed his restless watching of the riverbank along which they rode. The group was making as much noise as the caravan most likely had. He was not comfortable.

Archer spoke. "Take Ratha and scout, will you? If anyone is observing our progress, I would prefer to know."

Giri nodded. Moments later he and Ratha melted away into the trees.

The farther they rode from Whitewater, the more uncomfortable the townspeople felt. They weren't used to being so far from familiar places, and Archer began to wonder if they would bolt at the cry of a crow. Their voices grew quieter, until they were nearly silenced, until the only sound echoing around them was the tramp of their horses' feet on pine needles, dirt and pebbles. The almost partylike enjoyment of their start had given way to dread-filled quiet.

Pulling his steed to one side, Archer watched the single-file group pass, murmuring reassurances to the men. Tess was in the middle of the group, and he pulled in beside her.

"How are you?"

"I'm fine," she answered. "The woods smell so wonderful right now, in the cold air."

Indeed, the aroma of pine was strong, mixed with that particular, indescribable scent of nearby snow and ice.

"At least the trees are sheltering us from the worst of the wind." He was glad of that, for if the wind had chosen to follow the river gorge directly, he doubted that most of them would have come this far. "I don't ever remember it being this cold at this time of year," he said.

"What time of year is it?"

He looked at her, astonished by the idea that she might have forgotten such a simple thing. And that caused him to wonder what else she might have forgotten. "It's harvest time. But winter has come so early the frost has blackened the fields."

"That's not good."

"Most assuredly not good. Many will starve this winter." He scanned the column again, feeling the edginess of his companions as if it were a prickle in his own skin. "Tell me something of yourself," he said.

He saw her head bow, saw her hands tighten on the reins. For a few moments he thought she would refuse to answer him. Then, as if gathering her courage, she straightened and looked him dead in the eye. Her own eyes were as clear as a midsummer sky.

"I don't remember. I don't remember anything before I woke up and saw the...the slaughter."

He was astonished to realize just what she had meant when she said she might remember something. He had known men who had forgotten large parts of battles they had fought, or who had forgotten how they had come to be severely wounded, but never before had he met anyone without any memory at all.

"Nothing?" he asked.

She shook her head. Her lips quivered, then tightened, as if she were fighting down an overwhelming tide of emotion. When at last she spoke again, her voice was steady. "Speech is coming back to me rapidly," she said. "I trust the rest will come, as well."

"I'm sure it will, Lady." He studied her profile for a moment or

two, wondering why it was he kept feeling the itch of recognition.
He did not know this woman, of that he was sure. She must, therefore, remind him of someone, but the elusiveness of that knowledge was maddening, dancing just beyond his ken.

But some things always danced beyond his ken, it seemed. Distant things, sorrows that had burned a permanent ache of loss into
his being. Faded, almost vanished memories of other times and a
different way of life. A sense that what should have been had never
come to pass. The memory, from the distant mists of time, of the
loss of his beloved wife. A time he had long since forbidden himself to recall.

And this woman deepened that ache, as if she were somehow a
part of it. But that was impossible. His years outstretched many
lifetimes of men, and the ache was so far in the past, it preceded
all that had come to be.

He thought he had learned to live with the ache, with being
homeless, nameless, a wanderer who could never be one of those
he wandered among. A man set apart for reasons he barely recalled,
a man who was not man, apparently, given his agelessness.

But this woman reminded him of the ache and the yearning. Unsettled him.

'Twould be best to heed Giri's warning and put distrust before
trust with this woman, then. He needed a clear eye and a clear head
in the worrisome days to come.

For worrisome they would be. As they rode east along the river,
the silence grew deeper, as if the very trees themselves held their
breath. There was more behind this early winter than a foible of
nature. Beneath it a sense of huge power thrummed, a power that
had more than once raised the hairs on the back of his neck.

He could not yet say that it would endure, nor even guess what it might do. But ancient magicks were stirring, and his every sense was on alert to detect anything out of the ordinary. Somehow he recognized that thrum of power, that echo of immeasurable forces at work, though he could not say he knew it.

But he recognized it anyway, in the way the tips of his fingers would tingle and the hairs at his nape stand on end. He knew it in the way the pit of his stomach responded to it. He had met this force before.

The attack on the caravan had been abnormal. Of that there was no doubt. He'd seen such things before, but rarely did more than a few die, and never were the riches left behind. As near as he could tell, nothing had been stolen.

Which meant the attack was directed at a person or group of people. That it was born of vengeance, or something even darker. But it was not a robbery.

He wondered if anyone coming with him even guessed at the kind of darkness that was approaching, or if he and his two Anari friends were the only ones.

Somehow the woman Tess had escaped the massacre. And Giri was right. That alone, given the savagery of the attack, was cause for wonder and doubt.

"Is something wrong?" she asked him now.

He realized his silence had endured too long. "Nothing," he answered, though it was far from true. "I'm going to drop back and check on the rest of the column."

She nodded and returned her attention forward.

Column? Ragtag bunch of merchants, farmers and youths from Whitewater. He daren't let them become at all separated, for he doubted any of them knew how to fight. Defense would be all on him and the Anari.

He knew his skills and those of his two companions, and never doubted they could do the job, but 'twere still far better if they encountered no one at all.

Because they had to follow the trade road along the river, and because they were so many, most unaccustomed to riding over difficult ground, they neared their destination too late to hope for a return before dark. They would have to spend the night.

Archer looked up at the still-blue sky as the shadows deepened around them, knowing the sun had already fallen behind the mountains. Noting, with a sense of uneasiness approaching alarm, that no vultures circled in the sky overhead.

That could mean only one thing: someone was already searching among the remains of the caravan.

He halted the column and gave a whistle that sounded like a birdcall. Once such a sound would have seemed normal in these woods. Now, with no wildlife left to be found, it sounded both eerie and obvious.

Moments later, Giri, then Ratha, emerged seamlessly from the shadows, joining him.

"No vultures," said Archer. "Is someone at the caravan?"

Ratha shook his head. "Not a soul for leagues around us."

"So even the vultures have fled."

"*Everything* has fled," Giri said. "Nothing stirs in these woods any longer, not bird, not squirrel, not deer nor boar."

"It wasn't like that just yesterday," Archer remarked. Though there had been a paucity of life, they had still caught sight of the occasional squirrel and bird.

"No, 'tis far worse today," Ratha replied. "There is something foul afoot."

With that Archer agreed. "Did you make it as far as the caravan?"

"Aye," Giri answered. "Naught has changed. All is frozen as if in ice."

"Best we camp here," Archer decided. "We'll rescue what we can in the morning."

There was some grumbling in response to his decision, though he couldn't blame anyone for it. None had really expected to have to spend the night in the abandoned woods, though he had warned them they probably would.

Or perhaps they grumbled because the woods and the riverbank felt so…strange. As if they had left everything familiar behind and stepped into a different world where the threats were unknown.

As Archer guided the establishment of the camp, he mulled that over. He could only conclude that somehow, someway, they had indeed stepped out of the familiar.

And he had a terrible feeling that it would be a long time before they could go back.

Tom was at last enjoying the adventure he'd always longed for, and he wasn't about to let anything ruin it. In fact, he was quite de-lighted that everyone seemed so uneasy because the forest was empty of its normal inhabitants.

Actually *he* was quite glad to know they wouldn't run into any boar or bears, and if that meant doing without deer and birds, he was content. He'd never slept outdoors in his life, and cold though this night was, the big fire they'd built cast both light and warmth, and provided yet another opportunity for the men of Whitewa-ter to swap tall tales.

But he first had a mission. Carrying a carriage blanket made of fleece, he approached the Lady Tess. "Lady," he said awkwardly, "Sara sent this blanket and asked me to give it to you for the night."

The woman, who looked so alone and uncertain amidst the crowd of strangers, gave him a smile that made him feel at least six feet tall. "Thank you," she said, allowing him to spread it over her. "How kind of you and Sara."

"Thank Sara," he said, shuffling his feet awkwardly. "'Twas she who thought of it."

"And you who carried it and gave it to me. I thank you, too. I'm afraid I don't know your name."

"Tom. Tom Downey, the gatekeeper's son. Most call me Young Tom."

"Well, Young Tom Downey, I am pleased to make your acquaintance. I'm Tess." A flicker of memory flashed into her mind; the memory of a mockingbird in the morning. "Tess Birdsong."

He smiled bashfully. "Would you like something warm to drink? There's tea, and some mulled cider."

"Cider sounds wonderful."

Many of the men had brought skins of hard cider with them, a remedy against the cold, and Tom, thanks to Sara, had brought spices and a pot in which to heat it. Sara, in fact, was responsible for the fact that the party had eaten a hot meal this night. Tom's packhorse had been loaded, unlike the others, with viands and some cooking pots, with the result that he had been something of a hero a little while ago, as he'd cooked and served a meal they otherwise would have done without, relying instead on the strips of dried fish and jerky most had packed.

And now he could give the lady a tin cup full of piping hot mulled cider. She accepted it gratefully and held it close, as if savoring the warmth. She patted the ground beside her. "Tell me about yourself, Young Tom."

He sat, but felt nearly tongue-tied. "There's naught to tell," he said, when he could find his voice again. The woman was so beautiful and otherworldly, and he wasn't accustomed to conversing with strangers, especially beautiful ones.

"Ah, you must have done something during your years," she replied.

"Nothing of interest. My dad is the town gatekeeper. Mostly I help him."

"That's a very important job."

"I suppose."

She smiled gently. "But you long for greater adventures?"

"Doesn't everyone?"

"At your age, I suppose so. Right now I seem to be having the biggest adventure of my life, and I'd rather not be having it at all."

Tom considered the matter from her viewpoint, or at least what he could know of it from what he had seen since Archer brought her to the inn, and decided that perhaps, after all, some adventures were not worth having.

But this one was different, a trek down the river to places he had never before visited to recover food for his town, to assuage the hunger of his friends and neighbors over the winter. This was a good adventure.

"I'm sorry," he said presently. "You must be very unhappy."

"But that shouldn't make you unhappy," she said kindly. "You are here to help your entire town and should be proud."

"I am," he admitted. "This will probably be the most important thing I do in my entire life."

He looked shyly her way and saw her blue eyes grow distant, as if she were seeing beyond him, beyond the woods and the night.

"Somehow," she said after a moment, "I think you have far more important things to do, Young Tom."

"What do you mean?"

The vagueness vanished from her gaze and she looked at him as if startled. "Oh! Well, just that most people have far more important things to do in their life than they realize. So many of the things we do seem small, yet they're very important in the larger scheme."

"Oh." He wasn't sure what she meant but was reluctant to question her further. The word *small* made him uncertain that he wanted to know her meaning.

"Aye," said a deep voice from nearby. Archer approached them, and with a swirl that wrapped his cloak around him, he settled on the ground with them. "The small things, Lady. They matter beyond estimation."

The men closest to the fire, quite happy now that they were full of food and hard cider, were arguing about who had caught the biggest fish last summer. Archer ignored them. Ratha and Giri seemed to be nowhere about.

"Simply being true to one's word, Young Tom," Archer said. "That is of great importance. The raising of a child..." His voice hushed a bit; then he shook his head, as if trying to dislodge an annoying insect. "The love and care of one's wife. These things matter, Young Tom, for they are the essence of goodness."

Tom nodded, but even he could feel the disappointment that must be showing on his face.

Suddenly Archer laughed and clapped a hand to Tom's shoulder. "If you're lucky, lad, you'll never have to use a sword."

Tom nodded. While he wanted adventure, he was in no hurry to kill anyone.

"Unfortunately," Archer continued, "luck may not hold and that day may come. Something stirs. Something dark and evil."

Tom's eagerness grew. "What do you mean, Master Archer?"

"Would that I could say for certain. All I know is...there is a strangeness to the air. Something awakens that were better left slumbering."

He looked at them both. "Stay close to the fire."

Then he rose and disappeared into the darkness, his cape swirling about him.

Some seconds passed while the men at the fire continued to happily argue. Then Tess spoke.

"What do you know of Master Archer?"

Tom shook his head. "No one knows much. He comes from time to time to town. He's never made any trouble, and sometimes he tells the old tales to us. But what he does otherwise, none knows."

Tess nodded and peered into the darkness. Tom knew she couldn't see Archer any longer. No one could.

Fog crept into the woods from the bank of the river. Low, hugging the ground, dense enough to make men disappear beneath its blanket. The night's chill grew deeper, and the moon disappeared behind a cloud. The only light came from the fire, well stocked and burning brightly.

Well beyond its glow, Archer paused to speak with Giri. "Do you feel it?"

"Aye."

"Keep sharp."

Giri nodded, his back toward the fire, his nostrils flared as if he were on the scent of something foul. Archer slipped away into the darkness, his movements barely stirring the fog, and came upon Ratha, who was guarding the other side of the camp.

"It's staying away," Ratha told him quietly. "Whatever it is, it's too cautious to approach."

"Can you hear it?"

Ratha shook his head. "I can smell it."

"It wants something we have."

"Nothing ordinary, I warrant." Ratha shook his head and drew another deep breath.

"It knows we wait and watch."

"That would trouble me less if there were more of us."

Archer touched his shoulder. "We three are enough. It fears us."

"So far. I wish I knew what it is."

"Mayhap we'll never need to know. I'll keep on the move."

Ratha nodded, keeping his attention on the night and the fog that hovered just above the ground. The night itself might betray nothing, but movement in the fog could tell much of a story.

Archer was gone again. A caw, like that of the crow, carried on the night air. Giri, saying all was still well at his post. Ratha answered in kind.

So far, it was well enough.

Tess's sleep was disturbed. A nightmare kept returning to her, a dream of dark oily fingers slipping into her mind. Finally, able to bear it no longer, she shook herself awake and sat bolt upright. The fire still burned, lower now, and she was surrounded by sleeping bodies.

Shivering as the night air hit her back, she drew the carriage blanket around herself and tried to shake off the ill-effects of the nightmare.

Though she had no memory older than three days, she was still able to judge the scene around her as safe and normal. The fire burned, the people slept, people that she was coming to know. Even Young Tom was lost in the sleep of innocence.

But the dream would not quite go away, and uneasiness danced along her spine. Shuddering, she scooted closer to the fire, then wondered why she thought the light would make her any safer.

Or any warmer, for the chill she was feeling now came from within her. From some place so deep inside her she didn't know how to name it. Didn't know what it was.

"Is something wrong?"

The whisper startled her, and she jumped with a small cry, twisting to discover that Archer had come to squat beside her.

"My apologies," he murmured. "I didn't mean to startle you. Are you all right?"

"I had a nightmare. I can't seem to shake it off."

He nodded, his gaze darting around as if he were trying to watch the entire world at once. "Ratha, Giri and I are standing guard. You need not fear."

She shuddered again.

Hesitantly he reached out and touched her hand, where it clutched the blanket around her. "Tell me," he suggested quietly.

"It was as if something evil were trying to get inside me. Something evil and cold. And the feeling is still here."

He nodded but said nothing. On the other hand, he didn't tell her that she was being foolish.

Finally he looked at her again. "You're feeling it, too. There's something out there, but it dares not approach. You can rest safely."

"I don't think I'll sleep again tonight."

"Perhaps not. How quietly can you walk?"

She didn't know how to answer that. "I'm not sure."

He cocked his head. "Then it's best you stay here. Trust me, we're watching over the campsite."

"How can I help?" It was a stupid question, she thought, even as she asked it. She had no idea whether she knew how to use a weapon of any kind. No idea whether she had ever fought anyone or anything.

"Keep your back to the fire and watch," he said. "We need eyes."

She nodded, then watched him rise and melt away once again.

It was only then that she noticed the fog that surrounded the campsite, as if held at bay only by the fire. It clung low to the ground and was so thick that nothing could be seen through it. But while it surrounded the campers, it approached none of them.

Another shiver passed through her, and she wondered how long it would be before the sun rose.

Dawn came without further incident, much to everyone's relief. The party struggled through a quick breakfast, then set out on the last brief leg of the journey to the caravan.

The scene, when they came upon it in the clear morning light, was almost exactly as Tess recalled. The bodies were strewn about, untouched by carrion eaters. The river ran clear now, free of blood. The men of Whitewater at once began to burden their packhorses with as much undamaged food as they could carry. Then they began the bitter task of burying the dead.

Tess sat astride her horse, disappointed that there was nothing here that might wake her memory.

Archer drew his mount up beside her. "Do you remember anything?" he asked quietly, so that no one else would overhear.

She shook her head, feeling her heart squeeze with both disappointment and the horror of her earliest memory: the carnage she had seen here.

"Give it time, Lady," he said. "For now, come with me. I want to find some sign of who wrought this destruction."

Nodding, having nothing else to do with herself, having no personhood or even personality to guide her, she followed him.

"We'll ride downstream," he told her. "That would be the best place for the attackers to start from—the rear of the caravan."

"That makes sense."

"If anything about this makes sense."

"This doesn't happen often?"

"This *never* happens," he said flatly. "Few caravans are attacked, and those that are rarely suffer more than a few casualties and the loss of their goods. This is surpassing strange."

She gave a little laugh of unhappy amusement. "Like me, the woman from nowhere."

"Be at ease, Lady. You remembered how to speak. The rest will come."

"I'd be at ease if *anything* seemed familiar."

He raised a brow at her. "Are you saying riding that horse doesn't feel familiar?"

At that she gaped, and finally a trill of laughter escaped her. "You'll cheer me up in spite of myself."

"It's the small things that matter," he reminded her.

Then his attention began to focus more on their surroundings. They crossed the portage bridge, and he drew rein, staring up at something.

"What?" she asked.

"See those rocks?" He pointed at a bunch of high crags.

"Yes."

"The caravan would have passed beneath them. If one could gather his group up there, he'd be in the best possible position to know when to attack."

Tess looked around them. "I don't see any way to get up there."

"Not from the road. That would be too obvious. I'm going into the woods. If you'd like to stay here, that's fine."

"No, I want to come." She had to start carving something out of her new life, and staying behind every time someone did something would only make her exceptionally useless in the long run.

The old forest was deep and dark, with only little shards of sunlight dappling the ground here and there. It was easy enough to pass through, but still not the sort of place one would choose to ride.

"It would be easy to get lost in here," Tess said.

"Aye. But don't fear. My sense of direction is excellent."

Indeed it was, because in only a short time he had brought them round the tor and found a narrow, rocky path up its side, sufficient for them to ride single file.

But instead of leading them up it, he dismounted. "Wait here. I want to see the tracks."

She took the reins of his horse from him, although she suspected that was totally unnecessary. There was something about Archer and his horse that felt like a single entity.

She watched as he climbed the rock alongside the trail with booted feet as naturally as if he were a fly climbing a wall. Every so often he paused to look down on the dirt of the trail, to lean toward it as if studying something. Then he disappeared into the treetrops

She waited, growing increasingly aware of the silence of the woods around her. She might have no memory, but she knew woods were never this quiet. There was always the rustle of something moving about, and occasionally the sound of birdsong or the screech of some small animal protecting its territory. From time to time trees cracked and groaned like old men who had been still for too long.

But these woods were as silent as death. Not even a breeze seemed to stir the distant tops of the trees. She looked straight up, longing for even a small glimpse of the sky.

But it was as if the branches crowded in over her, jailing her.

Enough was enough, she decided abruptly. Sitting here like someone's handmaiden, holding the reins of a horse, was not the way she intended to continue this new life of hers.

Dismounting with ease—something else she knew!—she tethered both horses to a nearby pine trunk. Then, tucking the front of her slit skirt out of the way by threading it through her belt, she began to climb the tor, following the path Archer had used.

A thrill filled her when she realized that her hands felt comfortable grasping small crannies, when her toes seemed to know on their own how to wedge against the smallest protuberance. She had done this before. Often. Of that she was now certain.

Glancing at the narrow path beside her, she could see the imprint of many horses' hooves, most chewed up, but one or two clear as a bell. These horses had been shod. For some reason that surprised her.

The climb was strenuous but exhilarating. For the first time since her fateful awakening, she felt truly confident and alive, as if somehow she had made a connection with a deep part of herself. The brooding silence of the forest was forgotten as she mounted the tor.

Something clattered, and she realized it was a pebble falling down from above. She hoped it was Archer returning and not the thing that had terrified these woods into silence.

She was warm and breathing hard by the time she mounted the sun-drenched top of the tor. There she found a wide circle, surrounded by higher tongues of stone. Archer was squatting in the middle, looking at the black remains of a campfire. From it he picked up something small and white, and tucked it in his tunic.

He turned when he heard her.

"I thought I told you to remain below."

She clambered over the last rock. "I don't take orders well. I tethered the horses. What have you found?"

He put his hands on his hips, throwing back his cloak and revealing the long sword at his side. She could tell, somehow, that he was at once displeased and amused by her. In response, she tossed her head back and met him stare for stare. "Well?"

"The coals at the bottom of the firepit are still warm. Nothing unusual in that. They buried the fire before leaving."

"Or to hide themselves."

"Aye, or to hide themselves."

She looked around the dirt and the few hummocks of grass that dotted the area. "There were quite a few horses here, were there not?"

"So it appears. And quite a few men, as well." He walked over to her and guided her a few feet to the left. "However," he said, squatting down and pointing, "they left quite a bit of information."

"That the horses were shod?"

"That they were all shod by the same smith in Derden. See this crescent? I know who made these horseshoes."

"That will aid in finding them."

"Most certainly." He straightened. "Now come over here."

She followed him to the opposite side of the tor and at his direction peered between two tongues of rock.

"Lean just a little farther," he said, "and look down."

"I can see the road quite clearly."

"Exactly." He drew her back and pointed to the ground. "Archers lay here. As I see it, before they even went below to attack, they lined up here and began to shoot at the caravan from above."

She nodded, picturing it.

"It would have caused a great deal of confusion in the caravan. They would have rushed for the portage bridge, which is a bottleneck."

"Yes." Leaning forward to look through the rocks again, she picked out the bridge a short way upstream.

"Great disarray," Archer continued thoughtfully. "Perhaps before they had even crossed the portage, the archers had taken out most of the caravan's guards. By then everyone would have been screaming and struggling to get as far away as possible."

She straightened. "And other thieves were already waiting for them on the other side."

"Perhaps." He eyed her sharply. "Do you remember this?"

She shook her head. "It just makes sense. Terrify them with the archers, cause disarray in the caravan, and drive them headlong into the ambush."

His gaze was now definitely hard. "You think like a general."

She stood before him, arms hanging helplessly at her sides, no memories to guide her. When she spoke, the words sounded choked. "Maybe I was."

His face tightened with suspicion. "Maybe you were part of this."

"I don't know. Oh, God, I don't know."

She averted her face as memory of the slaughter she's awakened to overtook her, as nausea rose within her, and wrapped her arms around herself as if trying to hold something in. "Those poor people," she whispered brokenly. "Those poor, poor people!"

Then a single large tear rolled down her cheek.

7

Archer insisted on descending the tor first, so that he could catch Tess if she fell. There was, however, little danger of that. Clinging to the rocks felt as natural to her as riding a horse. Clearly it was something she had done many times in the past, although she couldn't begin to imagine why.

The forest still felt dark and haunted, the air thick with threat as they descended below the canopy to the ground. Somehow she was sure woods weren't supposed to feel this way, that at some past time she had enjoyed walks among trees such as these. But she couldn't summon a visual memory to support the feeling. It was just a feeling arising out of her unreachable past.

"How long have the woods been like this?" she asked as they rode back to rejoin the others.

"You mean the absence of the animals?"

"That and the sense of threat."

He turned in his saddle, looking at her with renewed interest. "You feel it?"

"How could anyone not?"

He studied her a moment, then returned his attention forward. "Many don't. Most don't. Oh, they've noticed that the animals seem to have fled. Everyone remarks on that, and it makes them uneasy. But I've heard no one else speak of the sense of threat."

"Maybe I'm crazy."

Gray eyes settled on her once again. "Or perhaps you're more sensitive than most. I feel it, too. It began recently, with the early snows. It was as if something dark began to move over the land."

She nodded and reached back to pull up the cowl on her wool cape. The wind was snaking down her neck, chilling her. The wind.

Suddenly she lifted her head. "There was no wind here before. Do you feel it?"

He lifted his head, looking upward toward the treetops, and she followed his gaze. In woods this thick, the wind rarely built any real strength below the trees, but she felt a definite push against her back.

"It's like it's trying to drive us out," she said. Then, for just an instant, the trees bent as if before a gale.

"Hurry," Archer said, and spurred his horse.

Her own mount followed immediately, barely needing the pressure of her heels. It was as if the mare wanted to escape this forest, too.

It was a relief to emerge from the woods back onto the road, at least from an emotional standpoint. Tess felt as if she had just left a heavy, oppressive mood behind. But the instant they hit the clearing of the river gorge, the wind became even stronger, blowing from the north as if seeking to lift them and carry them away.

Upriver they could see the men of Whitewater struggling against it to lift the last few sacks of grain onto the final packhorse.

Then Archer did something so strange that Tess would wonder about it for a long time. He stood in his stirrups, stared into the teeth of the wind and said, "Too late. I already found what I wanted."

Then he settled back into his saddle, and the two of them galloped across the portage bridge to their companions.

The wind battled them every step of the way. It blew straight into their faces as they headed north toward Whitewater, until they all hunched forward against their horses' necks. The animals themselves pushed into the wind with heads down and nickered sullenly from time to time.

And with each passing league, the wind grew icier. By early afternoon, snow began to fly, a promise of greater treachery ahead as it melted and dampened the road. On the tree limbs it stayed frozen, gradually whitening them into ghostly shapes.

Young Tom drew abreast of Tess, shivering within the deep wool of his gray cloak, and said, "The men are muttering that this is no natural storm."

"Why would they think that?"

"Because it came up so sudden. Because 'tis far too early in the year."

"What do you think?"

He shrugged. "Winter came early. Why shouldn't a blizzard come, as well?"

She nodded as if she accepted what he said, but she couldn't forget the way the wind had seemed to be pushing her out of the woods, a wind that she shouldn't have been feeling. Or the way

Archer had felt moved to speak into the teeth of it, as if it were some icy beast with a mind.

The youth spoke again. "The wind makes it feel as if we're traveling up a steep hill."

"Yes. I hope the horses will make it."

"These are good horses, Lady. Sturdy and strong, Whitewater bred. They pull plows and heavy carts when they're not being ridden."

She took hope from that, although these mounts were a long way from being Clydesdales. And where in the world had that comparison come from? What was a Clydesdale?

For long minutes, despair settled over her like a crushing cloak. How could she ever hope to get on if she remembered nothing? Her life had become like rattling around in a darkened, empty room, occasionally getting a glimpse through a window at people and events that didn't always seem fully real. As if a pane of glass separated her from everything else.

But that pane of glass had protected her from none of the horror she had felt amidst the caravan's carnage, nor had it protected her from the sting of fear and doubt when Archer had suspected her of being party to the raid and she hadn't even been able to defend herself.

Those feelings had come through loud and clear, putting a fresh ache in her heart and a near wish that she had died with others in the caravan.

As the despair rode her, making her thoughts darker and darker, she felt again the icy, oily fingers of her dream, trying to pry into brain as if they sought something there.

All of a sudden she felt terror. No dream, but reality. She was awake now, yet again she felt it. Ignoring Tom, she spurred to the head of the column and found Archer. Why she should feel any trust for him after his implications on the tor, she didn't know. All she knew was that she was certain no one else in this crew could help her.

"Archer." She gasped his name into the icy wind and snow.

He turned his cowled head, his face shadowed, his eyes a dim gleam within. "Lady?"

"I feel it again. As it was in my dream last night. As if something icy and ugly is trying to get within my mind...." She trailed off, feeling ridiculous for saying such things out loud, yet certain of what she was feeling.

"'Tis an ill wind," he answered. "It carries doom on its breath. But I have no magicks to help you, Lady. You must fight it yourself."

"But how?"

He bowed his head for long moments as if pondering. Still their horses struggled forward on the muddy road, taking them ever closer to Whitewater.

"Think," he said at last, "of a warm fire. Big and bright, so warm it stings your cheeks. Imagine you are sitting in the comfort of the inn and listening to my tale."

He reached over and took her rein. "Close your eyes, Lady. See the fire and listen. I will keep you with me."

So she closed her eyes, trying to ignore that awful, icy, oily feeling in her head, and pictured the blazing fire on the hearth of her room at the inn. Archer was sitting beside her, his voice talking quietly, so quietly that the occasional word disappeared in the roar of the fire.

"'Twas a time when the gods walked this earth," he was saying. "They each brought with them their own gifts, of which I will tell you another time, and created this beautiful world of rock, tree, water and grass.

"But they found it to be an empty garden, so little by little each of them created creatures to populate their garden. They made the birds of the sky in many varieties, and the animals that walk the ground, and the fish that swim in the waters.

"But still they felt 'twas not enough."

The image of the fire in Tess's mind was growing brighter and warmer, until the sting of ice on her cheeks felt like the sting of heat. The icy grasp on her mind began to ease, just a little.

"For the wild things, you see, cannot share in the awareness of the majesty of all that has been created by the gods. They live simply, their concerns rising no higher than surviving and reproducing. Some of the gods began to think that the garden would be very empty indeed if they could not share the joy and beauty of it...."

Some of his words disappeared, but Tess hardly noticed as peace began to steal through her. It was as if she was hearing something she had long known and since forgotten, a familiar, comfortable tale.

"...created the First Born, or, in their language, the Samari. The Samari were blessed with beauty and long life, and to them the gods gave some of their powers so that the Samari might not only share in the joy of the earth but might also add to its beauty.

"And for a long time, the Samari were content. They built a city of beautiful gardens that flowered the year round. Every work they did was designed to add beauty to their city. The world was full of love and music and life."

Just as Tess began to feel that the story was going to take a downturn, someone cried out, "We're home!"

Her eyes snapped open, and she saw that they were at the lip of the valley that cradled Whitewater and its blighted fields. At once the company no longer rode in a file but instead dashed forward as fast as their steeds and packhorses would allow.

Archer laughed, and passed the rein back to Tess. "A race, Lady?"

Without even answering, she dug her heels in, and her horse took off like the wind, most likely because it, too, recognized home and wanted to be stabled and fed as quickly as possible.

The gallop exhilarated her, driving all the ugliness from her mind, and she laughed into the teeth of the wind. For the first time since her shocking awakening among the dead, she was glad to be alive.

And the last of the icy touch in her mind withdrew.

Everyone gathered in the public room at the inn after unloading their burdens into the village storehouses. Even Tess joined them, sitting in a corner just close enough to the fire to keep warm, watching and absorbing the sight of so many men enjoying themselves with ale and food and much backslapping.

And so they should, she thought. Most of them probably had no idea just how great the threats against them had been. No idea that for some reason a dark power had held back far worse than the blizzard.

Although how she knew that, she had no idea.

Sara appeared before her, a heavy tray in her arms. "Tess, you haven't had a drop to drink or a bite to eat yet. Let me bring you something."

"You're busy, Sara."

"Not too busy to see to your needs as well as the rest of these jackasses. What will you drink?"

"Tea. Just tea."

"None of my dad's ale to warm you?"

"I'm sorry, but I don't drink it."

Sara seemed to find that extremely odd, but she said nothing more. "I'll be right back with your tea, and a bowl of stew, as well."

"Thank you."

Sara was as good as her word, returning very quickly with both a pot of tea and a bowl of thick mutton stew. Just as she laid them on the table, Archer slipped into the seat beside Tess. He'd abandoned his cloak, but not his long sword. It hung by his side as if it were part of him.

"What will it be, Master Archer?" Sara asked him.

"A tankard of your father's finest and a bowl of that wonderful stew, Sara. With, mayhap, a loaf of your bread."

Sara beamed at him and moved away through the crowd.

Archer tossed a few silver coins on the table, and Tess looked at them, feeling suddenly very awkward. "I have no money to pay with," she said, ashamed.

"I've paid," Archer said. "'Tis of no concern to me. I have plenty of silver. You're my responsibility, in any event."

"Your responsibility?" She didn't like the sound of that.

"Aye." He looked at her, his haunted gray eyes seeming to peer to her very soul. "I saved your life. That entails obligations."

"I don't want to be anyone's obligation!"

He shrugged. "It makes no matter to me. But the alternative is to walk out into the storm and freeze to death. So I suggest you let me pay your way until you can make arrangements you like better."

"I shall help here at the inn."

"I imagine you could if the Widow Lawd wouldn't feel threatened by your youth and beauty."

Tess drew back, aware that she was being needlessly contrary, but equally aware that pride demanded it. "The Widow Lawd?"

"Aye, she's set her cap for our good innkeeper."

"Oh."

Archer smiled faintly. "Be at ease, Lady. We'll work something out that will salve your pride. But first you must grow well."

The reminder that her memory was only three days old deflated both her pride and her resistance. She sighed and looked down into the thick bowl of mutton stew.

"'Twas little enough we brought back today," Archer murmured. "'Tis good to see everyone celebrate, but the food we recovered won't be enough to get this town through the winter."

"No, it won't." Tess swallowed hard, then looked at him. "I need to go east."

He stiffened. "Why do you say that?"

"Because the caravan came from the east. If I was with it…perhaps someone there will know who I am."

He nodded slowly, then made a gesture with his hand. Instantly Giri and Ratha separated from the group they were drinking with and came to join them at the table.

Archer spoke. "Do any of you know who Lantav is?"

The two dark warriors exchanged looks and shook their heads.

Tess joined them. "It doesn't sound at all familiar," she said. "But then, nothing does." She tried to make it sound humorous and apparently succeeded, because the three men all smiled at her.

Archer reached into his tunic and pulled out a scorched scrap of thick paper. "I found this in the brigands' fire. It's in the Old Language. Does it look familiar?"

Each of them studied it in turn, but none remembered having seen it before.

"It's the name Lantav. There's something very strange about discovering the Old Language on a scrap of parchment found in the thieves' fire. Strange indeed. Almost no one uses the Old Tongue anymore."

Ratha spoke, his voice so soft it barely carried above the crackle of the fire, let alone the thuds of tankards and the laughter of men. Tess wasn't certain she heard him correctly. In fact, she didn't want to believe she heard him correctly.

"Except wizards."

It was as if a hush fell across the table, a bubble that seemed to insulate them from the noise around them. Tess felt her heart flutter.

"Aye," said Archer finally. "Aye. We need to leave at dawn for Derda. I smell the stench of something that has been awakened from the sleep of centuries."

Tess wanted to rebel against his words, but she couldn't. She had felt it, too, in the forest. Inside her head. Whatever her past had been, she realized for the first time, with utter certainty, that her future was going to be very different.

"I'm going, too," she told Archer. "If I must, I'll go alone."

"I'm coming, as well," said a youthful voice. For the first time they all realized that Young Tom had been standing there, listening to their every word.

Archer looked at him, his mouth opening on what appeared to be a protest. Before he could speak it, Sara appeared from behind Tom.

"And I," she said firmly.

"Now look…"

She shook her head. "Master Archer, Tom and I must go. We must bring samples of my father's ale and see what food we can purchase, what trade we might be able to arrange. Else the people of this town will starve before the spring thaw. If we can't travel with you, we'll go by ourselves with Tess. But this is urgent. I must find some trade for us. And well you know I went to Derda to trade last year. I saw you there."

Slowly Archer nodded. He looked at Ratha and Giri, whose faces might have been carved of solid ebony, so expressionless were they.

Finally he said, "We'll go to Derda together. 'Twill be safer for you. But beyond that, I cannot promise. Our paths may diverge there."

"Then Tom will bring us back," Sara said firmly. "Nor will you find me a complete burden. I can swing a sword, you know."

For the first time, Tess saw Archer's full smile. "Aye, lass, I know it well, for I taught you."

"And I taught Tom."

Tess, feeling Archer's gaze turn to her, could only shrug. "I have no idea whatsoever if I can handle any kind of weapon. I know not what I may have to offer...except..." She closed her eyes as the memory of the little girl returned. "I may have some healing skills."

"Then," said Archer, "we leave at dawn for Derda."

The predawn air was so frigid that breath turned to clouds of ice the instant it escaped the mouth or nose. The horses stomped impatiently, as if they longed to be moving to warm themselves up. Young Tom arrived a few minutes late, looking as if he'd faced an emotional struggle at home. Bandylegs helped them pack the provisions, then hugged Sara as if he feared to let her go.

Yet let her go he did, standing in the doorway of his stable, looking after them, his breath making clouds in the air.

At the gate, Downey was awaiting them. He looked at his son, a look of deep pain on his face.

"Son…"

"I have to go, Father. The town will starve without trade, and I cannot let Sara go alone. I must go."

His father nodded slowly. "I've always known you would. I just…"

His voice trailed off; he obviously neither wanted to finish his thought nor explain what he'd just said. After a long moment, he pulled a long wrapped parcel from his cloak and handed it to Young Tom.

"Father, no," Tom said.

"You need it more than I," his father replied as Tom unwrapped the package.

Tom hefted the sword within, the sword he had more than once peeked at when he was sure his parents were not looking, more than once wondered why his father kept deep in his closet.

"Forged in the hot kilns of the Panthos Mountains, was that," his father said. "And tested more than once on pain of death. It has always proven its mettle. May you always do likewise, my son."

For a long moment Young Tom said nothing. Then, slowly, he nodded and stepped forward to hug his father. The cold wind made his tears sting as they rolled down his face. Finally his father pushed him away.

"It is time for you, my son," he said. "Time for you to emerge. Be well and know always that your home and my blessings lie waiting for you."

He pulled back the huge wooden door and made way for them. Tom stole a last glance at his mother, watching from the upstairs window, before he could look no more and turned his gaze ahead.

The sun was just beginning to crest the eastern hills.

No one seemed much inclined to speak as they made their way single-file along the frosty road beside the blackened fields. A little snow had fallen overnight, but not enough to hide the destruction the early winter had brought. It looked like a haphazard attempt to wipe the slate clean.

The reddish dawn light glinted off the frost, sparkling prisms of red and yellow, and even some blue. The horses lifted their feet high, prancing and sidling as if they longed for a run. But of course they could enjoy no such delight, as a long day lay ahead of them.

The creak of leather and the jingle of harness was a familiar sound to Tess, one that made her feel as if she were hovering on the edges of some happy memory. For once she didn't strain after it, content to wait and see if anything flickered in her mind.

But no images joined the happy feeling, and the sway of her mount beneath her began to remind her of how sleepy she still was. The night had been late, sleep had resisted coming to her, and rising had been far too early.

Sara rode beside her, a rather surprising sight this morn. She had cast aside her dresses for men's garb of leathern pants, boots, shirt and vest, and over all she wore a wool cloak of a mossy-green. Beneath one edge of it, the tip of her shortsword scabbard peeked out.

No one else, however, had seemed surprised by Sara's mode of dress, so it occurred to Tess that she might have made a faulty assumption that women must always wear dresses.

But of course she had been mistaken. She almost laughed at herself as she recalled what she herself was wearing: leather pants beneath a wool tunic that fell to her ankles. Not very different, when all was said and done, from what the men around her wore, except for its fineness and color.

And in the saddlebag behind her were more clothes which had belonged to Sara's mother. All of them white, for Bandylegs' wife had favored no other color.

"Sara?"

The girl looked at her. "Yes?"

"Would you mind telling me a little about your mother?"

"Of course not." Sara smiled. "She was beautiful, nigh on as beautiful as you. And as you can see, you are of similar build. It gave me a moment's start when I first came into the room at the inn and saw you dressed thusly."

"I'm sorry."

"No need. It happened six years ago, and I've grown accustomed to her absence." Sara sighed. "I still miss her, and think of her every day, but I've learned to live with it. We don't know whether she was taken, or whether she chose to leave. Or if she's still alive. She just disappeared during the Harvest Festival, and we never found sign of her anywhere. Dad and I hoped for a long time that she might return, but…"

Sara looked down at her gloved hands for a few moments. "Well, she hasn't," she said finally. "But her memory is as clear to me as yesterday. She laughed and sang a lot. I think she was one of the happiest people I ever knew. My earliest memories are of sitting on her lap while she sang to me. And at festivals…oh, *everyone* wanted her to sing."

"Do you sing?"

Sara shook her head. "I haven't the voice for it. I take after my father mostly."

"She sings very well," Young Tom said, coming up beside them. "And she's every bit as beautiful as her mother."

Sara blushed. "Where did that come from, Tom?"

He looked rather astonished. "I don't know."

Sara eyed Tess with a twinkle in her eye. "Tom usually has very little to say around me. Sometimes I wonder if he's tongue-tied."

It was Tom's turn to blush.

"But I think," Sara said mercilessly, "that he will discover his tongue on this trip. See, it has already started!"

Tess laughed along with Sara, and, finally, a beet-faced Tom joined them.

All of a sudden, however, the sound of their laughter seemed too loud. It seemed to echo back from the hills, and when it returned it no longer sounded like happiness but something darker and uglier. The awareness seemed to strike all three of them at once, and they fell abruptly quiet.

The three of them somehow edged their mounts closer together, and Tess was not ashamed that she looked around them, half expecting to see that someone was mocking them. No other being was in sight, however, except their cloaked and hooded companions.

The sun crested the top of the hills and began to climb, but it brought no more light to the day as a mist filled the air, cold and damp. It wasn't long before the forest closed in on the narrow, icy road, and the daylight became twilight, the hour impossible to tell.

Only two days ago they had passed along this same road to collect what they could from the caravan. Today it felt entirely different, as if they had crossed some kind of threshold to a different world. Apparently Sara felt it, too, for she surprised Tess by reaching out to grip her hand.

Tess immediately looked at her. "Are you all right?"

"I'm fine," the girl answered. "But the woods are not."

Tess was inclined to agree with her. Part of her sought to rationalize the feeling as due to the eerie nature of the light owing to the mist and the thickness of the wood, but rationalization was not working this morning. She felt that something was amiss as surely as she had felt that cold oiliness in her brain only yesterday.

Just behind them, Ratha began to sing. He had a deep voice, and the tune was melancholy and wistful, although Tess couldn't begin to understand the words.

Telahnoh gahza Anahar, Telahnoh ah fohkee.

Ayanoh torhah Anahar, Telahno ah fohkee.

But whatever he sang, it seemed somehow to lighten the air around them. From time to time, from just ahead, Giri's voice would join in on what seemed to be a chorus. Even the horses joined in, timing their gaits to the song.

Ahneroh ona Anahar, Ahnferoh enta nigh,
Ahnferoh ona Anahar, Intari sola zigh.

Tess relaxed in her saddle and gave herself up to the rhythms of the journey and the sound of the music. Finally she turned to Sara and whispered, "What are they singing?"

"I'm not well skilled in their tongue, ma'am," Sara said. "But from what I can tell, it is a song of freedom."

"'Tis a longing for freedom," Archer said, having appeared at their sides. "Translation is awkward, but I shall try. 'I long to see, oh Anahar, I long for your embrace. To kiss your portals, Anahar, I long for your embrace.' And the chorus, 'May freedom bless brave Anahar, Free men we all shall be. May freedom bless brave Anahar, until the sun we see.'"

"Who is Anahar?" Tess asked.

"Not who," Archer said. "Where. It is the most holy city of the Anari people. A people long since enslaved and yearning for free air."

The pain in his voice cut to her heart, and she found herself joining in the chorus when it came round again.

Ahnferoh ona Anahar, Ahnferoh enta nigh,
Ahnferoh ona Anahar, Intari sola zigh.

Hours later they passed the place where the caravan had been attacked. They all grew tense and watchful, but nothing happened.

It was as if everything held its breath.

Awaiting a better time, thought Tess, then wondered where such a thought had come from.

Even so, they remained untroubled through the rest of the day and made camp in a dell near the river, surrounded by a protecting wall of trees. Sara insisted on cooking for them, and turned dried fish and other items into a thick, warming stew, just what was needed against the deepening cold of the night.

But it was afterward, as they all—except for Ratha and Giri— sat around the fire, waiting for sleep to call to them, that Archer began to speak.

"I have kept something from you," he said, looking at Tom, Sara and Tess. "I believe Ratha and Giri have already realized, but perhaps not."

Since Ratha and Giri were posting guard at some distance from the fire, they couldn't answer for themselves. Tess, however, could speak her own thoughts.

"How delightful," she said. "Secrets that wait until we're all deep in the woods and far down the trail."

He looked at her, firelight catching only bits of his features beneath his hood, but making his eyes glint.

"I said nothing," he replied firmly, "because there was no point in upsetting the good people of Whitewater. It's not as if they could do aught about it, nor do I believe it will ever be directed against them."

"And just what is 'it'?"

"The Bane," he said simply.

Both Tom and Sara gasped. Tess, having no idea whatsoever of his meaning, merely looked at them, then back at Archer. "Which is?" she asked.

He sighed and reached for a stick of kindling. With it, he began to draw idly in the pine needles and dirt.

Tom could no longer hold himself in. "It's an ancient poison, my lady. From the olden times, when the immortals walked the land. But I thought that was mere legend!"

"Aye, lad, and myths oft bear truth," Archer replied.

"Will you please explain?" Tess said. "You must all remember, I have no memory older than a few days."

Archer grew thoughtful, as if trying to decide where to begin. Finally he spoke, and a rhythm and rhyme gave tuneless, sorrowful voice to an ancient song.

"'The fairer day has passed away, and rage is painted on the sky, of love surpassed that may not last, and rage, and rage, upon us fast, the Bane that First may die.

"'Found cursed deep in earth asleep, and winnowed from the soil, it tears the soul and then the whole, and rage, and rage, upon us toll, the Bane that they may die.

"''Tis evil in the heart of sin, and rage is painted on the land, of spite untold and sight too bold, and rage, and rage, upon us fold, the Bane of Dederand.'"

For long moments there was no sound save the crackle of the fire. They sat as enthralled by the burden that seemed to be carried by the song.

"The poison," Tom explained, "was created to kill the Firstborn, or so the legend tells. The tales tell of a war over the love of a woman, and an evil people from Dederand who sought to slay the Firstborn and claim their divine birthright. For this, they created the Bane."

"How do you know the Bane poison has been rediscovered?" Tess's head felt as if it were whirling with snippets of information that didn't quite fit.

"Because all of the bodies of the caravan were flattening, Lady," Archer said. "Their flesh was hollowed within them. The poison,

'It tears the soul and then the whole.' Anyone touched with the poison will die and eventually simply disappear as the poison finishes its cursed work."

Sara nodded. "My mother spoke of that, when she would tell me the old tales. Only she called it Bane Dread."

Archer shook his head sharply. "Bane Dread was a sword, forged in the poison for a special evil, and the gods curse the day on which it was made." Then, in a swift movement, he rose and left them by the fire.

Tess sat stiffly, feeling as if chords deep within her had somehow been plucked, but she could find nothing else within herself. The void of her past was as big and empty as ever.

But Archer… Something about this seriously disturbed him, and for a man who had so far appeared imperturbable, that meant something.

Sinking into thought, she lowered her head and scarcely noticed that Tom and Sara quietly slipped away from the fire, too.

There was something she was reaching for, something just out of her grasp. Something in that dark emptiness of mind that she had awakened with.

But it eluded her, dancing just beyond her grasp as if toying with her. She sat on before the fire, arms wrapped around her knees, head bowed, seeking whatever it was that had stirred within her.

Because, for the first time, she felt she had touched upon a memory that was too important, too critical, to be allowed to hide behind the veils of her amnesia.

But those veils remained, seeming more like iron walls now than ever before.

9

"Lady."

The whisper startled Tess awake. She was stiff from sitting by the fire with her knees drawn up and head bowed, and for a moment her neck shrieked a complaint as she lifted her head and turned toward the whisper. It was Archer.

He put a finger to his lips, warning her to silence, then motioned with a hand that she should follow him.

He reached out, taking her hands, and pulled her to her feet. Every muscle in her body ached at the change of posture, but she bit back a natural urge to let a quiet complaint escape. Instead, with Archer still holding her hand, she let him lead her into the darkness of the wood, away from the fire. There the horses were waiting, as were Tom and Sara.

With an ease that astonished her, Archer lifted Tess by her waist onto the back of her horse.

Again he lifted his finger to his mouth, then whispered, "Run as fast as you can back to Whitewater if any ill befalls us."

He looked at Tom in particular. "See to it, Tom."

The youth nodded, though he didn't seem to like the responsibility too much. Or perhaps he didn't feel adequate. It seemed to Tess that the boy was about to grow up very fast.

She rubbed the sleep from her eyes and stifled a yawn. Beneath her the horse was unnaturally still, the only motion the pricking of its ears. The other horses were equally still, and Tess wondered crazily if some sort of spell had been cast over them.

Archer pulled Tess's cloak closer around her, covering any white that showed, making her, she realized, nearly invisible.

"Now stay," he whispered, "unless we fall."

Then he disappeared into the silence of the night. Through the curtain of the trees, Tess could just barely make out the glow of the fire, which had burned down considerably. Nothing, anywhere, seemed to move.

Had the brigands found them?

It struck her then that she must be mad, riding off into the unknown with three men she hardly knew, and a youth and a girl who had barely reached adulthood—and all in the name of finding out who she was?

The assumption that she had come from the east with the caravan and thus might find something in Derda to jog her memory was about as good as assuming she had been heading west for a reason, and that remaining in Whitewater would bring back everything.

When she lost her memory, had she also lost her judgment? Probably. Without memories, how could one lay claim to any wisdom?

Just then Sara clutched her arm so tight that even through multiple layers of wool, Tess could feel her nails. She looked immediately at the young woman and saw she was staring off to the left.

Tess followed the look and drew a sharp breath at what she saw.

Not ten feet away stood a snow wolf. Its coat was of purest white, and its eyes gleamed an eerie gold. It stood watching them, just as they watched it, drawing no closer.

A sound drew Tess's attention, and she saw that Tom was slowly drawing his sword. At once she reached out and stopped him, though she wasn't quite sure why. It just seemed to her that if they didn't threaten the animal, it wouldn't threaten them.

It was a large wolf. From Tess's hidden memory came the certainty that she had never seen a wolf as large as this. It might easily have attacked and killed them all.

Yet it stood there, simply watching. Waiting.

And it looked directly at Tess. She found herself meeting its gaze, staring into golden eyes that were like a crystal ball, that made things inside her whirl and spin, as if trying to fit together into some picture that would make sense.

Almost before she knew it, she was dismounting.

"Tess!" Sara hissed her name.

One of the wolf's ears twitched at the sound, yet it made no other move. Tess ignored Sara's concern, drawn by a power that seemed to override everything.

She reached the ground and moved away from the horses. Never once did the wolf's gaze leave her. As she drew closer, she realized that its head was nearly as high as her breast. A huge beast indeed. But somehow, no thought of fear came to her. As if mesmerized, she leaned forward and extended her hand palm upward.

The wolf's eyes darted quickly, as if gauging the distance between Tess and the others. Then its long legs moved, a slow, almost regal stride, and it came toward Tess.

For long moments they stared into each other's eyes. Deep inside Tess was an electric sparkle of recognition, though she could not identify it.

And the wolf nuzzled her palm. Reaching out, she dared to touch its head and scratch. At that, the wolf bowed to her, stretching its long front legs until its chest met the ground.

"You're a good wolf," Tess heard herself murmur as she squatted and scratched behind the creature's ear. "A beautiful, wondrous creature."

The wolf's tail gave one brief wag.

"I don't believe this," Sara said quietly. "She must be a wizard."

"Or the wolf was drawn to her for some other reason," Tom said.

Just then a clatter broke out nearby, followed by the shouts of men. Tess instantly recognized Giri's voice, then Ratha's.

The sound brought the wolf instantly to its feet, and it melted away into the woods.

"Tess!" Sara was insistent. "Get back on your horse. Now!"

Tess obeyed, recalled to reality with a sharpness that seemed almost dislocating. At once she hurried back to the horses and mounted hers.

"I don't like this," Tom said. "Why should they fight for *us?* They could be hurt. We should stand beside them."

"Archer knows what he's doing," Sara argued. "He's fought many more battles than we have. We might only hinder him."

Tom shook his head impatiently.

"Remember," Tess said, "that if we join in, he will worry about us. That might distract him."

Tom nodded unhappily, accepting the inevitable, but he drew his sword, as if determined to be prepared should any vile brigand come their way. After a moment, Sara did the same.

At that moment, a wolf's howl arose from the woods. It was answered almost immediately by other howls, in an eerie, nerve-tightening harmony. How many voices answered Tess could not tell, but it sounded like many.

She stiffened, half expecting to see the wolves come from the trees at them.

But instead, shouts came from the right, where the fighting had begun. Growls and snaps joined the cacophony, and shouts changed to shrieks of terror and agony.

"That does it," said Tom and turned his horse.

Sara reached out and stopped him. "You have your orders, Tom. Do not leave us unprotected."

Tom's obvious frustration dimmed, and then Tess watched him swell with something like...pride? Had she not been so tense, she might have laughed at Sara's easy manipulation of the lad's emotion.

More shouts reached them, along with the clang of steel on steel.

Finally none of them could take the suspense any longer, and without a word, as one, they picked their way through the darkened woods up a rise.

What greeted them was an image from Tess's nightmares. The pale moonlight washed away all color, leaving writhing white bodies on black-speckled snow in the battle's wake as three black forms steadily hacked their way forward. Archer was the tallest of the three, Tess knew, with Ratha and Giri on his flanks, their swords swirling and slicing in an uncanny rhythm that made it nigh impossible for any of their enemy to move in against them.

Like a drill team, Tess thought, then wondered whence that thought had come, for she had no idea what the words meant. Yet another wisp of memory, as dim and intangible as the clouds that scudded across the sky.

Archer and the Anari moved inexorably forward, as efficient as if they were harvesting wheat, except this wheat fought back, with equal courage if not equal skill. And sooner or later, Tess realized, their courage and sheer weight of numbers would take a toll.

Tom drew a breath, and both Tess and Sara reached over to place a hand atop his pommel.

"You would never reach them," Sara whispered.

"And if you did, in this light they would mistake you for the enemy," Tess added.

"Aye," Tom answered, a sliver of disgust in his voice.

Some part of Tess's mind registered the great exertion required by her three companions' fighting style and knew they could not keep it up for long. Their swords flew in great arcs, each scything down and forward as its neighbor swirled overhead to build momentum, like interlocked blades in a deadly and terrible machine. So long as their enemies massed in front of them, they could do naught but die. But if any should arise from those left lying behind....

The thought had no sooner formed in Tess's mind than one of the bodies behind them moved, finding his breath despite the horrific gash across his chest, somehow drawing himself to his feet and hefting a sword. With a howl that might have come from the depths of hell itself, he hurled himself at Archer's exposed back.

"Archer!" Tom screamed.

Tess knew the warning would come too late, even had Archer been able to hear it above the scream and clang of battle. The brigand had little strength left, that was obvious, but it took little strength to drive a sword into flesh. Archer stood no chance.

In that instant, a white blur burst from the woods, swift, silent and savage. The lead wolf launched itself at the man behind Archer, gleaming white fangs sinking into the flesh of his throat as it tumbled with him to the ground. It gave a mighty shake of its shoulders, and with a ripping *crack* that was audible even over the din, the man's head flew and rolled across the snow.

The other wolves had taken the brigands in the flank, and now grim courage gave way. The brigands broke ranks and fled into the woods, the now howling wolves hard upon their heels, their blood-chilling chorus broken only by the occasional dying scream.

Gradually the howls and shrieks grew distant. Then there was no sound at all, save the panting of three men who now leaned on their swords.

Tess spurred her mount forward. "Are you all right?" she demanded of the three of them.

"Thanks to the wolves," Ratha said. Two dozen corpses littered the field in various stages of dismemberment. "We were far outnumbered."

"Therefore," said Archer, straightening, "we depart *now*."

Then he looked up at the three on their horses. "You take orders very well."

Tom was having none of it. "We could not stay back when you were at risk. And the wolves…one of them came up and bowed to Lady Tess! Before they came here to attack the brigands."

Archer looked up at her, his face so deeply shadowed that it might have been carved from wood. "Indeed."

"Yes," said Tom excitedly. "It was the most wondrous thing to behold. We thought it might hurt us, but she dismounted and it came to her, nuzzled her hand and bowed down. I have never seen the like."

"I have," said Archer, and there was an unmistakable note of bitter sorrow in his voice. "Indeed I have. Now, let's pack and leave this place before those murderers return."

At least the light of the crescent moon reached the road enough to light their way. They moved as swiftly as they could, trusting to their mounts' sense of the ground. They had been on their way only a short while when snow began to fall, at first a few sparkling flakes, then a heavier swirl that caught the moonlight, brightening the night, and making the shadows beneath the trees around them seem even darker and more threatening.

The setting was so surreal, and Tess was so tired, that she half wondered if she were dreaming. But she knew she was not, for never in a dream had physical sensation seemed so real. The movements of the horse between her legs, the gentle creaking of the saddle, the fur inside the gloves she wore...all assured her that she was awake.

But her mind seemed to be dreaming anyway, and her thoughts kept returning to the huge wolf. She had felt so drawn to it, so pulled, as if some external force had directed her. She was amazed that she had not felt even the least quiver of concern or fear, especially as she approached and as it came to her.

Somehow she had known the animal offered her no threat. Somehow it had seemed as if...as if their meeting had been destined.

That feeling made her long to see the wolf once more, to confirm that the experience had been real. To confirm that she hadn't merely suffered a deranged hallucination of some kind.

But the others had seen it, too. That ought to reassure her, but somehow it did not. Deep within her, that chord had been plucked yet again, as if there was something she ought to remember.

Some words, perhaps, or some tune, that would call the wolf to her.

The thought was so strange that it shattered her preoccupation. Surely she couldn't be thinking in terms of magic? Yet that was exactly what she was doing. How could she know of such things? She wasn't even sure if there *was* such a thing as magic, though all the folk around her seemed to believe that it existed to some degree or other.

Had Tom been right when he had said she must be a wizard?

But no, that didn't feel right. It didn't feel right at all. Frowning, she hunched deeper into her cloak as the snowfall grew thicker.

Archer's voice startled her out of her unhappy thoughts. "Lady, where did you learn to call the wolves?"

She looked at him, sure her utter helplessness must be visible in every line of her. "I don't remember. I'm not sure I did anything at all. I mean…the wolf just appeared."

"But you approached it. Few would have the nerve to do that."

"I know. But…it was as if it called to me. I couldn't resist it."

"Hmmm."

Tess was quite certain she didn't like the hint of suspicion in his response, but she had no idea how to argue against it. When one wasn't even sure of one's own past, it was like standing on the very tip of a precipice, unable to take a step in any direction.

He was, she thought, by any account a striking man. What her comparison might be, she couldn't remember, but she knew good bearing when she saw it. He sat his horse with his back straight, and he walked with such confidence that she could not imagine any root or hole might dare to get in his way. His features were well-formed, too, fine yet firm. Regal, she thought. He was regal.

But his eyes… Sometimes meeting his gaze was almost painful, as if those gray eyes held secrets and sorrows older than time.

"Do you travel much?" she asked him, curiosity overcoming caution.

"All the time."

The idea shocked her. "You have no home?"

Several minutes passed in silence. "Once I had a home," he said finally. "But no more."

"That's sad."

He turned her way. "You have no home, either," he reminded her.

"That's different."

"How so?"

"I am sure I have a home somewhere. I need only to find it. Or remember it."

"How can you know that when you don't remember?"

She shook her head. "I don't know. It's a feeling deep within me. I had a home. And I'm going to find it."

"Perhaps in Derda," he said.

"Possibly. I hope it is that quick and easy."

"That is why you chose to come on this journey," he reminded her.

"Yes." She paused. "What is Derda like?"

"It is a large town, perhaps even a city, given its size. It's a commercial city where traders meet. Derda has always provided a large market for Bandylegs' ale."

"Then perhaps Sara will be able to obtain food for her town."

"'Tis a small hope, Lady," he said quietly. "Once the winter sets in, there is almost no trade to the north, because the river freezes and the deep snows make overland travel too difficult."

Tess looked ahead toward Sara and Tom, who were now riding side by side, apparently involved in some deep conversation. Or at least Sara was, for Tess could see she was talking quite animatedly, though quietly, and Tom's head was bent toward her, as if he were listening. For some reason, their youth filled her with sadness.

"When the sun rises," Archer said, "we'll stop for a few hours. We're all in need of some sleep."

"At times I think I may fall asleep in the saddle."

He looked her way, and one of his rare smiles creased the corners of his eyes. "I will catch you if you start to fall."

It was a promise, but she was unsure whether she should believe it. What, after all, did she know of these people?

Then again, what, after all, did she know of herself?

10

Tess...

The whisper seemed to entwine with her dreams, the voice almost-remembered.

Tess...

She jolted awake, sitting bolt upright to discover she had been sleeping with the rest of the party in a grassy, sun-soaked dell. Giri alone was awake, on the far side of the dell, leaning against a tree and quietly whittling at a piece of wood. The faint *snick* of his knife against the wood was almost inaudible from where she was.

Around her, in a pinwheel pattern, the others slept, not a one of them close enough to have whispered in her ear.

A dream, she thought. It was just part of a dream. It had to be. Even the horses appeared undisturbed as they grazed and rested in a cluster twenty feet away.

She rubbed the sleep from her eyes and tried to banish the feeling that the whisper had been real, that someone had been calling to her.

Rising quietly so as not to disturb her companions, she backed away from them, then began to walk the outer edges of the dell, trying to stay in the warmth of the sunlight, but not always able. There was a briskness to the air, mediated only by the sun's rays. Autumn days, she thought. Some of the trees near the edge of the clearing weren't pines but instead leafy. Their leaves seemed to hold the gold of sunlight within them.

But not even that stirred a memory within her. Uneasiness stalked her, an unwelcome companion. Yes, she had felt uneasy and even frightened almost constantly since awaking among the slaughtered caravan, but this was a new feeling. Where before she had simply been an unknown woman who had lost her memory, now she had the distinct feeling that someone, somewhere, knew who she was. Someone who had just tried to call to her.

She shook her head and paused in her pacing to stare into the trees. Ridiculous, she told herself. Logically, no such thing was possible. She had simply experienced a very vivid dream. Her reactions were scrambled because she had amnesia.

But some part of her wasn't buying that at all. Closing her eyes, she sought to define the feeling at the base of her brain, the feeling of a presence. A presence that knew her name.

Perhaps it was merely her own lost memory calling to her. But the idea didn't fit, didn't feel right. It was something else.

Then, with a snap as if something had broken, the feeling was gone. Gone as if it had never been. Even the air seemed to lighten in an instant.

She must be losing her mind.

Turning back toward the circle of her companions, she saw that they, too, were stirring, making ready to begin the next leg of their trek. Relief filled her. Activity would keep her from wandering these strange paths of mind.

The next two days passed without incident, much to everyone's relief, although Archer and his Anari friends continued to maintain a high level of alertness.

The air grew warmer, allowing them to shed their cloaks, at least when the sun was high, although signs of autumn were all around them in the colorful leaves and the browned grasses.

At night, however, it was as if a malicious chill crept over the land, lowering temperatures rapidly, until frost began to settle on everything. They huddled close around the campfire and shared tales, at first light and lively ones of recent events in Whitewater.

But then Giri, sitting with them one evening after night had cast its cloak over the world, reached forward and stirred the fire, sending a shower of sparks upward.

"Derda," he said, "is not a good place for my kind."

"Your kind?" Tess questioned.

"The Anari. We of the dark skin, though 'tis not that which causes us trouble."

"No," said young Tom eagerly, as if he had heard the story before. "Your land was conquered."

"Aye. Three generations ago. Before then my people were great builders, constructing temples and dwellings of the most magnificent kind. Stone workers, we were."

"More than mere stoneworkers." Archer's voice reached them from the darkness. "Master masons, with a skill no other race has ever possessed. And from this art came wealth and beauty."

Giri nodded slowly. "And little enough of it left since the Bozandari invaded. They razed what they could, leaving nothing but rubble behind them. Rubble and our temple. That they could not destroy, however hard they tried."

"And then?" Tess asked. The sorrow in Giri's voice was so palpable that she wanted to reach out and hug him.

"Those among us still alive were taken into slavery so that we could glorify the cities of the Bozandar kings with our masonry." In the firelight, his teeth gleamed suddenly, a small smile. "Somehow, it seems, we cannot build quite as well beyond our former borders. Some skill was surely lost during the conquest." Then he laughed, a sad laugh, but humorous all the same.

Archer squatted beside Tess, holding his hands out toward the fire. They bore, she noticed, many scars, as if he had fought many battles. "I doubt the Bozandari have the eye or the sense to notice the difference."

"Aye," said Giri. "Some small revenge, eh?"

"The day will come," Archer assured him. "The day will come when all your countrymen will be free."

"'Tis good we are a patient people," Giri replied. "But those who work with stone must be."

"Who are these Bozandari?" Tess asked, trying to fill in her picture of the world.

"Their capital," Archer explained, "sits on the Enalon Sea at the Strait of Bozan. They therefore control all trade, whether by land or sea. They grew wealthy by taxing all that passed through, then used the wealth to raise a powerful army. They long since took over Sedestano, at the north end of the sea, and Lorense, up the Adasen River from there, and more recently they took over Derda, though that was a bloodless invasion."

Giri nodded. "No reason for a fight. Derda never stood a chance."

"So now they are an empire encompassing the entire Adasen Basin, the western shores of the Enalon Sea, and south into the Green Desert and the homelands of the Anari."

"Why not Whitewater, too?" Tom asked.

Archer smiled. "So far Whitewater is protected by its position on the trade route. If the Bozandari moved against your town, Tom, they might find themselves in a clash with the northwestern kingdoms, for whom Whitewater is an essential point on the mountain caravan trail."

Tom nodded slowly.

"Which only means," Sara observed, "that eventually they'll try to take us, when they feel strong enough."

Tom sighed. "I can't imagine Whitewater being that important to anyone."

"Well, it is," Archer said. "But that is of no significance to our current mission. The important thing is to find out who is behind this attack on a caravan."

Tess's skin chilled. "To find out who is *behind* it? You don't think this was a random act?"

"Clearly not. The slaughter, the use of bane poison…" He shook his head. "We must find who is behind this. We *must*."

"But what do you think is going on?"

"I'm not sure. What I *do* know is that the bane poison disappeared…a very long time ago. Centuries, in fact. If someone has rediscovered it, they can only have done so for some reason other than robbery."

"But that wouldn't explain why they attacked a caravan with it," Tess argued. "It doesn't make sense."

"It makes sense if they were looking for someone in particular."

His gray gaze settled on her, and she felt ice reach to her very bones. "Why...why would you think...?"

There was no escaping his stare, nor the look in his eyes that seemed to say she was central to the mystery. That she might in some way be a source of great trouble.

"The snow wolf bowed to you, Lady."

The answer was as enigmatic as it was irrefutable. Within her cloak, Tess shivered in dread, and then came that strange touch in her mind, that sense that someone was trying to reach her. She shuddered again. "But I don't know *why!*"

He nodded slowly and settled cross-legged beside her. "I believe you."

She supposed she ought to be grateful for that much, at least, but the utter frustration of being unable to recall the least thing from her past, combined with the horrifying sense that Archer might be right, that *she* might have been in some way the cause of that slaughter...

He reached out and clasped her shoulder, as if to reassure her. Then, his hand still heavy on her, he began to talk.

"In long ago times, so long ago that it was before the time of men, so long ago that men think the tales are merely stories to amuse, a great schism occurred among the Firstborn, or Samari, as they called themselves in their own tongue. At that time the king wanted to step down and pass his mantle to one of his sons. But in order for one of them to succeed him, that son needed to be wed to one of the Ilduin. And thus began the troubles."

"Ilduin," said Tom, his voice excited. "Tell us about the Ilduin."

"The Ilduin..." Archer repeated the words, his voice so full of sorrow that to hear it was enough to cause the hearts of his listeners to ache. His hand fell from Tess's shoulder.

"The Ilduin," he said again, his voice stronger, "were the hearthstone of the Samari. They were women gifted with great power by the gods, and together they caused the Samari to thrive and create great wonders. Only a handful they were, never more than twenty, never less than nine. Their daughters might or might not inherit their powers, but always the powers were passed mother to daughter."

"What kind of powers?" Tom asked.

Archer's eyes looked hollow. "All the powers of creation. One might be a great healer, another might have a gift for making things grow. But together…together they were the warp and woof of the Samari world. Together they could reach out and touch the very fabric beneath creation and reshape it as needed. It was told in those times that eventually one would come, The Weaver, she who would be able to join all of their powers in herself and meld reality to her will."

"I've heard of her," Sara said. "My mother called her Theriel. The White Lady."

For a long time Archer sat in silence. "Mayhap," he said finally. "It was said that she could do great magicks without the aid of her sister Ilduin. She was in fact so powerful that one of the king's sons determined she must be his. But as it happened, she preferred and wed the other son. And thus began the war of the Samari, the war that ended the First Times. And bane poison was the tool by which it happened."

Tess spoke tentatively. "And now this poison has returned?"

"Aye." He looked at her. "It is no small magick, this poison, and to make it one must have the assistance of an Ilduin."

The silence around the flames was suddenly so profound that even the fire seemed to have lost its voice. Then Archer turned and looked at Tess.

"And," he said, "one must have great magick to avoid it."

She protested instantly. "I don't know anything about magick."

"You don't know anything about yourself."

The truth of that followed her as they mounted and rode, and kept her awake well into the night.

Had she somehow been involved in that attack? She could not find within herself even the slenderest belief that she could have done such harm.

But what if she had been the object of the attack? And what if the voice that had called to her was still trying to find her?

What if she brought all her companions to their death?

They had left the last of the hills and forest behind, and were now crossing the grasslands of the Great Adasen Basin, still traveling alongside the river, but in far more exposed country.

Tess wasn't sure if she liked that. The woods had guarded depths in which any kind of attacker might hide, but out here hiding places were few, only an occasional scattering of bushes or trees.

"Derda lies not far ahead," Ratha told Tess as he rode beside her for a while. He alone of Archer's original party did not seem to be suspicious of her. "Another day, perhaps."

"Good." After six days in the saddle, she was beginning to feel sore. "I'm not accustomed to riding such long distances."

He smiled at her. "You will grow used to it, Lady."

"Where does your country lie?"

He pointed to his right. "Far, far to the south, beyond Bozandar, in a land where the kiss of the sun is a daily blessing and the desert blooms green in the spring. A land of dangerous beauty, where rugged rock faces whisper with the morning breeze. Nearer the sea, the lowlands are lush and sweet year-round. The lowland Anari are a bit paler to our eyes, though perhaps not to yours. My people come from the high desert, where it is said that on a clear night, one can touch the moon. For centuries my people walked among that land, waiting for the rock to invite us, then gathering and shaping its invitation to our needs."

"So you didn't just quarry from the mountains?"

"Every stone has its own nature, Lady. A good mason waits for the stone to find him."

She nodded. "It's not something I seem to know anything about. But then, I seem to know very little about anything."

He flashed a gleaming smile. "Your memory will return."

"I hope so. I feel so rootless." She hesitated, then asked, "Do you think Archer is right? That I may be a threat?"

"I feel no evil in you, Lady. But I think it may be necessary for us to protect you."

"I don't want anyone to get hurt on my account."

He nodded, his eyes as dark as a moonless night. "That may not be your choice, Lady."

"I know." She stared glumly at a spot between her mount's ears. "Unfortunately."

 **11**

Giri rode out to scout when they made camp just before nightfall. When he returned, it was dark, and a frigid wind was blowing out of the north. With no trees to block it, it whipped around them and cut through their clothing like an icy scythe. They huddled close to the firepit Tom and Ratha had dug, waiting for one of Sara's miraculous stews to finish simmering. But even the delight of smelling the stew was denied them as the bitter wind snatched the aromas and carried them away into the night.

After seeing to his mount, Giri joined them.

"The early winter," he said as he knelt by the fire and rubbed his hands together to warm them, "has taken its toll here, as well. I found abandoned farmsteads and crops dead in the fields."

Archer muttered a word that sounded like an oath.

"But as near as I can tell, no one follows us. Those who attacked us in the woods evidently have no stomach for following us into the open."

Archer nodded. "We might thank the wolves for that." His gaze fell on Tess, once again making her uneasy, as if she had committed some sin she could not remember. Perhaps, for this man, her simple existence was sin enough.

"They may have ridden past us into Derda," Archer said. "Those that remain. We'll need to keep a sharp eye out for them while we try to discover who sent them."

Giri nodded. "Although, as time passes, I find myself more interested in *why* they were sent than in who sent them."

"I suspect the answer to both questions lies in the same place, my friend."

With their stomachs eventually full of hot fish stew, they all lay down to sleep as best they could in the cold. After a little while, Tess heard a rustle near her and opened her eyes to find that Sara was coming to lie beside her.

"Cold?" Tess asked, keeping her voice low, so as not to disturb the others.

"Aye, but who isn't?" Sara whispered back. She lay down facing Tess, and between them a small pocket of warmth began to grow. "I told you how my mother disappeared?"

"Yes. I'm so sorry about that, Sara."

"'Twas a long time ago, Tess. But…I grow troubled."

"About what?"

"It's…" Sara's whisper trailed off into a sigh. "You will think I'm mad."

"I don't see how you can be any more mad than I am."

Sara's smile gleamed in the starlight. "You are not mad at all."

"Then neither are you."

A soft little laugh escaped Sara. "Well then, I shall tell you. But you *will* think me mad. It's that…well…the farther we travel?"

"Yes?"

"The more I...feel...my mother is still alive."

The words came out in a rapid rush; then Sara fell silent, as if awaiting judgment.

Tess reached out and gripped Sara's hand. "I hope she is."

"I know I'm being foolish...."

Tess squeezed her hand. "I won't say that, Sara, and neither should you. In fact...in fact, I've had the feeling off and on that someone is calling to me. We may both be experiencing different versions of the same thing."

"Whatever it is," Sara said almost inaudibly, "it must be some form of magick. We need to keep together, Tess. It might be some evil calling to us."

"I know. But I have no way to judge. Without memory..."

Now it was Sara who squeezed *her* hand. "I have memory, and yours will return. I'm sure of it. But if we keep together and watch out for one another, we'll be all right."

Clinging to that thought, and to each other's hands they finally fell asleep.

Tess's sleep was fitful, however, filled with strange images of golden threads all crisscrossing each other, and voices without faces that called her name. One face did float into her dreams, however. It was a face almost identical to Archer's, yet his hair was blond, and the lines that etched his face were not those of sorrow and weariness, but of something darker and more frightening. He was looking for something, and Tess curled herself into an invisible ball, terrified that he might see her.

Then the voice called to her again, this time gentle and reassuring. *"Tess..."*

And with that she somehow fell into a more restful slumber.

* * *

By midmorning it was evident that something was seriously wrong in Derda. The walls of the city came into view, but around them were huddled dark masses, almost as if in a siege, and smoke seemed to be billowing from somewhere to the east, carrying with it the smell of burnt flesh. When the north wind allowed the smell to reach them, the horses grew nervous and whinnied as they tried to sidle away from it. The riders pulled the corners of their cloaks over their faces, trying to keep the stench out.

Finally Archer drew rein, and everyone stopped behind him.

"Something is terribly wrong here," he said. "I'm not sure we should go any closer without first scouting."

"Have they been attacked?" Tom asked.

"I think not. Judging by the abandoned farmsteads Giri found, I suspect famine has driven many more to the city than the city can contain. There may be illness...."

Tess spurred forward, suddenly sure of herself, as she hadn't been since the moment of awakening. "If there is illness, I must go. I can help."

Archer studied her, as if trying to read the future in her face. At last he spoke. "I cannot allow you to go alone." Then he looked around at the rest of the party. "But you must all be aware that if pestilence has struck the city, we have no protection."

"Keep your mouth and nose covered with your cloak," Tess said. "And wash your hands any time you touch something. But if many are sick, then helping hands are too few."

"I know something of healing," Sara said. "I will go with Tess."

"I, too," said Tom, who would rather have his head cleaved from his shoulders than be separated from Sara.

"Then we all go," said Archer.

Ratha and Giri nodded agreement.

Tess looked around at them all and felt her heart swell with warmth toward them. She had been blessed to fall in with these people. Singularly blessed.

"Thank you," she said. "Thank you." Then she spurred her mount toward the city, knowing nothing else but that she must help the ill.

The picture grew uglier the closer to Derda they drew. Around the walls a tent city had sprung into being, but these were no weathertight tents. They were built of pieces of cloth strung over ropes, or raised in the middle by various implements. None was tall enough for a man to stand beneath, and the ground all around had been trampled to dust and mud.

The faces of those occupying the tent city were hopeless and silent, and more gaunt than they should have been.

"There is something grievously wrong," Archer said. "Even with the barren fields here, there should be food aplenty. Even untilled, the rich soil of the Basin grows more in a year than could be consumed by all the Bozandari peoples. No one should be starving, except perhaps by men's greed."

It grew worse the closer they came to the city's open gates. Death carts began to pass them, with bodies laden high, headed toward the smoky area in the east.

Finally Archer bent in his saddle and stopped one of the men leading a cart. "Friend," he said, "what terrible thing has happened here?"

"The early winter. Famine." The man's gaze was hollow, his tone flat. "Our fields are barren, and that which we did harvest carries death within it. Our stores are empty." He looked at the party, one after another. "Take my advice. Leave now. This place has fallen into evil times."

But the party continued toward the gate, and Tess felt sorrow weighing ever heavier on her heart as she saw children too listless to play simply lying or sitting beside mothers who didn't move.

Nor did matters improve within the city. Every street was lined with beggars who held out bowls and pled for something to eat.

"I would empty our packs," Sara said, "but none of what we carry can be eaten without cooking."

"Save what we have," said Archer. "We'll find a better way of using it to help."

To Tess's eye, it seemed that the primary problem was starvation and its accompanying illnesses, but not a pestilence of any kind. Yet. That would come soon enough if nothing were done to improve matters.

They reached an inn at last, and there found not only rooms, but an innkeeper and his family who seemed to be avoiding the starvation that surrounded them. The sight of the portly man's good health sparked Tess's anger, but she bit back words of reproof.

He greeted them warmly, apparently glad to see paying guests. "No one comes to Derda anymore, since the famine," he told them as he bustled them upstairs. "Only the starving in search of food."

"It seems," said Archer, "that the situation has grown dire very fast."

The innkeeper paused as he was unlocking a door. "Aye, 'twas fast indeed. As near as I can tell, the distant field hands were the first to fall ill from their harvest. And without them to work… We started living on our stores and whatever the local farms might produce. But then came the killing frosts. By that time we had little enough left in our stores, and the people began to come from everywhere seeking food."

He opened the door and led them into a private parlor. "The room for the ladies is through that door." He pointed to a door off the parlor. "The gentlemen will be across the hall." He handed them keys. "I can feed you, but only lightly. The repasts I used to serve my guests are no longer possible."

Archer nodded. "Does anyone know why the crops are making people sick?"

The innkeeper hesitated and cast a nervous eye about. "I'm sure I don't know. Perhaps someone else might have an idea." Then he slipped out quickly, as if he feared another question.

Archer turned to Ratha and Giri. "Take care of our mounts, and bring all our possessions up here. Then you and I will begin to search out this mystery."

The Anari nodded and left the parlor. Tom went along to assist.

Archer turned to Tess and Sara. "Ladies, please remain here for now. We need to know more before you can safely help anyone."

Tess started to protest, but Sara touched her arm. "We'll remain here. For now."

After Archer had left, Tess turned to Sara. "These people need help now!"

"I know," Sara said. "But what can we do with any surety if we know nothing of the situation? And…" She hesitated. "Tess? Don't you feel it?"

It? Tess flopped into a nicely padded chair near the fire, seeking the first real warmth she had felt since leaving Whitewater. Sara took the chair opposite her, and for a while the two of them simply soaked up the heat until they felt warm enough to doff their cloaks.

Closing her eyes as the warmth began to relax her entire body, Tess tried to empty her mind of all the concerns that had filled it since she first saw the state of affairs in Derda. For someone who'd had little enough to occupy her thoughts not so long ago, that proved to be surprisingly difficult.

The call she had been feeling seemed to have vanished, and she was surprised to realize that she missed it. In some strange way it had been almost comforting.

But in that moment she realized that something else had taken its place. Not as obvious as what she had felt before, as if the oily blackness had developed some finesse. But it was there, lurking in some tiny place, and from it radiated a darkness that seemed to shadow this entire town.

Her eyes popped open. "My God! What is it?"

"'Tis the worst evil I've ever felt," Sara replied. "What has happened here was done for a purpose."

Tess rose from her chair and strode to the mullioned window, looking out on the streets below. Everywhere her eye met horror. "Who could do such a thing? And why?"

Sara had no answers. A few minutes later the men returned, laden with saddles and packs, which they set in a corner of the room. All of them then headed for the fire, seeking the same warmth that Tess and Sara had.

"Something unnatural is involved here," Archer said, echoing the thoughts Sara and Tess had shared. "It is as if the earth itself decided to kill these people. They speak of farmers around the basin baking bread that burned their bellies and brought sores to their faces. Yet when Ratha and Giri and I passed through here just a few weeks ago, on our way to Whitewater, it seemed a land of plenty."

Tess spoke. "Perhaps the food is being stolen? Taken downriver?"

Archer shook his head. "Lady Tess, imagine rippling field upon rippling field, for as far as the eye can see in any direction, broken only by the occasional farmhouse or village. That is the Great Basin. In the summertime, it is like looking upon a great, pale green sea. All of the Bozandari together could no more steal it than they could steal a mountain, or an ocean."

Giri spoke. "It seems we may have passed through too soon, my lord."

It was the first time Tess had ever heard anyone call Archer that, and it seemed that for a moment he stiffened, as if rejecting the title. Or as if concerned what others might think upon hearing it.

"Mayhap," he said finally. "Certainly we are out of touch with what has happened in these parts. Perhaps malignant disease spread among the fields, malice bred into the crops themselves. Nothing else could destroy so great a bounty."

He paused, as if tracing the deadly plague in his mind's eye. "It would have begun along the rim, where the earth rises up into the hill country. The harvest comes early there, brought in before the cold strips the fields. Those who grew sick would have moved into the valley for help, riding the tide as the disease washed over the fields. Sooner or later, they would all arrive here, those that survived. Too many hungry mouths, too little food. And the healthy fields that remained would have been left to wither for want of hands to glean them."

"And," said Ratha, "the people here could not have prepared their larders for the winter. The wagons came laden not with rich, warm grains, but with sick, hungry mouths."

Archer squatted before the fire and stirred it, causing the flames to leap higher and renewed warmth to spread through the room. "The thing that troubles my mind, however, is the scale of it all. Crops blight, yes, but not in such great numbers, and not so quickly. Something swept these people in here...to die."

Sara and Tess exchanged looks, but for some reason neither of them mentioned the feeling they had, that some dark power loomed over Derda.

Perhaps they both felt foolish about talking of such things. Or perhaps they feared that mentioning their feelings too often would draw unwanted attention from the looming darkness.

Tess was not sure why, but her tongue remained motionless, as if cloven to the roof of her mouth.

12

Early in the morning, the men set out in various directions to learn what they could of affairs in Derda and the surrounding area. Archer's stated mission was to visit the blacksmith who had shod the horses of the brigands who attacked the caravan.

Left on their own at the inn, Tess and Sara decided they weren't about to sit by the fire and do nothing.

"After all," Tess said, "I was the one who insisted we come into town to help these people. In conditions like these, with so many malnourished people crowded together, it's only a matter of time before disease starts to sweep through the population...if it hasn't already."

Sara agreed wholeheartedly. "Let's go out and see if we can find some other women who want to help us."

"We need to teach them," Tess agreed. "Sterile procedures. Cleanliness." Her own knowledge of the subject surprised her momentarily, given that she could remember nothing about her past.

Then she realized that there were many things she remembered how to do, from speaking to clothing herself, even though she could remember no particular details of her past.

And for one moment, with a deep pang, she remembered the child's life she had tried to save. Perhaps this time she could accomplish more.

They spoke first to the innkeeper about what they hoped to do. He proved surprisingly helpful.

"'Tis a good idea," he said at once when he heard their plan. "I've been worrying mightily about all the vagrants in the streets, but mostly about the young ones. If disease starts among them, none of us will be safe."

A pragmatic, self-centered view, but useful nonetheless.

He drew them a little map on the back of a tattered piece of parchment. "Go see this woman, Mistress Alconti. She's known as a healer and will probably be able to help you get started."

The streets were even worse than Tess remembered from the evening before, perhaps because people had come out from the places where they had been hiding from the chill and now sought the sun with fervor. They wouldn't get much of it, for already dark clouds were building to the northeast, promising either frigid rain or snow before the day was over.

As they walked farther into the center of the city, the homeless began to thin out noticeably. It seemed that some effort was being made to keep the streets clear of them near the larger homes and businesses. Though never a beautiful city, Tess could tell it had once been a scene to warm heart and hearth. Thatched roofs smeared with pitch glistened deep yellow against the sunlight over sturdy, stone cottages. Like Whitewater, every home had its garden, and perhaps only that had kept these people alive thus far. Nearer the city center, the homes were larger, and likewise their gardens. The people here might well have grown enough to keep their families alive through the winter, if they could ignore the suffering of those around them, and if their guards could prevent the poor from stealing. So far, they had managed. It was as if they had passed through a gate beyond which the ill and starving were not permitted.

"Typical," muttered Tess under her breath. Though how she knew it was not unusual for the wealthier to protect themselves from the sight of the poor, she could not say.

The people about on these streets were healthier and better fed. Occasionally they passed soldiers who eyed them suspiciously from haggard faces, then let them pass.

At last they came to a house set by itself among flower gardens that must have been beautiful in the spring and summer but now bore the forlorn gaze of autumn. This house was surrounded by a gate, but the gate was open, and a slow stream of sickly people passed through it, headed for a pavilion on the south side of the house.

Instinctively Tess and Sara followed them, and found an older woman directing a handful of other women in the treatment of sores and other illnesses.

"Mistress Alcanti?" Tess asked.

The older woman turned at once to them, her graying hair tumbling from a knot on the back of her head, her face lined with fatigue and sorrow. "I am Landra Alcanti. But you'll have to wait your turn, ladies."

"We haven't come for healing," Tess replied. "We have come to help. In fact, we are hoping you can help us to find enough people to deal with the afflicted in the outer reaches of the city and beyond the walls."

The woman regarded them with jaded eyes. "There is more to

be done than there are hands to do it. And precious little to help too many."

As she spoke, she drew Tess and Sara away from the pavilion, pausing once to make a remark about a dressing one of her helpers was applying. When she had brought them to the front door of her house, she asked them to come in.

Inside, all was pleasant, with stone floors, and beautiful tapestries covering the sandstone walls. The entry hall soared above them for two stories, and a stairway curved upward to the rooms above.

"This is a beautiful house," Tess said sincerely.

"Aye, and far more than I need, but it is passed through the family and will go to my children, if they survive this plague." Mistress Alcanti shook her head sadly and guided the two women into a sitting room off the entry hall. "I'm sorry I can't offer you refreshment, but apart from the small amount of food my household will need for the winter, I have given the rest away."

For the first time since arriving in Derda, Tess felt a warm, almost beatific touch in her mind. "You are a good woman, Mistress Alcanti."

Mistress Alcanti waved her hand dismissively. "One does what one should, I always say. Please call me Landra. And you are?"

"Tess Birdsong and Sara Deepwell from Whitewater," Sara answered promptly. "I'm Sara."

"Any relation to Bandylegs Deepwell?" Landra asked.

"He is my father."

Landra Alcantari paused, studying Sara, then clapped her hands with pleasure. "Oh my...you were the little girl pulling at your mother's skirts as she bustled through the rooms. In my younger days I often stopped at the inn. Now look at you. Your father always made us so welcome, and he was such a good storyteller. How does he fare?"

"He fares well," Sara answered with a smile. "And he still tells a good story."

"And your mother, dear woman?"

Sara's face shadowed. "She disappeared six years ago."

Landra's face fell. "Oh, my dear girl, I am *so* sorry! I'd heard nothing about that. She was the kindest soul."

Sara thanked her and looked down at her hands for a few moments, as if trying to gather herself. Meeting someone who had known her mother seemed to have shaken her from her usual composure.

"Well," said Landra presently, lowering her voice, "I brought you in here for reasons beyond mere courtesy. I need to warn you."

Tess looked sharply at her. "Warn us?"

"Yes. I don't know what has really brought you here, but you cannot leave soon enough. I can tell by looking at you that you haven't truly been touched by what is going on here…but I fear if you stay long, it will put its mark on you as it has on nearly everyone."

"Mark?"

Landra sighed and looked around, as if to be certain no one listened. "There are so many rumors afoot these days that one hardly knows what to believe. But the one I hear most often is about a wizard to the east who has cast a spell of death and disease."

She leaned forward, lowering her voice even further. "There are things that some of us can sense. In you I sense the ability to feel these things, too. Am I wrong?"

Sara and Tess exchanged glances. Finally Tess answered, "We sense…something."

"Aye, I thought so. It was something about you."

"What is it?" Sara asked.

Landra shook her head and spread her hands. "I am not certain. It...or perhaps *they.* I cannot tell. Sometimes I think it is one evil shadow cast by one evil mind, then I sense another mind and I am no longer certain. I do know that..."

She hesitated again, and finally rose and went to close the door of the sitting room. When she returned to them, she drew her chair closer. "Ladies, you must promise not to speak of this in Derda. It is something only I know. But someone must leave this town with the knowledge, because I fear this evil will spread."

"What evil?" Tess asked.

"Most of our governing council is dead. They appeared to die of natural causes, and when I saw the first of them, so I thought, too. But when I was called to see the rest of them after they died... I knew it was nothing natural that had brought them to their end. I believe they were murdered, though I don't know how or by whom.

"And of the council members who remain...when I go into their presence I feel as if a dark shadow moves over my vision. Something more than famine and illness has infected Derda."

When Tess and Sara left Landra Alcanti's house a short while later, they felt they had learned much without learning anything at all.

"It is that shadow I mentioned to you earlier," Sara said to Tess. "But it does us no good if we don't know what it is."

"I know."

The promised storm was blowing in, whipping through the streets and stirring up dust devils. The cold it brought was an icy bite, causing them to shiver within their cloaks. As they passed from the wealthy part of the city toward the inn, they noticed again that many of the homeless had disappeared and the streets were clearer. There must have been warmer niches within which to hide from the wind, which was a good thing, because the streets seemed to funnel and strengthen it.

"I doubt this would be a good time to go outside the walls," Sara said sadly, her words snatched from her mouth as soon as they started to emerge. "Everyone will be hunkered down."

"Tomorrow morning we will start to help, first thing," Tess promised.

But it wasn't even that long. A block from the inn they came upon a woman with two young children. She was weeping, and begged them for help.

"My boys," she said. "My boys are so ill, and the cold will kill them."

Neither Sara nor Tess hesitated. They each scooped up a child and told the mother to come with them.

At the inn, their host was less than pleased.

"You can't bring them in here," he said. "They're ill! And they can't pay!"

"I'll pay for them," Sara said.

"Nor have you any other custom to worry about," Tess told him sharply. "Make way before these boys die."

He grumbled but stepped back, allowing them entrance to the public room. There they placed the boys on one of the tables near the fire. Their mother stood nearby, still weeping.

"Gruel," Tess said to the innkeeper. "These boys need gruel. Make it thin."

Grumbling even louder now, he stomped away.

Gently, Tess and Sara unwrapped the boys from the tattered

blankets in which they were swaddled. They were appallingly thin, their bones showing in their arms and legs, their ribs protruding. Their lips were covered with sores, which had broken, run and finally scabbed over.

"We've had no food for more than a week," their mother sobbed. "And before that it was barely more. Their father...their father was killed when—" A sob broke her voice. "When some men stole our last measure of grain. He tried to stop them...."

Sara went to her and helped her to sit in a chair near the fire. "Warm yourself," she said gently. "There will be food for you, too."

Tess was looking over the boys carefully, her mind automatically cataloging the symptoms. While the sores were ugly, they were not born of infectious disease. They were the signs of severe malnutrition. The boys themselves watched her passively, as if they didn't have the energy to make even a small sound. No more than five or six, they looked even younger now. Her heart felt like breaking.

"Hot water," she said to Sara. "And dressings. We must clean these wounds before they become infected."

Sara hurried off to do her bidding, and from the rear of the inn came sounds of disagreement. Nonetheless, Sara returned with a sheet under one arm and a kettle full of water. "The gruel will be here soon."

The water was warm, apparently having already been sitting by the kitchen fire, but Sara set it near the blaze on the public room's hearth, and soon it was steaming. Together she and Tess tore sheets, washed sores with water as warm as the boys could stand, dabbing gently until the boys' mouths could open freely.

"I need to make some salve," Sara said. "My mother taught me herbs and mosses to mix to prevent infection. But first I must find them."

"Not now," Tess said as the wind battered at the inn's windows and the clatter of sleet joined it. "For now the cleaning will be enough."

The gruel arrived, three bowls of it, but the boys' mother left hers untouched as she tended to her sons, coaxing them to drink each spoonful.

Tess stood back watching, feeling something stirring deep within her. But this time it was not the sense of darkness and evil she had earlier felt. This was a brighter, lighter feeling, a vibration like the note of a musical instrument. It thrummed within her and seemed to grow, filling her.

Almost before she knew what she was doing, she approached the boys again and laid a hand on each of their mouths. As she did so, words she didn't recognize passed her lips.

"Sa lassi mar loda."

Sara turned to stare at her, but Tess was in the grip of something she could not control.

"Sa lassi mar loda."

Then, when she had finished touching the wounds, the thrumming inside her eased and a fatigue almost too great to bear fell upon her. She collapsed into a chair, and the world went away.

Archer's day proved nearly fruitless, as did those of Tom and the Anari. Everywhere they went, they were greeted with suspicion, although when Derda had become so suspicious Archer could not imagine. A trade town, it should have been accustomed to the comings and goings of strangers, but not now.

No one seemed to know what had become of the smith whose crest was a crescent moon. His shop was now a mass of seething humanity seeking warmth near the furnace that had once tempered steel. Those who had the strength to answer questions had no information to share, and none of the surrounding shopkeepers seemed inclined to answer.

Toward the end of the afternoon, Archer realized that he was being followed by a pair of town guards. He decided he'd stirred up enough buzz for one day and headed to the fountain where he'd promised to meet Giri, Ratha and Tom. Only Tom awaited him.

"They left me here," Tom told Archer as the cold wind of the storm whipped about them. Sleet came in a stinging wave and cut at their faces. They drew up their hoods. "Giri said he could find out more among the slaves, and that it would be easier without me."

"He may be right," Archer answered. "I've certainly learned nothing. Let's go back to the inn before the guards decide to clap us in irons. They've been trailing me for more than an hour now."

Tom nodded, and with heads bowed into the wind, they headed toward the inn.

"I doubt the brigands came from here," Archer told Tom as they strode along the streets.

"Me too," Tom said. "I doubt any of the people here are strong enough to have done such a thing. Even those who look better fed don't seem to be well."

"I've noticed. And people are fearful in such an unusual way. I swear some of them seemed to think the wind could hear their words."

"Aye," said Tom. "This entire city feels haunted."

Archer ruminated for a minute. "That is an excellent choice of word, Young Tom. That is exactly how this place feels. Haunted. By evil."

13

Tess awoke to find herself being carried up the inn stairs by Archer. As her eyes fluttered and she stirred, he murmured, "Shh. I'm just taking you up to your room."

"What happened?" she asked groggily.

"I thought perhaps you could tell me. Sara said you fainted."

He pushed his way through the parlor door. A fire was burning on the hearth. "Do you want to sit before the fire or go to bed?"

"By the fire, please." His arms were strong and comforting as they carried her, and she realized with a sudden twist of despair that it was the first real comfort she had felt since awaking among the slaughter of the caravan. All too soon he set her on the padded chair before the fire and withdrew. It was as if she had briefly known the warmth of the walls of home, only to have them snatched away, so that she found herself standing alone once again on an icy pinnacle.

She tried to convince herself that she was being foolish, but her throat tightened anyway, and her eyes stung with tears she refused to shed. The day had been long and difficult, she told herself. She was simply tired. She wasn't truly feeling despair.

"Lady."

Reluctantly Tess looked at Archer. Even his visage was coming to signify comfort to her, and that was a dangerous thing, because she had clearly seen how reluctant he was to fully trust her.

"Lady," he said again, "Sara tells me…she said you spoke strange words as you touched the sick children. Right before you fainted."

Tess lowered her head. "I…I don't know what exactly I did or said. I have only a vague memory."

"Aye?" He squatted before her, looking up into her face, giving her no means of escape. "What happened? What do you remember of it?"

Tess shook her head and closed her eyes, trying to recall. "It was… Oh, it sounds mad!"

"My definition of madness may be narrower than you think. Tell me."

She had a sudden urge to tell him to stuff his head in a bucket. It wasn't as if she'd done something purposefully. At least…

That was when a spear of fear stabbed her. Her eyes snapped open. "It was as if…as if a hum started inside me. I could feel it. And this tone sounded in my head, so beautiful and musical. I was compelled to reach out and touch the children's wounds, to speak those words. My God, Archer, did someone take over my mind?"

His expression was grim. "If someone did, it was not for ill, which is more than I can say for the rest of what is happening in this town. The children are already feeling better."

He rose and took two short steps across the room before turning with a swirl of his cape. "Sara says you haven't eaten all day.

She'll be up soon with a meal for you. You don't look well, Tess. You look as ashen as some of the people on the streets."

"If I do, it's from the cold. It was terrible out there."

"No," he interrupted. "It is not from the cold." Once again he came to her and knelt before her, this time taking her hands. "Listen to me, Lady. There are many kinds of magicks in this world, though few know how to use them. They are left from times long forgotten, but they are still there. Some have the ability to channel the magick and suffer not at all for it. Others must use their own life force. It seems to me that whatever you did downstairs, you drew on your own strength to do it."

She nodded, understanding him but not at all sure she believed him.

"Heed this warning, Lady. If you must draw on your own strength to do something, you risk your life. You must not do it again too soon. And you must learn to take control of it. Otherwise, next time, you might lose more than your memory."

He gave her hands a quick squeeze, then left the parlor.

Alone with her own thoughts, Tess discovered that she knew only one thing for sure: somehow she had fallen into madness, and the whole world had fallen with her.

Magick? How could she possibly know any magick?

And if she had any magick, why hadn't she been able to save that poor little girl's life?

Bowing her head, bent by fatigue, fear and hunger, she gave in to tears.

Sara entered the room twenty minutes later, bearing a tray. She started chattering the instant she laid eyes on Tess. "Can you believe it? Our lovely host has fired all his kitchen maids and serving maids because he didn't want to have to feed them! Of all the heartless creatures."

Tess wiped furtively at her cheeks. "I think he's a confused man."

"Well, Archer silenced him with a few gold pieces, and the woman and her two boys will have a room for now, at least, and some warm food in their bellies. But, my lady, we would never tolerate such in Whitewater. What we have, we all share in times of hardship."

She set the tray on a small table. "Can you eat something, Tess? You really need the nourishment."

Tess nodded and rose to go sit at the table. "Have you eaten?"

"Most certainly. The others are below eating, also."

"I'm sorry you have to take care of me so much."

Sara laughed. "Oh, you are just so much trouble, needing a little food every now and then."

Tess felt herself smiling back. The despair she had been feeling began to fade, especially as warm soup and fresh bread began to fill her stomach.

Sara sat across from her and poured them each a cup of tea. "I don't know what you did down there, Tess, but those children…well, it's very nearly a miracle. They're eating like hungry little piglets and already getting into mischief."

A pang of panic struck Tess. "I did nothing."

"I saw you do it," Sara said firmly. "But I won't trouble you about it. Archer says that you mustn't use your magick very often or you will grow ill and die. The way you fainted! My word, I swear my heart stopped."

But then, as if realizing she had just done what she had promised not to do, Sara squeezed Tess's hand. "I'm sorry. Enough of that. When you get your memory back, such things will sort themselves out. In the meantime, we shan't worry about them."

As if Tess could do anything else. A power she didn't know she had and didn't know how to control was in and of itself enough to worry about. But the black oily feeling at the back of her brain was growing again, too, as if taking advantage of her current physical weakness. What was that all about? How did it fit with what everyone was saying she had done for those children?

And who the hell was she?

But Sara was determined to keep her distracted with chatter, and Tess was more than willing to let her. She listened to the update from Archer and the others, which seemed to indicate they had as yet learned nothing. The food filled her with warmth, and finally with a sense of well-being, and she was able to settle again before the fire and listen to the storm rage outside as if it had nothing at all to do with her.

But deep within, some voice said it had everything to do with her.

The storm worsened throughout the night, sleet beating angrily at the windows as if the very heavens raged at the world. The old inn, built of wood in days almost forgotten, creaked before each blast of the storm's icy breath and occasionally shuddered as if it, too, were trying to hunker down.

Unable to sleep, in part because of the fury outside, and in part because she couldn't stop thinking of those outside in this weather, particularly those beyond the town walls who wouldn't even be able to keep their ragged tents from blowing down, Tess rose and dressed. Her mind filled with images of the hundreds, if not thousands, who would be dead by morn.

Torn by the anguish the very thought gave her, she crept out of the room, trying not to wake Sara, who slept in the trundle bed.

But apparently Sara could not sleep, either. "Where are you going?"

"To save what lives I can."

"Wait for me."

Sara dressed swiftly, an easy thing to accomplish when, for the sake of warmth, she had worn most of her clothing to bed. Together the two left the parlor and headed downstairs.

The fire burned low in the public rooms, and no one stirred. Tess paused to open the wood box and load more logs onto the fire. Almost as soon as they touched the coals, they ignited.

"What is your plan?" Sara asked.

"To bring as many people off the street and into these rooms as I can."

Sara laughed quietly. "Our host will probably throw us all out."

"Then let him try."

Chin set, Tess marched to the door and with Sara's help lifted the heavy bar. At once the door blew open, as if the wind had been but waiting for an opportunity to reach inside.

Together they stepped out into the street, glazed now with ice. At first they could see no one, but as they slipped and slid their way to the narrow passages between buildings, they began to find shivering bundles of people all huddled together to share what warmth their own bodies made.

"Come to the inn," Tess told them, pointing. "I have left the door open. Come to the inn, and bring any others you find."

Aching, shaking bodies began to move as directed, helping one another to balance on the ice, to bring along children, who seemed worst off of all.

The two women continued their mission until they, too, could not stop shivering and their hands felt as numb as the ice that coated everything. Only then did they make their way back to the inn, bent into a glacial wind that seemed determined to stop their progress.

"By the gods!" said Archer's angry voice, and suddenly strong arms were around them both, sweeping them to the inn's door. "You could have died out here! Why did you not wake us to help?"

Neither Sara nor Tess could speak a word. Their mouths seemed unwilling to obey any command from their brains.

But Archer seemed to expect no answer. With his great strength, he half carried them both back to the inn and through the door into the public rooms. Behind them, someone slammed the door shut and barred it.

Tess barely had the strength to look around her, but she saw that the public rooms were crowded, until hardly another soul could be squeezed in. The fire leapt in lively warmth, and gaunt faces looked back at her with such gratitude that her heart almost broke.

But Archer continued hauling them toward the stairs and up to the parlor. There he put each woman in a chair directly before the fire. He piled on more wood, until the blaze made their icy skin feel as if it were burning.

"Stay here. Tom will bring you tea and gruel. And I need to go deal with our host, who is still screaming that he will call the soldiers against us."

Tess tried to say she was sorry for causing him trouble, but her lips still would not form words. He astonished her then by placing his warm, strong hand on her forehead. "Next time," he repeated more gently, "tell me in advance."

She managed a shaky nod. He was right, of course. It would have been better to have had his help.

"I'll be back," he promised. "After I deal with the landlord, I will see to your refugees."

She managed at last to speak, though the words sounded rubbery. "So many will die tonight."

He nodded. "I know." Then he left them.

Tom appeared moments later, carrying a tray with two large bowls of gruel and a large pot of steaming tea. "This will warm you," he said, setting the tray near the hearth. Then he brought them each a bowl of warm gruel, not too hot to hold, just right to eat.

He sat near them, as if he had decided they needed to be watched over. "Our host is an angry man," he told them. "He was the first to wake as the people began to fill the public rooms. When he told them to leave, they told him a lady in white had sent them. Then he knew who was responsible, and he came to wake Archer."

"I cannot say I'm sorry," Tess said, her spoon halfway to her mouth.

"Nor should you," Tom agreed. "Archer told our host to calm down, that he would be paid for the disruption, then set out to find the two of you. After that the man stopped arguing with everyone who came in the door, but he was still grumbling quite noisily."

"He's afraid," Sara said. "He's afraid all these people will take everything he has left to get his family through the winter. He's afraid he will starve—like them."

"An understandable fear," Tess said. "But I could not leave those people out there."

Sleet rattled against the window again, loudly, and somewhere a shutter banged. The building creaked and groaned.

"This is no common weather," Tom said, looking over his shoulder at the windows. "I have seen ice storms before, but this is more violent than any I can recall. This kind of wind rarely comes even with a thunderstorm, and when it does, it does not last this long."

Sara spoke. "This entire winter is unnatural. We all know that. Even the beasts that stay through the winter have vanished somewhere. These poor people can't even hope to go out to hunt for meat."

Archer returned as Tess and Sara finished their gruel and began to sip the tea Tom had been keeping hot by the fire. The warmth of both food and fire had driven away their chills, and comfort began to seep back into their bodies.

"All is settled," Archer said, sitting on a trestle near the hearth. "Ratha and Giri will keep an eye on the peace downstairs. The inn is bursting to its very rafters with refugees, but our host has agreed to make enough gruel for everyone. What is to become of them on the morrow is uncertain. They cannot remain here."

Tess nodded slowly. "Tomorrow," she said, feeling suddenly as if she were drifting away on some current of thought that pulled her along, "there will be very few refugees left except those that are here."

Her words cast a pall over the room, punctuated only by the fury that battered the windows.

Another shudder passed through Tess as her eyes drooped closed. In her heart, in places seldom explored, she sensed that the fury had a name.

14

The storm blew itself out just before dawn, and the sun's rising brought amazing relief. Before it had cleared the rooftops, the ice was melting, water dripping until small rivers began to run in the streets.

Archer opened a window in the parlor, and a warm breeze blew in, so at odds with the night before and all the preceding days that it felt like another world.

It might have caused rejoicing among the party except that the damage had been done. They all knew that many had died overnight.

"This thaw will be a problem," Archer said, having realized something that hadn't yet occurred to the rest of them. "All the ice that fell overnight is going to turn the ground into a mire."

"It's just one plague after another," muttered Giri. "Ratha and I must go out. We have some information to pursue. The people downstairs are still mostly asleep with exhaustion, but I expect it will not be long before they're herded out onto the street again."

Archer nodded. "Go take care of your business. I'll see what I can do about affairs here. Tom? Come with me."

At the door he paused and looked back at Tess and Sara, who had slept as much as they had been able by the fire.

"Both of you stay here," he said flatly. "Don't defy me this time. With so much death out there, matters could turn ugly very soon. Breakfast will be brought up to you."

Then he was gone, leaving the two groggy-eyed women to look at each other.

"I suppose he's right," Sara said reluctantly.

"I'm sure he is." Tess tucked her hands beneath the blanket someone had spread over her, needing warmth despite the promise of a pleasant day. "I don't want to see what's out there, Sara. Somehow I know what it will be like, and I don't want to see it."

Sara nodded. "I fear it, too. I can't bear to think of all those children."

"Nor I. In fact, I'm starting to feel very angry."

"At what?"

"At whoever or whatever is behind this. A wizard, Mistress Alcanti said yesterday. If that's indeed what it is, then he deserves to be consigned to eternal fire."

Sara winced and made a silencing motion. "The air might carry your words."

The superstition at once surprised Tess and seemed to hold the possibility of truth. But with her life so upended, who was she to judge the truth of anything? "Well, if he hears my words, then let him mark them," she said angrily. "The crops are despoiled, many have already died of starvation, the storm, I am sure, took most of the refugees, and now starvation may well take the rest. Who would do such a thing? What kind of mind and heart?"

"I would prefer not to know."

At that moment the door opened and Tom stepped in, bearing their breakfast tray. "I can't stay," he said apologetically, his eyes on Sara. "Archer needs me."

"That's all right," Sara assured him, smiling. "How are the people downstairs?"

"Well, that's part of what I'm needed for. I'll tell you later."

Then he was gone, the door closing firmly behind him.

Tess tossed off her blanket and her cloak, and strode to the window to look down on the street. A river was running down the center of it now, and ice lingered only in the deepest shadows. From too cold to too warm, so fast. Something was most definitely amiss, and she wondered if that oily feeling at the back of her mind was related to it.

There were not enough people willing, or able, to do the work, to carry all the dead far from the town. Instead funeral pyres were built outside the walls, bodies thrown upon them like kindling. Nearly everyone who had been outside the walls overnight had died. Within the city, only a few more of the shelterless had survived.

Derda's refugee problem had vanished overnight, leaving the survivors, both citizen and refugee, stunned by the scope of the devastation. The city reeked of the stench from the pyres, but people kept up the body removal until well past exhaustion, for failure to clear away the dead would lead to plague.

Along with the deaths of the refugees had gone any hope that, come spring, the farms of the great basin would once again yield abundance, for now there was no one left to plant and reap.

Archer and Tom, moving among the tired, dirt- and soot-streaked populace, helping where they could, memories seared into their minds that would never leave. Tom's youth vanished from his face forever.

It was then, when the survivors were worn to the bone and full of limitless despair, that two names began to be whispered, almost as if they were carried on the warm breeze.

"Lantav."

"Glassidor."

But even as Archer heard them, they never seemed to come from anyone right around him. When he asked who Lantav was, people grew glassy-eyed and silent. When he asked about Glassidor, they drew away from him.

Finally he drew a man aside and asked where he might find Lantav.

At once the man began to tremble like a leaf in a storm. "I don't know what you're talking about!"

He pulled hard away, and Archer let him go.

Tom spoke, his eyes wide and hollow. "I think if we can find this man, we may find many answers."

"It would seem so." Archer stood a moment lost in thought. "I thought I knew all the remaining mages. Perhaps I was wrong."

"Perhaps this one concealed himself until he was ready to act?"

Archer nodded slowly. "I cannot tell you, Tom, how very much that thought disturbs me."

Ratha and Giri moved freely among the slaves and bondsmen. The people of Derda were not accustomed to seeing Anari in any other role and did not even suspect that these two were freemen. Throughout the morning they worked alongside other Anari, carrying the dead from the city. As they worked, they quietly asked questions. Because they were among their countrymen, some of their questions even received answers, however indirectly.

"There is rumor," one man told them as they pushed a laden cart toward the city gate. "Only rumor."

"Of what?" Speaking their own language gave them some privacy.

"Take care," said another Anari nearby. "Someone always listens."

The man who had begun speaking nodded and lowered his voice. "It is said there is a great wizard in Lorense. I do not know if this is true."

"I've heard it, too," whispered another man. "They call it the hive. It is said he has raised a group of—"

"Hush!" The command came from a man nearby, and all fell silent as they passed through the gate, the guards watching them with deadened eyes.

Then came the truly difficult part of pushing the heavy cart through mire already made worse by the passage of so many other carts. The air was stifling with the stench from the pyres, and the sun beat hotly upon them as if it would burn them, too.

When at last they unloaded their cart, they turned about and headed back to the city to seek more victims.

"'Tis said," the first man whispered, "that they all share one mind. I do not know how this can be."

"It can't" said the other, looking over his shoulder. "'Tis not possible."

"I know," said the first man. "I know. But that is what I hear. That and whispers of assassins…"

After that, no one would say anything more. Satisfied they had learned all they could, Ratha and Giri departed to return to the inn.

They had barely turned the first corner when they saw the man against the wall, his attacker lunging in with a gleaming blade. Ratha and Giri had left their swords at the inn—the better to pass unnoticed among a slave people—but their instincts and training fired as if led by a single thought.

They rushed forward, Ratha moving between the attacker and the already sagging young man against the wall, while Giri expertly grabbed the attacker's knife hand and spun it backward, until the blade dropped into the mud. The man's eyes widened, but Giri continued to twist, his face an impassive mask, until the man's wrist snapped audibly and his scream cut through the unnatural silence that had engulfed them.

Giri released the man's wrist and he fled, none the richer and much the poorer for his attempt at robbery. But it was too late for his victim. The young man who had been attacked lay bleeding and barely breathing. Ratha knelt beside him, knowing there was nothing he could do.

At that moment, a cry rang out. "Murderers! Murderers! They have killed my son."

There could be no doubt who the man screaming about his son could mean. Ratha and Giri exchanged only the quickest looks before taking flight into a warren of twisting streets, away from the inn.

Being Anari in the Bonzandari Kingdom meant only that anything they might say in their own defense would be disbelieved. Slaves, after all, could never be trusted.

The night's tragedy seemed to have brought a new awareness to Derda. Or perhaps it was that so few refugees were left, they no longer frightened anyone. But for the first time, doors opened and food was shared with those who remained. And those who had worked so hard to clear the streets were rewarded with the heartiest meals of all.

"One would like to think there's been a change of heart," Archer said as the evening began to fall over the city. The heat of the day still lingered, welcomed by all who ventured out. "But I can understand why those with families are so protective of their stores. I cannot say I would give away food if it might cause my children to starve."

"I know," Tess said sadly. "'Tis the great sorrow of this. All might die if none are selfish."

"'Tis not only the sorrow, 'tis the evil," Archer replied. "Hearts have been twisted by this. Some will never again be generous."

"And so many dead." A lone tear trickled down Tess's cheek as she closed her eyes. She could feel it, as if this place had been scarred forever by recent events. It was as if the very ground cried out in protest. Some part of her wished she had the power to reach out and mend the world, to soothe the sorrow that had blighted it and made this place so unholy.

"I still feel it," she said.

"Feel what?"

"We have both been feeling it," Sara offered. "The evil. An evil pall lies over this place."

"And it does not rise from within," Tess said. She opened her eyes and wiped away the tear. "I am certain of it."

Archer nodded and turned back to the window, where the sky was reddened not only by sunset but by the pyres that would burn for days. "I have learned a little, though I am not quite sure what it means. I will not speak of it, but I may have to leave you for a while."

Tess stood up and went to stand beside him at the window. "If you leave us, it will not be here."

He looked at her. "Why?"

"Because the evil stays with me. Because if I stay here..." She shook her head. "Words cannot describe it. This place is ill for me. I will be surrounded by the very thing I most need protection from."

"What is that?"

She spread her hands, anguish from the day, last night, all the days since she had awakened among the slaughter, filling her voice. "By the gods, I do not know. I do not *know!* If I could be granted but one glimmer of memory..."

Archer enfolded her in his arm, tucking her head to his chest as he continued to stare out at the reddened sky. "I will not leave you, then, Lady. But the dangers and horrors to come may well make what we have seen here seem small by comparison."

Tess lifted her face and looked up at him. "It hunts me," she whispered. "I do not know how or why, or even what, but it hunts me."

He nodded and brushed a strand of hair back from her cheek. "I know," he said. "It may be that you are part of it. What if that should prove to be?"

"Then I hope you will kill me with one blow of your blade."

He searched her eyes, then spoke. "If I find that to be true, be sure I will."

Sara began to protest. "Archer, she cannot be—"

Her words were cut off sharply as the door to the parlor slammed open. Ratha and Giri stepped inside, closing and bolting the door.

"Draw the curtains," Giri said.

Archer at once complied, closing out the red sky and falling night. He did not put his arm around Tess again, a loss she felt to her very core.

"We are hunted," Ratha said. "We came upon a thief stealing from a young man. By the time we drove him off, the young man was mortally wounded and his father claimed that we were the killers. We have been evading pursuit all afternoon."

Archer reacted instantly. "Then we leave now. Immediately. Sara, wake Tom, if you please. Ratha, Giri, start loading our horses. Tess, gather what you can carry and bring it to the stables. Sara, you and Tom do the same. I'll meet you at the stables. First I must deal with our host."

The sky was dark now, as they stood in the stables with their mounts, awaiting Archer. The evening was warm, and fires reddened the horizon, but mercifully the wind blew the smell away from them.

The streets outside were quiet, as if the day's horror and labor had caused everyone to disappear indoors. The countless homeless who had greeted them on their arrival no longer lined the damp thoroughfares. There had been a cleansing of the very worst kind.

Archer appeared finally and swung up into his saddle. "Let us go. Ratha, Giri, you stay behind and keep your swords out of sight. I will probably need to pass you off as my slaves and the rest of you as my family. Let us try to do this without any trouble, for this town has enough fatherless children."

Their ride down the streets toward the north gate drew no attention. No one was out, and no one opened a window out of curiosity at the sound of clopping hooves. Perhaps Derda had no curiosity left.

There were two guards at the gate, playing dice with a leather cup. Only one of them bothered to look up.

"Whither go you?"

"Whitewater," Archer answered. "My wife—" he gestured to Tess "—has learned that her mother is ill."

The guard rose, walking past him to look at the others. "Your children?" he asked, indicating Sara and Tom.

"Aye," said Archer. "And my slaves."

It was there that the guard paused, looking at the two Anari who, wrapped in their cloaks despite the evening's warmth, were trying to look small and humble, no easy feat for such large, proud men.

"You heard of the merchant's son who was murdered by slaves?" the guard asked, still looking at the Anari.

"Aye, a tragedy that is," Archer said. "More owners need to keep a better eye on their slaves."

The guard nodded and turned from the Anari. "There be many who would agree tonight." He looked at Tess. "May your mother recover, Mistress."

"Thank you."

Archer tossed a coin to each of the men. "I hope this can buy some food for your families' bellies," he said. "'Tis my hope I can bring back food from Whitewater when we return."

The guard shook his head mournfully. "Would that you could, Master, but I be doubting it. I cannot see how Whitewater can be any better off, what with the crops turning to poison in the fields."

"Well, if they *are* having better luck, I shall bring some food back for you."

"Thankee." The guard waved them on and returned to his dice game, the silver coin already tucked away.

15

Through the darkness they rode west, back the way they had originally come.

"We retrace our steps for a while," Archer explained when they were out of hearing of the guards. "'Twould be best for any who might watch to believe we go to Whitewater."

The darkness blessedly hid the worst of what had happened outside the walls, and gradually even the pyres grew distant and dim. For the first time on their trek they filled every one of the water bags they carried with them. Then Archer turned them from the Adasen River and led them northeast, across blighted fields and past empty farmhouses. It was, Tess thought, as if the entire world had died.

Archer and the Anari no longer carried their weapons concealed beneath their cloaks or bound to their horses. Their swords now rode in scabbards over their backs, where they could be instantly reached. They also carried quivers full of arrows and, over their shoulders, long bows. They bristled with weapons, it seemed, and Tess suspected she could not see all of them.

Tom, too, had thrown back his cloak to bare his sword, as had Sara. Tess alone carried no weapon, nor did she desire one. She doubted she would know how to use one, and did not believe she would even try.

When the night was in its deepest hours, there was a change in the air, a sense of presence so strong that Tess's scalp prickled with it. The horses, who had been plodding steadily along, grew nervous, snorting and tossing their heads, and sidling as if to move away from something.

"We are not alone," Archer said. He drew Tess up near him and motioned the others to close in, except for Ratha and Giri, whom he motioned to scout to either side.

The two Anari seemed to vanish into the dark. Tom struggled to hold the packhorses, who grew more restive by the moment.

"Tie them to your saddle," Archer told him. Sara bent over to help, slipping the lead ropes through the loops at the back of Tom's saddle. Once they were tied, Tom spurred his own mount forward, drawing the leads tight, which seemed to have a calming effect on the pack mares.

"Let us keep going," Archer said quietly. "Remain alert for any movement around us."

With only starlight above and blackened fields to either side, the darkness was an almost impenetrable cloak over the world. The horses must be picking their way by instinct, Tess thought, as her eyes roved the depthless black around her.

The feeling of a presence continued to grow, until it was an almost crushing sensation. In her mind, Tess felt little pinpricks, as if something were trying to get in. From some deep reservoir, she found the will to block it, though she did not know what it was.

Then she saw them, a pair of glowing red eyes. They blinked out the very next instant.

"There!" she said, gasping the word. "I saw eyes."

Archer at once turned in his saddle and looked. With his hand, he gestured everyone to halt.

In the silence they heard a rustle and a quiet crack, as if something broke underfoot. Whatever it was, it was very near.

Archer called out, "To me!" and moments later the Anari emerged from the shadows, ranging themselves in a protective triad with Archer around Tess, Tom and Sara.

For long, nerve-stretching minutes they waited. The breeze blowing over the dead plain was silent.

Then, from their left, came a slithering sound. Tess turned her head quickly and saw again the red eyes, just as they winked out.

"I saw it," Archer murmured as she opened her mouth to tell him.

"What is it?" she whispered back.

"I don't know."

That was comforting, so comforting, in fact, that Tess wished for the first time that she had a sword. A knife. Anything for self-defense.

Then, out of the night, came the hissing call. "Tessss…"

Tess's heart stopped. It was not the voice of her dream, not that that made any difference. Something out there knew her and was calling her, and all she could feel was a sense of dread evil. Her hands tightened on her reins until they ached, and she wanted to close her eyes, as if that would make it all go away.

"Tessss…"

"It seems," said Archer, his voice harsh, "that you have a friend out there."

"No friend," she gasped. "No friend. Kill it or kill me, but do not let it take me."

Sara's hand was suddenly on her arm, comforting her. "Archer, you cannot believe she would be part of something that feels so evil. You *cannot!* I have felt nothing but good in her since the day you brought her to Whitewater."

Tom, too, sprang to her defense. "Have you thought, Master Archer, that she might have escaped this evil once before? And that now it seeks to take her back?"

For a second that seemed endless, Archer was still as stone. "Aye," he said finally. "We must keep her at our center and keep moving. 'Twill be difficult, but we cannot wait here indefinitely for this *thing* to have its way with us."

"At least," said Ratha, "we now know what we carry that draws danger to us."

"A surprisingly philosophical thought," Giri retorted.

"Well, 'tis always good to know what needs to be protected."

"Oh, aye."

Tess found herself at the center of a wall of horses and swords.

"Tesss…come…" The hissing came out of the night again.

Tess, suddenly fearing for her companions even more than herself, said, "Please, don't risk yourselves for me. 'Twould be better to kill me now and have done with this."

Archer turned his steed and leaned toward her. "But, my lady, you forget. This evil is spreading across our world. And now it seems you may be the key to it. We will protect you, for the sake of others if not for yours."

It was a harsh statement, and its dagger plunged deep into Tess's breast. But even in her anguish, she recognized the justice of his words. More hung in the balance, evidently, than herself. In which case... In which case she needed to survive, if only to help discover what lay behind all the death and blight that had fallen over the world.

The group began to move forward again, Tess at its center. Head down, she wondered why the gods had done this to her. Why she had been deprived of memories that might be useful and dropped among strangers who doubted her. And why she appeared to be the object of such evil.

What could she have done?

Never had her despair been deeper.

At dawn they stopped at an abandoned farmhouse. Nothing was locked, so they entered and took advantage of its amenities. Their pursuer had given up as the first gray light appeared in the east, and now for a time they would have relative peace.

Tess was sent to sleep in a small upstairs room on a bare cot. How the others disposed themselves she did not know, nor, at that point, did she care. Exhaustion and despair had left her lifeless, and as soon as she stretched out, she fell into a deep, dreamless sleep.

Tom and Sara offered to take the first watch. After first checking everything out, Archer and the Anari settled on the floor, wrapped in their cloaks, and soon slept.

Tom and Sara sat outside on a bench, from time to time walking around the outside of the building. As far as the eye could see, nothing blocked their view until the mountains in the north and the forested hills to the east, both of which were hazy in the far distance.

Tom, who had grown in confidence during the journey, now reverted to the bashful youth because he was alone in Sara's presence. She laughed gently, and reached out to take his hand and hold it.

He blushed to the very roots of his hair.

"Tom, my dear sweet Tom," she said softly, and brushed a wisp of hair back from his face. "Must you be so shy with me?"

He was now so completely tongue-tied that she took pity on him and looked away from him to the world beyond, although she still clasped his hand.

"'Tis a lovely morning," she said. "The loveliest in a long while." Unlike yesterday, when heat had battered them, this morning held gentle warmth, not unlike the promise of spring. "I wish I believed it would last, although it comes too late."

Tom managed an affirmative sound.

"The natural winter still faces us."

"You think…the weather we have had is unnatural?"

"Surely." She looked at him, her face shadowing. "I know you cannot feel it, but every breath of the icy wind carries with it the stench of the unholy."

His eyes widened a bit, but he seemed to be growing less bashful. "You are like your mother."

"So it seems. Slightly fey, despite my practical nature, sensing things others cannot. I must tell you, it has actually been a relief to meet Tess. She senses these things, too, and I no longer feel so lonely or odd."

"You feel odd?" Tom appeared appalled. "But, Sara, you are so…so perfect!" His face reddened again, and he looked away.

She laughed gently and squeezed his hand. "We don't talk enough. You are always so shy, and I am always so busy. So we will talk now, while we keep watch, and I will tell you of my mother. Things no one else knows."

Tom waited, eyes alert, his attention so tightly focused on her that she realized she was going to have to be the one who kept watch while they talked.

She felt flattered as she never before in her life had felt flattered. She was not one of Whitewater's pretty lasses whom the boys always sought after. She was built sturdily, like her father, though with a sweet face. Tom was the only lad who had ever really noticed her, and now she would test him with some truths that might send him into flight from her. But it must be done, because she could not encourage his attentions unless he could accept her as she was.

"My mother," she said quietly, "had gifts. Gifts beyond her talent for healing, which everyone knew about. The poultices and draughts she used were only part of her ability. It was, she always said, her prayers that did most of the work."

Tom nodded, willing to accept this, it seemed. But of course, after what they had seen over the last week, all of them were more willing to accept things beyond normal ken.

"Anyway, she did other things, too, which no one knew about. At night, when the fields were first sown, she would walk among them, blessing them so they would grow well. And sometimes, when the fishermen would complain of poor catches, she would go to the river and sing a small song, and soon the fish would be plentiful again."

"That's amazing," said Tom.

"She told me of these things, because she said I had gifts, too. But I do not know what they are, Tom. She was gone before she could teach me. All I know is that I can feel evil when it is near."

Impulsively he put his arm around her shoulders, and with a sense of vast relief, she leaned into him. "I do not frighten you?"

"You frighten me, Sara, but not because you have gifts."

A little chuckle escaped her, and she allowed herself to enjoy the sensation of being held, of resting her cheek on a strong chest. Because, for all that he was still a stripling, Tom's work with his father had built a great deal of strength in his body. Strength that was comforting.

"I'm sure," he said, "that you'll find your gifts when the time is right. And perhaps I'll find mine."

She looked up at him. "You have gifts?"

"I do not know. I know only that I am not meant to be a gate-keeper for the rest of my days."

She nodded, her eyes holding his. "I believe that, Tom. Greater things lie ahead of you."

Somehow, as if magic filled the air and compelled them, their faces drew closer until their lips met. The first touch was tentative, uncertain, but then Tom's other arm closed around her and their kiss deepened, as they learned together the first lessons of love.

Wildness grew within Sara, and she wanted things she could hardly name. Wanted his hands to move over her, wanted her hands to move over him.

At that moment they were startled apart by a boom of thunder louder than any they had ever heard. It rolled on and on beneath a blue sky, causing the very air to vibrate, causing the ground beneath them to tremble and the house behind them to shake.

They both leapt to their feet and looked around. In an instant they were joined by Archer and the Anari.

"There!" Tom cried, pointing to the western mountains.

A plume of smoke so huge that it could be seen even at this great distance rose from a peak that had once been snowcapped.

"By the gods," breathed Ratha. "It's Moranir, Earth's Root!"

Archer nodded. "So it is. It rumbles for the first time in..." He shrugged. "I cannot remember anymore how long it has been."

"Aye," said Giri, his tone altered. "'Tis part of the great prophecy."

"Prophecy?" asked Tom.

"Aye." Giri's voice fell into a singsong rhythm.

> "The Earth Root trembles, smoke and fire
> Awash upon the peace of dreams
> Where evil sleeps amid its pyre
> Life unbearing, life uncaring
> Rises in its patient screams.
>
> The firstborn son of Firstborn king,
> Alight upon the land of old
> The sword within his hand will sing
> Fear unbearing, fear uncaring
> Rises raging hard and bold.
>
> White Lady lost is Weaver found
> Adrift within a war of night
> To move within the space of sound
> Time uncaring, time unbearing,
> Rises glowing inner light.
>
> The foundling son will see beyond
> Asleep within a heart unknown
> To see the ripples on the pond
> Speech uncaring, speech unbearing,
> Rises with a sight not shown.
>
> The darkling ones will then be free
> Alive within a land of blood
> To fell an ancient enemy

Death uncaring, death unbearing
Rising as a raging flood.

The battle joined in bitter spires
Aloft within a darkened sky
The One whose anger never tires
Gods uncaring, gods unbearing
Rising up that all may die."

For a long time no one moved or made a sound. The rumbling of the erupting mountain continued to roll over them as if it had no end.

Sara looked at Tom and once again took his hand. "It is," she said finally, "a terrible time when prophecies come to pass."

10

From a window in her room under the eaves, Tess could see the erupting mountain. The plume of gray smoke rose to the clouds and beyond, and before long, within the plume could be seen the red of fire. Around her in the room everything shook a little, and the window glass vibrated against her fingertips.

At first she watched in simple amazement, sure she had never before seen such a thing. Then uneasiness began to fill her as she saw the gray cloud spread, coming directly toward them. With such distance, the approach seemed slow, but for it to be visible to her over all these miles, it must be moving very fast.

Quickly she pulled on her boots, gathered her cloak and headed downstairs. She found the rest of the party gathered in the farm-yard, watching the spectacle.

"That smoke is coming this way," she said.

"Aye," agreed Archer. "It comes swiftly."

"We have to leave."

"I doubt we can outrun it." He turned to look at the rest of them. "We must seal up the farmhouse and remain inside. Bring the horses in, as well. That foul cloud may carry death."

Every window was checked to be sure it was sealed tight. Where holes were found, they wadded pieces of cloth tightly into them. They managed, by removing all the furnishings and then maneuvering the beasts carefully, to fit all the horses in the rear room. Their steeds had little space to move, but that did not seem to trouble them, especially when Giri found hay in the barn and used a wagon to bring it to them.

"I hope this is none of the poisoned growth," he muttered. "But it seems too old."

Then they sealed the doors. There were only two, but they proved more problematic than the windows, for there were large gaps above and below and along the edges. Ratha made a paste of water and dirt, and used it to seal the openings when cloth failed to be sufficient.

The fireplace was left until last, for they needed air. Giri bound hay in some shirts he had found, planning to stuff it up the chimney when the cloud nearly reached them.

"That is all we can do," Archer said finally.

It wasn't going to be pleasant. Already the air in the house was growing stale and laden with the smell of the horses. But a look out the western window showed that the cloud was within miles of them now, and that it filled the sky, growing larger as it approached.

"How can it move so fast?" Tom asked, watching the approach.

Giri answered. "Earth's Root has power beyond imagining. When it shakes and blows its billows of smoke, 'tis said the smoke and burning mud can move faster than the wind."

"Aye," agreed Archer. "Much faster than the wind. Now would be a good time to plug that chimney, Giri."

At once the Anari moved to do so, stuffing his bundled hay in as tightly as he could.

Only minutes later, a gray cloud rolled over them, hiding everything from view. The entire house shook before its force, and from the back room the horses whinnied and stomped.

Staring out the window near the settle on which she sat, Tess thought it looked like an impenetrable fog, but a fog that roared with rage. Then she saw large indeterminate objects among the cloud, objects that hit the house with thuds and bangs that made her nerves stretch.

"I hate this," Sara announced. Tom at once put his arm around her. Tess looked at her with concern, as Sara always seemed so in control and unafraid.

But now the young woman's face was pale even in the dim light that managed to penetrate the cloud that roiled around the house.

The roar that came with it began to make thunderclaps, and outside the window in the near-night made by the cloud, she began to see lightning. At first it was only small crackles of light, but then came nearly blinding bolts, as if she sat within a thunderstorm.

Watching the fury without, Tess began to feel strange, as if she were somehow rising out of herself. Maybe the cloud was getting inside.

She looked around at the others, but they all seemed to be normal, looking out the windows with expressions ranging from grimness to, in Sara's case, outright fear. Then she turned her attention back to the window and to the bolts of lightning.

The lightness continued to fill her, making her feel as if she could bob above the very ground without touching it. Something inside her wanted to reach out to those bolts of lightning, to gather them to her and twist them into…into what?

But even as her rational mind rebelled against the thought, something inside her kept urging her, telling her to take the power...take the power....

She was leaning toward the window, her entire being stretching toward it, when she heard her name called.

"Tess!"

She jerked and looked around to find Archer staring at her.

"Are you all right?" he asked.

Uncertain how to respond, she shrugged. Then, needing to be alone, she climbed the stairs to the tiny attic room and sat on the edge of the bed, staring out the window, seeing the lightning...wanting the lightning.

But solitude was not to be hers. Archer followed her.

"What is going on?" he demanded.

"Why are you always sure something is going on?" Her voice was tense, strained, even a bit resentful. "I'm tired of you looking at me with constant suspicion. What have I done to earn your distrust?"

He hesitated, stooped in the doorway, a large man, too large for the room. Then he entered all the way and sat cross-legged on the floor. The cot was so low and Archer so tall that their heads were almost on a level. Outside the lightning continued to flash in the cloud, and something banged against the roof.

"I am," he said presently, "perhaps an overly cautious man. But I have seen much in my life, and it has taught me to give my trust sparingly."

"I'm not asking for your trust! I'm simply asking that you not always act as if I may be about to do some terrible thing. Archer, I have no memory older than twelve days! At this point the only things I know about myself are what has happened in those days, and they are exactly the same things you know about me. Must you always look at me as if I'm about to turn into a threat before your very eyes?"

His gray gaze never wavered. "Lady, may I remind you that your lack of memory is of itself a great concern? Especially when I sense power in you. The power to which the snow wolf bows. The power to heal two little boys. If you are a mage and have forgotten your own powers, what might you do with them unwittingly?"

That she could not answer, especially when she remembered how the lightning had seemed to call to her, telling her to take the power. She lowered her head and twisted her fingers together.

"There are few mages left," he continued. "Some little power of the Ilduin remains behind, but it is rarer than ice in the summer. Sara doesn't know this, but her own mother was an Ilduin, but even her powers were limited and untaught. You may yet be another Ilduin. I do not know."

He sighed and drummed his fingers on his thigh. "These are difficult times. I thought I knew all the mages, but now we apparently face one I have never heard of, Lantav Glassidor."

"You can't think I'm one of them."

"I do not know. Somehow you escaped the slaughter of the caravan. Yet I think that if you belonged to this mage, he would long since have regained your mind. If he can find you."

A chill crept down her spine, and horror began to fill her. "I feel…I always feel this dark, oily presence at the back of my mind, as if someone is trying to get into me. And in my dreams…oh, Archer, in my dreams my name is called. Except…except that feels very different. Not evil at all. It's as if someone who cares about me calls for me."

A deafening clap of thunder caused her to wince and bend to

her knees as if she feared the house would collapse around her. It shook to its very foundations but remained standing.

"It would be safer downstairs," Archer said. "Come. Rejoin us."

But as he started to rise, she stopped him with a hand on his arm. "If it seeks me," she said, "then I am better off dead. I meant what I said before."

He nodded. "I know you did."

As quickly as it had hit, the storm died. The world without was transformed, everything covered with a layer of gray dust, though it was not deep. The wind had continued to carry the worst of it on to the east, leaving little behind.

"It will get worse as we travel east," Archer remarked. "All the dust and dirt had to fall somewhere."

To the west, Moranir was now glowing fiery red at its peak, apparently far from finished. Overhead, the sky was still gray, and almost as if in answer to Archer's words, it began to rain, bringing more ash down with it.

The group returned inside.

"With any luck at all," Giri remarked, "the rain will wash away the dust."

They unstopped the chimney, throwing the hay to the horses, and built a small fire on the hearth, since the overcast had turned the day chilly.

"Well," said Sara, "since we must stay here a while, I may as well make us a meal."

Since there was yet no way to replenish their supplies, they had begun to eat very sparingly. Soups and stews were thinner by far, but enough to warm the stomach and stop the pangs of hunger. Ratha more than once evinced the hope that once they reached the

Tolora River north of Lorense, they would find some decent hunting or trapping.

"Let us hope we haven't been misdirected," Archer replied. "We need to find those brigands, and I suspect that when we find them, we'll find the cause behind all the evil that has befallen us."

"Aye," said Ratha. "In Derda they hesitated even to whisper his name. Apparently the people have been aware of this mage's growing power for some time. But why would he seek to destroy so much?"

"Can you think of a better way to take control of everything?" Giri asked his brother. "Only think of it. Even the Bozandari Kingdom would fall eventually before such power."

Ratha harrumphed. "Pardon me, but I don't see the joy of ruling over a dead kingdom."

"But you are not evil," Sara said. She stirred the pot, which was beginning to bubble on the fire. "Evil has its own ways and desires."

"Well said," Archer agreed. "Well said indeed."

"But evil," Tess added, "always thinks it is right. And therein lies the true danger."

"How so?" asked Ratha.

Tess hesitated, for who was she to speak when she remembered so little? But a tiny certainty grew within her, and the words came. "The evil one will always have what he believes to be a good reason for his acts. He may think he is saving the world, or bettering it. He may think he is opposing some other evil. The danger lies in his belief. He will be ardent, determined, convinced of his own wisdom. And those who support him will be the same."

"Excellent words of warning," Archer agreed. "Let us not trip into this lightly."

"What troubled me," Giri said after a few minutes, "was the way

the person I spoke to in Derda seemed to believe that there is a..."
He hesitated. "I cannot recall the word for it. Did he call it a hive?"

Ratha nodded. "'Twas the word he used. This mage has apparently created one mind among his followers, so that each knows instantly whatever another knows. So that he can control them with a thought."

"But even as we were told this, it seemed the man who spoke was embarrassed to say it. As if it must be a lie he was repeating."

Archer's chin settled on his chest for several moments; then he looked at them again. "Once the Ilduin had such a mind. All of them, no matter where they were, could share thoughts instantly or work spells together. I find it hard to believe that anyone else could create such a thing."

"Why?" asked Sara.

"Because the Ilduin held special gifts, innate gifts shared by no one else. Others could do magicks, but to do what the Ilduin did...none other could ever do so."

"Then mayhap," said Giri, "this mage has found himself an Ilduin."

"No Ilduin could be thus perverted," Archer said flatly.

"Not in the first times, perhaps," said Ratha. "But these are no longer the first times, and the Ilduin no longer hold sway over all matters."

Outside the rain continued to pour, and inside the gloom settled deeper.

17

"I'd like to hear more about the first times," Tom said. "You seem to know so much about them, yet I've heard so very little."

"Yes," said Sara. "In Whitewater, when we are shut inside by the weather, we occupy our time telling tales. 'Twould be a pleasure if you could tell us tales we have not heard before."

Ratha and Giri looked at one another, then at Archer.

For long moments Archer remained still. Tess thought a sudden tightness around his eyes spoke volumes: the telling of the tales would be no pleasure for him.

"The old tales are sorrowful," he told them. "Many tell of the end of the first times. But perhaps in that they carry a lesson to others."

He lowered his head for a minute, then began to speak.

"The White Lady was the greatest healer of the Firstborn city of Dederand. She had only to lay her hands upon a broken limb or a wound to make it whole. Eventually her fame spread to the Samari High King in Samarand, and he invited her to practice her art in his city, as well. In time, the King was so impressed with her gentleness and wisdom that he invited her to sit upon his council.

"At council she met the King's two sons, Annuvil and Ardred. Annuvil was the elder, dark of coloring. Ardred, the younger, was fair and full of beauty. He was loved by all who knew him, including his brother Annuvil."

Archer paused, as if lost in thought. Sara went to one of the packs and offered him a skin of ale. He took a long drink, then passed it back with thanks.

"The brothers both fell in love with the White Lady, but she would not favor one over the other. For years matters continued thus, and the brothers argued between themselves often and mightily. This might have been of little account, except that the brothers each ruled a city. Ardred ruled Dederand, and Annuvil ruled Samarand. Factions began to appear, especially in Dederand, in support of Ardred against his brother.

"The High King, despairing, decided he must force the White Lady to choose, or peace would be lost.

"So the King called the lady to his chamber one day and, unbeknownst to her, hid his sons behind a screen so they could hear her words themselves.

"'Lady,' he said, 'you must choose one of my sons to wed.'

"'I cannot, my lord,' she replied.

"'Have you no preference, then?'

"'That must remain my secret, my lord.'

"'But, Lady,' said the King, 'this will lead to war if my sons are not reconciled. Surely you cannot wish to be the cause of war.'

"'Then I must leave Samarand, my lord, forever.'

"The King was a great deal perplexed, and he asked, 'Lady, why can you not choose?'

"She sighed heavily, they say, and replied, 'My lord, if I choose Annuvil, Ardred will kill him, and I cannot choose Ardred.'

"Thus the brothers knew where her heart lay. Ardred disappeared from the kingdom for a time, and Annuvil married the lady in joy and celebration."

Archer paused, and the sound of the rain seemed to grow louder. Then he continued with the tale.

"Ardred returned eventually, to sow seeds of discord and raise factions among the Dederandi against Samarand and the High King. He was beautiful to behold, and many believed his poisonous lies."

"So it came to war as the lady thought it would," Sara said.

"Aye," Archer said heavily. "It came to war, and war came to destruction. Ratha and Giri here have seen the Plain of Dederand. They can tell you how evil the war was."

Giri spoke. "Where once there was a beautiful Firstborn city, there is now a plain of black glass that stretches as far as the eye may see and beyond."

"Such power!" said Tom.

"Such evil," Archer replied. "'Twas during this war that bane poison came to be, and that Bane Dread was forged."

"And the White Lady?" Sara asked. "What became of her?"

Archer shook his head. "None know. She disappeared forever. And with her passing, the Ilduin seemed to lose much of their power, as if the gods cursed the Firstborn for their evil. The Firstborn faded into the distant past, replaced by men."

"As if we are so much better," Giri remarked.

Archer surprised them all by laughing. "At least, Giri, you have not yet learned how to turn a beautiful mountain into a plain of glass. You must count your blessings."

Giri laughed with him, and the somber mood lifted.

Sara's stew was flavorful and warm, though thin, and sated hungry bellies, creating a sense of well-being for the first time since...Tess suddenly found she could not remember the last time she had actually felt this good.

Of course, that wasn't saying much, given the shortness of her memory, but she was willing to accept the feeling now and embrace it. The room was warm from the fire, and sleep—deep, much needed sleep—overtook her. She was vaguely aware that someone lifted her feet from the floor onto the lumpy settle, and that her cloak was thrown over her.

Then the world vanished completely.

She stood in a woodland dell, alone. Above, the sky boasted a blue that nearly hurt her eyes. Around her, trees laughed playfully in a gentle breeze, their leaves a multitude of green hues, with occasional flashes of gold. Beneath her feet the grass was warm and soft.

From the woods came a snow-white wolf, larger than most of his kind. Golden eyes looked back at her with affection. The wolf came to her and bowed low, speaking a wordless howl of greeting. Bending, she buried her fingers in his soft white ruff and felt the life pulsing in his neck.

She murmured to him, and he settled at her feet, as if he belonged there and always would.

Then she felt her sisters. She could not see them, but she could feel them. They spoke to her, their voices gentle murmurs. "I am here.... I am here...."

They were with her now, all of them, and joy filled her entire being.

Then, slowly, she lifted her arms, ready to begin the chant.

But the words would not come. Puzzled, she tried again, but still it was as if they had been hidden from her, though she had known them forever.

Distressed, she squatted by the wolf and touched him, feeling suddenly cut off and alone.

Then, without warning, day became night. The wolf vanished, as did the touch of her sisters.

All but one.

That one cried out, "Tess! Flee!"

Tess jerked awake, her heart hammering, gasping as if she had just run a race. The settle beneath her felt lumpier than before, painfully so.

Needing to shake off the fear that had filled her in the last moments of the dream, she forced herself to sit up.

Outside it was still raining and seemed to be darkening toward night. Around her on the floor the others slept...except for Archer. He sat by the fire, watching over them all.

"Bad dream?" he asked quietly.

She managed a nod. "Terrible."

"At least you managed to get a few hours of sleep. Do you think you can try to get some more?"

"Not yet. Not yet..."

She looked out the window again, wondering why her sleep was so plagued. Was she trying to remember her past?

Then Sara, who was sleeping nearby, made a small sound of sorrow and sat bolt upright. "Oh!" she said, looking around. "Oh!"

"Nightmare?" Archer asked.

"Not exactly." But Sara pushed herself to her feet anyway, as if quite certain she did not want to go back to sleep.

"Come sit beside me," Tess invited. "I, too, just woke from a nightmare."

Sara complied readily, tucking her legs beneath her. "It is strange how disordered my dreams are becoming. They have changed since we started this journey."

"How so?" Archer asked.

"I haven't dreamt of my mother in years. But now nearly every time I sleep, I see her. And she is not happy. That bothers me. I can't imagine why I would think she is not happy."

Tess had no answers, nor, it seemed, did Archer. Tess put her arm around the younger woman and gave her a hug. "Dreams are strange," was all she could offer. "This time the voice calling my name told me to flee. Now where, I ask you, am I supposed to flee?"

The question drew a small smile from Sara and even a chuckle from Archer.

"If I had a memory of any kind, it's possible I might know the answer to that. Then again, I might not. I think, Sara, that we are all terribly on edge. 'Tis hardly surprising that we have frightful dreams."

Sara nodded. "This journey has been far from easy, and we have seen some terrible things."

"Horrible things," Tess agreed. "I wish I could lose my memory of Derda as easily as I have lost all the rest of it."

"I fear," said Sara sadly, "that we will see even worse. The prophecies have long told of a terrible time to come, and now Moranir awakens."

"Aye," said Archer quietly. "Aye." He turned and looked out the window, as if he might see beyond the deepening darkness. "Moranir shakes. It has been told since time out of mind that one day the mountain would shake the world."

Tess replied. "It seems to have done that today."

"It has rumbled before," Archer said. "I've seen rivers of burning rock and mud run down its sides. But never since the dawn of time has it exploded like this."

Tess wondered how he could say that with such certainty, but who was she to question him? There was clearly an oral tradition that she had forgotten, one that everyone held to be true. And certainly, if the mountain had erupted like this before, it would have made its way into some tale or song.

Archer turned from the window and rubbed his eyes briefly. "If this rain does not stop soon, the land will be a mire. Nothing grows. The water will mix with the mud and make the ground too treacherous to travel. I do not care to stay here much longer. If we are being watched or tracked, staying here could well give our pursuers a chance to attack."

Tess remembered the red eyes she had seen in the dark before they arrived at the farmhouse. Archer was right. Something was indeed following them. She closed her eyes, as if she might reach out with her other senses and discover whether their pursuer was out there somewhere.

Sara spoke. "How can our pursuer have survived this day?"

"Much as we did," said Archer.

She sighed. "True, I had not thought of that."

Tom, on the other side of the fireplace, stirred and sat up, yawning widely and stretching. "Is it time to go?"

"No," said Sara gently. "I'm sorry we disturbed you."

"You did not," he answered, smiling at her. "I'm feeling quite rested. But when I heard you talking, I thought you might be discussing plans to leave." He glanced toward the window. "I guess not. It's still raining?"

"Teeming," Tess replied. "It wouldn't surprise me if it started to come under the door."

"Please, no," Sara said. "The floor is the only place we have to sleep."

"Try the bed upstairs," Tess suggested. "It's actually quite comfortable, and I don't intend to keep it to myself just because everyone was so kind as to put me there when we arrived."

"Thank you. Maybe I will—later."

Turning, Archer hung a pot of water over the fire and sprinkled some tea leaves into it. "I wonder if the rain outside is clean enough yet to drink."

"I'll check," said Tom, rising instantly. He took up one of the other cooking pots and went to the door. When he opened it, the sound of steady rain grew louder. It was indeed a heavy rainfall.

A few minutes later he stepped back in, soaked around the shoulders. "It smells all right," he said, bending his head toward the pot. "And it appears clean."

"Water the horses," Archer suggested. "Then we'll collect some more."

The dampness was making the odor of the horses even more noticeable than before. While Tom watered them, Ratha and Giri undertook to clean up after them. They opened a window while they did so, and for a little while the wind entered the house with them, whistling as it found its way out beneath the front door. The air was moist, chilly, but very fresh smelling. Whatever damage the cloud from Moranir had caused, the rain seemed to have cleansed it.

A sudden chill whipped through Tess. At first she thought it was the breeze, but then she realized that it was more.

"Close the window," she said abruptly. "Now. Please!"

Archer at once called out to the Anari, "Ratha, Giri! Close the window. Now!"

A slam came from the back room, and Giri appeared in the doorway. "What is wrong?"

Archer looked at Tess.

"Can't you feel it?" she asked, imploring. All she wanted was for someone to tell her she wasn't going crazy. Because right now, every cell in her body said they weren't alone any longer.

"Please, doesn't anyone feel it?"

Sara's huge eyes turned toward her. "There is something out there."

18

Giri looked at Tess. "You think our enemies have found us?"

She nodded. "Don't ask me how."

He glanced over at Ratha, who nodded silently. The Anari believed her without needing to know how.

"Assassins couldn't have moved through that cloud of ash," Tom said. "No one could."

"Perhaps not," Giri said. "But something did."

Now it was Archer who rose to challenge her. "Lady, I question not your honesty when I say that Tom is right. The blast from Moranir was beyond that which any alive could bear. I doubt not your conviction in your feelings, but reason betrays them."

"Then reason stands betrayed, my lord," Giri said. "There are things of this world that even you have not yet seen. Things my people have spoken of since the dawn of stories. Things we do not share with any other."

"From within the mountain," Ratha said, nodding.

"Your secrets may be the death of us all," Archer said, looking at them. "If you know of the evil that has come upon us, tell us now."

Giri looked at Ratha, uncertainty written on his face. His brother mirrored that same indecision. The Anari were a people of secrets, vows taken almost in the womb and repeated through childhood, matters that were not to be shared with any outside their people upon pain of *Keh-Bal,* the most feared of Anari punishments. The offender would be carried into the desert in the height of the summer sun and left: alone, naked, without water or tools. Exiled into the desert, to be swallowed up by the sands in the desert's own time and manner, no grave at which a family could mourn, his name never to be uttered again.

Now one of those secrets approached with stealth and malice, its approach detected by the lady's gift. A gift for which that secret was said to thirst as a man in the sun thirsts for water. To tell the others would be to violate his vows. Not to tell them would be to sentence his lord and his friends to a death beyond all deaths.

Giri was already in exile from his people. His friends were here. And likely his vow would not matter, for likely none of them would live out this day. He and Ratha had made a vow to Archer, a vow of eternal loyalty, even unto death. Even, he now realized, unto *Keh-Bal.*

He looked once more at Ratha and saw that his brother had reached the same conclusion. Taking a deep breath to steel himself against the conflict within, he spoke.

"Within each angry mountain lives what the Anari call the *Lao-Sou,* a race spawned by the great fire that rained at the end of the First Days. Before they left, the gods chained the *Lao-Sou* deep within the mountains, that they might never cause harm. We Anari come from the stone and the mountain, and we feel its life. That is how we build. But there were mountains upon which we would not tread, stones whose life we would never share, because we could feel the *Lao-Sou* within them, yearning to be set free."

"When Moranir exploded," Ratha said, joining in, lest Giri be alone in betrayal, "it must have opened the door to one of these evil beasts. It will now seek its mother, the womb from which the great fire was born."

"Me?" Tess asked. She looked disbelieving.

Giri nodded. "You. And even fair Sara. It knows your power, even if you do not, and it seeks what you have. We cannot outrun it. And I fear we cannot fight it."

"What are you saying?" Archer asked. "What is this...this *Lao-Sou*?"

Giri looked at Ratha, hoping against hope that his brother knew more than he, but Ratha shook his head.

"We do not know for sure," Giri said. "Some say it comes as a fiery serpent. Others say it lives in the form of a man. None have seen it. We have only felt its dark presence within the ground."

Tom rose, walking to the window. "All that lives can die. All that breathes can bleed. All that burns can starve."

Tom turned to them, and for an instant his face was as that of an old man whose life had drawn its stories in the lines on his face. "I know this to be true."

For a moment the room was silent. Then Archer's face hardened as he sprang into action. "Come, quickly. Coals from the fire. Quickly."

Giri nodded, reaching for the coal hamper beside the fireplace, knowing what Archer had in mind. With the mud and ash covering the ground, it would be difficult. But Giri knew beyond knowing that this was their only hope.

Ratha helped him shovel the brightest coals into the bucket, and

Giri hefted it, gritting his teeth against the heat that seared into his hand.

"The door," Giri said, already moving toward it. "Open the door!"

Archer pulled the door open and called the others to follow him. Working quickly, they swept aside as much of the sodden ash as they could, while Giri spread the coals upon the bare dead grass beneath. Their work continued as he returned to hand the bucket to Ratha, who quickly refilled it with the last of the embers from the fire. Perhaps it would be enough.

Rushing back outside, he found that the grass had already begun to smoke beneath the coals he had spread, and the others had already cleared more for him to burn. By the time he had finished spreading coals over the newly cleared grass, the first fires had already grown to open flames.

Now Ratha joined them with the coal shovel, reaching into the flames to scoop the embers back into the bucket, to be spread farther along as the others worked feverishly to expose more grass. Soon there was a ring of fire burning around the house, drying the ash before it, leaving the earth charred in its wake.

Within minutes the ring had burned itself out, leaving a black ring around the house.

"A fire break," Tess said. "I know about this. It stops the advancing fire, because there is nothing left to burn. If it's wide enough."

"Where did you learn these things?" Giri asked.

She shook her head. "I don't know."

"We call it *laesoh-rahlee,*" Giri said. "The ring of life. Brushfires are common in the Anari lands. The ring of life will protect a village. If, as you said, it's wide enough."

"This isn't as wide as a *laesoh-rahlee,*" Ratha said. "But it is all we can do. A village together can bring more coals. And brushfires happen in the dry season. We have done all we can. Now we wait for the *Lao-Sou*."

"And then?" Sara asked.

"We let it starve," Giri said. "If we are right, if you and Lady Tess have Ilduin blood, the *Lao-Sou* will be unable to leave, fixed by its thirst for Ilduin power, even as it burns around it everything that it might eat. When all is gone, it must wither and die. Consumed by its own unbending desire."

"And if it jumps the fire break?" Tess asked. "What then? Can we fight it?"

Giri looked down. "Perhaps. But I don't know how."

It came upon them an hour later, visible first as a bright spot on the horizon at the base of Moranir, growing more quickly than Tom could believe. Still reeling from the import of his earlier pronouncement, which seemed to have come from beyond his own knowledge or experience, he watched its approach with perverse fascination.

As it grew nearer, he began to make out features, although they changed as quickly as he could identify them. One moment it bore the appearance of a fiery lion, then a lion with a man's face, then that face on a jackal's body, and then with the head of a snake. It was as if he were watching a cloud twist in the wind. But this was no idle cloud, nor was it twisting at the whim of a breeze. It was alive.

And it had intent. Evil intent.

At Tess's insistence, they had drawn water from the well outside the house and set full pails within the firebreak, in case any sparks should take light inside the circle. The roof of the house itself was already sodden from the rains, but at Tess's direction they wet it even more.

It seemed impossible that after so much rain anything could burn, but their own firebreak proved that it could.

And still the *Lao-Sou* bore down on them, nearing the ring of blackened earth, shouting with an infernal roar. Tom fought the terror rising in his chest and felt his slick palm slide over the hilt of his sword. Tess and Sara needed him and the others to be strong, to be brave. Tom doubted he was up to the test.

"Courage," Archer said, resting a hand on Tom's shoulder, "is not the absence of fear. Courage is pressing on despite fear. Stand ready beside me."

Tom nodded. He and Archer and the Anari were posted outside the house, Tess and Sara within it. If the *Lao-Sou* was coming for their Ilduin blood, it was better that they were not in sight to goad it on. Not that it seemed to need goading.

It drew up on haunches like those of a horse and flailed at the air above the *laesoh-rahlee,* then pawed at the blackened earth, howling in rage.

"Steady!" Archer yelled, drawing his sword. "Give it time to starve."

Tom had no trouble obeying that order. The prospect of charging into battle with this beast turned his blood to water and his knees to jelly. He stood beside Archer, with the Anari on either flank, moving in unison with them as they tracked the *Lao-Sou* around the perimeter of the house. It was seeking a break in the *laesoh-rahlee,* but there were no breaks to be found.

Now nearer in shape to a giant lizard, it clawed at the ground, looking for fuel beneath the burnt grass. Its eyes fixed on Tom's, and he felt his heart lurch. It knew. It knew he had spoken the words that had led to the barrier that now held it at bay.

"*Arrgohn-arraaatha-morrrdoo!*" it cried.

Archer's reached out with his free hand and grabbed the front of Tom's tunic.

"What did it say?" Tom screamed, yelling to be heard over its incessant roar.

"It was the Ancient Tongue," Archer said. "'Death to all of you.' Or 'Death to all that is you.' It can mean both. And it doubtless meant both."

"Its fire is said to consume not only the body but the eternal soul," Ratha said.

"No beast on this earth has that power," Archer said. "The gods would not permit it."

"Perhaps that is why they chained these deep within the mountains," Ratha said. "The *Lao-Sou* are hell itself."

"That which lives can die," Tom repeated, tightening his grip on his sword. "That which breathes can bleed. That which burns can starve. This beast is not hell. It only wishes it were."

It was having to scrabble through the ash-covered ground outside the ring for fuel, moving around the house. And as soon as its claws touched fresh grass, the grass ignited and was consumed in an instant. It needed to eat constantly to stay alive, and there was only so much food to be had if it was to stay there to attack Tess and Sara.

Minute by minute, it grew weaker.

Minute by minute, Tom felt his courage grow.

If the *laesoh-rahlee* had not been wide enough to start with, the *Lao-Sou* was doing the rest of their work for them. With each orbit around the house, it widened the ring of lifeless earth. And now, when it tried to move within the barrier it had helped to build, it flickered down almost instantly and had to jump back.

"It will not flee," Archer said. "But it may blacken these fields for leagues around us. Let it come forward from the north, and we will move upon it while it is weakened."

"With what?" Ratha asked. "Of what good are swords against such a beast."

"None whatever," Archer said. "But the well is on the north side. Tom, get the women. Tell them to stand by the well. You will stand before them. Let us goad this thing into an attack."

Sara had huddled with Tess inside the house, listening to the roar outside, wondering what was happening. Archer had ordered them not to step outside nor even to look out a window, lest the sight of them encourage the *Lao-Sou* to jump over the protective ring.

The not knowing was tearing her apart, and her heart leapt when she saw Tom in the doorway.

"Archer wants you," he said. "Both of you."

Sara nodded immediately, for nothing could be worse than sitting there, blind to what was happening outside, wondering what was happening. Tess, however, hesitated.

"Are you sure that's a good idea?" she said.

Tom's face was as if set in stone. "Archer thinks so. And I think his plan will work."

Reluctantly, Tess rose and joined hands with Sara, walking behind Tom. He led them around to the north side of the house, but Sara's eyes were on the *Lao-Sou* that stood beyond the ring, its rage seemingly multiplied by their appearance.

Never had she seen so hideous a creature. With each roar it changed form, each more terrible and perverse than the last, each a greater blight of nature. This beast was pure evil, as fully as if it had been spawned from the soul of a hateful god. Tess pulled Sara along, following Tom to the well, where Archer and the Anari joined them.

The *Lao-Sou* no longer circled the ever-widening perimeter, fixed by its raging desire for what it could now see. Moment by moment it would claw at the earth around it for more food, and moment by moment the harvest grew ever leaner. Finally it could take no more and leapt onto the blackened earth that separated them, grasping what embers it could find, gasping as its power diminished with every stride.

"Get behind the well!" Archer shouted. "Tom, with me. Ratha and Giri, to the left. We'll channel it toward them."

Desperate beyond all reason, the starving beast came on, too hungry now to challenge the swords to either side, its eyes fixed solely on the two women behind the well. Yet with each step it grew more sluggish, flickering at its fringes, its roar dimming.

Archer and Tom kept pace to its right, while the Anari mirrored them to its left, leaving it no maneuvering room. Each lurching lunge weakened it, until finally there was but one lunge left to make: directly over the well and onto the objects of its desire.

The heat of the beast was still greater than even the oven in her father's inn, and Sara put a hand up to shield her face. Tess, however, did not. She seemed to stare into its eyes with a steel resolve that found a match deep within Sara's fear.

Sara lowered her hand and fixed her eyes on the beast, silently willing it to jump. It hesitated, uncertain whether it could make the leap, gasping, desperate, hungry and obsessed.

Finally its own all-consuming desire left it no choice, and it sprang from haunches that flamed bright with the strain of a last effort. It had gathered what strength it had remaining and focused it with deadly intent. It would clear the well, Sara could now see. It would consume them all.

"*Arrtah erlahsenah!*" Archer shouted, holding forth his sword.

And in that moment Sara felt a kick within her belly, rising up, rushing from her mouth like water bursting from a dam. Tess seemed to stiffen at the same instant, and their voices came out as one.

"Arrtah erlahsenah!"

The howling wind exploded upon them, halting the *Lao-Sou* in midair. For a moment the rush of air made the creature flare even brighter, but then it tumbled into the opening, grasping at the edges of the well, blackening the stones, screaming in anger and pain, until its last sickening scream rose with a rush of steam and faded on the wind.

They stood as one frozen until the rain began to fall again. Then Archer hurried them all back into the house, where he told Tom to build a fresh fire. Tom obeyed, laying tinder and logs in the fireplace, then taking out his flint. After a couple of strikes, the tinder began to burn.

The women huddled together on the settle, looking frightened. Ratha and Giri stood in a dim corner, as impassive as Archer had ever seen them, which meant their faces might well have been carved from stone. The last time he had seen that look on them, they had been on the auction block in Bozandar.

He lowered himself to the wooden bench beside the fire and looked at the women again. "It seems we carry a cargo more precious than most. I suspected it, but now I am certain. Ilduin."

Sara was quick to shake her head. "Not Ilduin. We may carry some small bit of the gift but… No, we cannot be the powerful ones you speak about."

Archer cocked his head to one side. "Really? And in my telling of tales, did I not say the Ilduin were rare, and that only every so often would the powers appear in a woman, even though her own mother was Ilduin."

Sara shook her head. "No, Archer, you didn't. I have no powers. Except that I can sense evil."

"And Tess heals."

Tess's head jerked up. "That was just once, and I'm not sure I did anything at all. Remember, that little girl I tried to save died in my arms."

"You are both unschooled as to your abilities. And, Lady," he added to Tess, "the snow wolf bowed to you."

"And," added Ratha, "the *Lao-sou* came looking for you. It was willing to die to reach you."

"So," Tess retorted sharply, "just where does this get us? Sara and I may carry something in our blood, but it has done us and everyone else very little good. If it has done anything at all, it has brought fearsome trouble our way."

Sara nodded agreement and moved closer to Tess. Archer noted it, and realized the women felt as if they were being attacked.

He softened his tone. "This is no criticism of you, ladies. But when one carries a valuable treasure, it is best to know it. It allows one to prepare better for the dangers of the journey."

"We are not treasures," Sara said. "We are merely women."

"Women, aye, but much more than that also. At least in the eyes of someone else. If Lantav Glassidor is using an Ilduin to magnify his powers, then he undoubtedly seeks more Ilduin to use. It may be that we carry you toward even greater danger."

"Aye," agreed Giri. "Mayhap we should take them back."

"And leave them unguarded?" It was Tom who sprang to his feet, the fire now burning behind him. "I will not do that."

Tess spoke, looking straight at Archer, who felt again a pang for something lost as their eyes met. "Wherever you leave us, we will be sought. And wherever we are sought, there will be death. For others. Remember the caravan."

"I have not forgotten. 'Twas the reason we set out."

Silence fell over the room, except for the hiss and pop of the fire.

Finally Archer spoke. "'Tis not my intent to leave the ladies behind. But we must be prepared to face again what we have faced tonight, and possibly far worse. We still do not know what tracked us two nights ago. Someone wants them. We must protect them. 'Twill not be an easy task."

He turned from them toward the fire, seeking its warmth. He wished to say no more, for discussion would be fruitless. For whatever reason, the gods had chosen this moment in time to bring these two women together. To bring this party together. Thus there was nothing to do but bear up as best they could until they had done whatever it was the gods wanted.

It was a simple calculus, but it was one he had learned at great cost.

Tess spoke. "Ratha? Giri? Do you know why the *Lao-sou* seek Ilduin?"

"And how do you know they do?" Sara added.

The brothers exchanged looks as if silently deciding who would answer.

Finally Ratha spoke. "We know only what the old tales tell us, and that is not much. Why they seek the Ilduin, I do not know."

"I do," said Archer heavily. His head was bent forward, and he had pulled up his cowl. His face was hidden within. "At the end of the Firstborn war, Ardred created the *Lao-sou* out of the fires of Dederand and sent them forth to destroy the Ilduin in retaliation for the destruction. Only the intervention of the gods saved the world from their wrath. I did not know, however, that they still existed. Until you told us otherwise, I thought the gods had destroyed them."

"But if the gods bound them," Sara asked, "how is that one got free?"

"The mountain erupted," Ratha said. "One escaped."

"No," said Archer. "One was freed. The question is, who freed it?"

The rain stopped during the night, and in the gray morning light the Anari tested the ground. It was still muddy, but they felt it safe to set forth.

The horses seemed to have had quite enough of being stabled in a small room. They were restive and eager to go. For the first mile or so, their riders had to fight to keep them from breaking into a headlong gallop.

But then their mounts settled into a safer pace, given the unknown potential for treachery beneath their feet. In some places the mire sucked at the horses' hooves, in others it was dryer. The entire landscape was gray now, with rivulets running through the remaining ash, but considering how the mountain had erupted yesterday, there was surprisingly little of the gray stuff remaining.

"It will have been washed into the rivers by the rain," Giri said. "And those downstream will have little to drink for a while."

"As if those people have not suffered enough," Archer said. Anger was growing in him, a hot coal in his belly, ready to erupt into flame at the first provocation.

These were times he had hoped never to see, yet here they were, and here he was. His memory was so long that much of it had become misty with time, or had even vanished. Most of the time he thought that a blessing. But right now he wished it were clearer, so that he could have more information to draw on.

He glanced toward Tess, saw her riding with her head bowed as if lost in thought. He wasn't sure about her, though he believed she had no memory. Over the time they had been so much together, she would have betrayed herself in some way if she were lying.

But that still left the mystery of her past and her true identity. That she carried Ilduin blood he had little doubt. But the carrying of that blood did not necessarily make one a good person, nor even promise the gift of magic.

And Ilduin had been perverted before.

So far he had seen only good in her. But that still did not ease him. Who could say what she might truly prove to be once she regained her memory?

The wolf. The snow wolf had bowed to her. He almost couldn't bear the ache that bloomed in him. The wolf had bowed only once before, to one woman, and her name was a painful scar on his heart.

His gaze slipped from her to Tom. The lad was growing up by the minute, maturing right before their eyes. His bearing grew increasingly sure, and his face reflected understanding beyond his years.

Then there was Sara. An innkeeper's daughter who daily grew, as well, her horizons expanding beyond Whitewater and the inn.

This journey was changing them all, he thought. He hoped it would be toward the good.

But with each passing league, they drew closer to the Tolora River, to the place where they would turn south toward Lorense.

The place where they hoped to discover the truth about Lantav Glassidor.

They had all better be ready.

Tom and Sara brought up the rear, side by side, holding hands. It would have been easy, so easy, for Tom to forget everything other than Sara. She drew his gaze as if she were a brilliant flame in the dark. Her hand within his felt warm, but it also seemed magical, as if her merest touch had the power to elevate him.

But he forced himself to remain alert to the world around them, for he knew Sara's life might depend upon him.

That awareness at once cowed him and made him feel stronger, for he knew, beyond any shadow of a doubt, that he was willing to die for her. And once he realized that, there was very little that frightened him anymore.

He felt as if he had stepped over an important threshold, one that had changed him forever.

He glanced at Sara again, smiling, and when she smiled back at him, his heart leapt for joy.

Periodically Ratha and Giri left the group to scout. Sometimes they rode in different directions, sometimes they rode together. This time they spurred ahead as one, searching out dangers that might await them. The world was a barren place, however, for the next several leagues. They then separated, one to the right and one to the left, heading back around the party to come up from the rear.

Toward nightfall, as the winter chill descended again, they found another abandoned farmhouse in which to spend the night. Together they guided the others to it.

It was a much bigger farmhouse, obviously the property of a prosperous landholder. To see it thus abandoned was saddening, and all stepped within as if entering a shrine.

Inside, the feeling was even stronger, for it was obvious someone had cherished this dwelling for generations. Glancing about her, Sara saw the same kind of love she had seen at the inn, everything burnished with age and care.

While the Anari took care of the horses in a nearby stable, Tom lit a fire in the central room and Sara rummaged around in her bags for something to cook for their supper. They had not eaten all day, and the cold had left them all shivering.

Then they all froze as they heard a creak from upstairs.

For a moment nothing more, then another creak.

Archer at once put his finger to his lips. The others nodded. Tom responded to Archer's gesture, drawing his sword and placing himself between the stairway and the two women.

Then, with amazing stealth, Archer crept toward the stairway, his own sword in hand, and began to climb.

Before he reached the second stair, a pair of feet appeared on the top stair, all but toes covered by a long skirt.

"Oh my," said an old woman's voice. "You don't need that, sir. I'm all alone and couldn't hurt a fly! Take anything you want. There's little enough left, unless you would like the furniture."

Archer stepped back down the two stairs and lowered his sword. "I mean you no harm, lady. We thought this place was abandoned."

The woman's feet began descending. "Well, it is, except for me. There isn't anything on earth that could make me go to Lorense these days, although my children were in enough of a hurry when the crops failed."

She emerged into view finally, a tiny woman with a mound of silky gray hair on her head, her cheeks pink with health, although her face was lined by many years.

"Oh my!" she said, smiling. "I have company. Two such beautiful young ladies and two handsome men. You can't know how lonely it has been here."

Archer helped her down the last few steps and guided her toward the rocker she indicated. Then he asked, "You won't mind if I look around upstairs?"

She waved her hand. "Be my guest. You won't find anyone else, sad to say. But why do you fear so much?"

"That," replied Archer, "is a long story."

The woman clapped her hands. "Then you must tell me all about it!"

Archer gave her a small bow, then returned to climb the stairs like a cat, making no sound. Tom, meanwhile, lowered his sword, as well, but kept himself between the stairway and the women. Neither was he ready to relax.

"You must have seen some very bad things, to be so cautious," the woman said. "I am Silver Haddon, and I have lived on this farm since birth. My father built it from nothing, and now my sons and daughters have abandoned it because of a bad winter."

"Why did you not go with them?" Tess asked.

"Because there has always been a Haddon on these lands. If I am to be the last one, so be it." She shook her head, a birdlike movement. "They have children to feed. I do not. I have my preserves from last year to keep me going, and 'tis quite enough for one. Even enough for a few guests." Her eyes twinkled.

"I hope," said Sara, "that your family did not go to Derda."

"My dear, no. They also have a house in Lorense, because they do not like to winter on the farm, and thanks to my husband, they can afford not to. Although, to my way of thinking, Lorense is the last place they should want to be."

"Why is that?"

The woman shook her head. "Later. I will speak of these things later, once we have learned more about one another. 'Tis not safe to speak loosely these days."

Archer returned before too long, his sword once again sheathed. "We are alone," he said, then nodded to Ratha and Giri, who were standing at the door. The two Anari gave him a small bow and stepped inside.

"Why?" asked Giri later, as they checked the surrounding land and buildings, and fed the horses, "would the family leave its matriarch here alone?"

"I am not of these people," was Ratha's answer. "Ask me not to explain their ways."

Giri snorted. "Aye, 'tis just like you to deny having an opinion, when you know you always have one."

Ratha shrugged. "She is the matriarch. If she refuses to go, who will make her?"

"It passes strange," Giri said as they stepped out of the stable once more into the frigid air. The icy wind had risen and now whipped their cloaks about them with the sound of half-filled sails on a Neri ship.

Ratha eyed his brother. Overhead, stars winked beyond counting, but no moon had yet risen. "If you are asking if I am uneasy, I will not deny it."

"The woman?"

"The situation."

Giri suddenly laughed and clapped his brother on the shoulder. "If we ever feel easy, wake me up, brother, for I will either be asleep or dead."

20

Silver Haddon proved to be a delightful hostess. She took Sara and Tess into her larder, and together they emerged with jars of jams and dried fruits. Bread they made from flour, which Silver promised them was from last year's crop, because this year's had failed well before harvest.

"And a good thing, too," Silver said. "We heard of those who sickened from eating the bits that survived, so we plowed our fields under. My lads were good. They gave as much as we could of last year's reapings to our workers, and I have saved, as you see, just a little more than I need for myself. 'Tis glad I am to share it with you."

"You're very generous, mistress," Sara said.

"I'll have you calling me Silver, if you don't mind. Generous? Not at all. One has obligations, you know."

Tess somehow knew how to make bread, even if her mind couldn't recall. She began kneading the dough without instruction.

"I see you remember something," Sara said, smiling.

"My hands do."

Sara laughed.

Silver looked perplexed. "Why would she not be remembering how to make bread?"

Sara flushed and looked at Tess, wishing she had not brought up the subject, for surely it must trouble her. But Tess gave her a gentle smile and said, "Well, Silver, I seem to have lost my memory."

"Oh, dear!" Silver appeared appalled. "My poor woman! Memories are life's greatest joy. I can't think what I would do without mine."

"Perhaps mine were not so good," Tess said, working the dough.

Silver sighed. "Sad to say, for some that is true."

Five loaves of hot bread were served at the plain plank table in the kitchen, along with jam and dried fruit, and plenty of good, strong tea. Even Silver ate as if she were famished, and blushed when she caught Sara looking at her.

"I haven't been making bread for myself," she said. "It seems a great deal of work for one woman my size, and I can never finish a loaf before it is stale. That's wasteful. Nor can I turn it into pudding, because my last milk cow has died. So I have been nibbling at the fruit, and occasionally enjoying a spoonful or two of the jam, along with a pickle every now and then. But one gets tired of it. Company makes a meal so much more enjoyable."

Sara jumped up from the table and returned with one of her father's ale skins. "I have something special for you, Silver. My father's ale."

She filled a mug for everyone at the table with Bandylegs' finest, and soon the conversation was flowing as freely as the food.

Ratha treated them all to a bawdy song, and for a while everyone was laughing and telling jokes. But then as if something dark suddenly fell over them, the conversation turned more serious.

Tom and Sara told Silver of their journey from Whitewater, omitting the worst, including the terrible things that had happened in Derda. Nothing was said about the *Lao-sou,* either.

"Heed my advice," Silver said, as she emptied her second mug of ale. "Don't be going into Lorense."

"Why?" asked Archer. He had so far remained mostly silent.

Silver hesitated visibly. When she spoke, her voice had lowered, as if she feared being heard outside the room. "You understand, I have not gone there. I would not go with my family and begged them to stay with me, though we might hunger through the winter. But they did not heed me."

"Heed you about what?" Tom asked.

"They are only stories, but they are fearsome stories," she said quietly. "I tremble even to repeat them, though I tell myself they cannot be wholly true."

All eating and drinking had stopped, and every head turned her way, awaiting each word.

"There are rumors," she said, her eyes darting about, as if to make sure every window was shuttered and every door closed. "Rumors of a mage of great power. 'Tis said that if one falls under his spell, one will never again be free. I have heard that he can read minds, this wizard, the minds of all who come under his control. That he need not even speak a word, for he speaks into their minds."

Ratha nodded. "So we have heard, mistress."

Silver nodded, her expression somber. "I fear for my sons and grandsons. I warned them of the danger, and they laughed at me. Few of our youngsters believe in such things as magick anymore, Master Ratha. Few indeed. But I fear we are falling on times long foretold. The time when mage will fight mage, laying the earth to waste. The time when the Weaver shall come and change all."

She sighed and leaned back in her chair. "I hear that if you cross this mage, one of his assassins will steal up on you in the night, invisible, and kill you. I hear that the people of Lorense live in terrible fear and will hardly come out of their homes. I hear, too, that Lorense alone has been spared this blight and early winter."

Her eyes fell on each of them in turn. "If that is true, then the tales of the mage are true. If so, his power is beyond any reckoning since the First Times, when the Firstborn knew such power."

Archer nodded, his expression grim. "So it appears."

Silver looked hard at him. "Your eyes tell of many miles and many years, Master Archer, though you seem passing young. I tell you now, whatever comes to us now surpasses anything man has ever seen. There are tales of bane-bears in the woods, of creatures created by evil magic who have no names at all and can hardly be described. There are things that are nothing but bloodlust on foot.

"Always has there been some magick in this world, though it has shrunk from what it once was. But this mage…he has somehow found the way to open doors that were closed at the end of the First Times. And thus I stay here and hope my sons and daughters escape his evil eye."

Silver claimed then that she was tired and longed to rest before the fire. Sara and Tess immediately went to her aid and saw that she was tucked beneath a blanket in the padded rocking chair she chose. She sat there rocking, watching the flames, until her eyes drooped closed.

None disturbed her.

* * *

In the kitchen, Sara and Tess began to clean up from dinner with Tom's help. Bread into the breadbox, jams and pickles back onto the larder shelf, dried fruit back in its tin. Crumbs were swept away and tossed into the kitchen fire.

Archer and the Anari, meanwhile, disappeared outside into the dark. Prowling, Tom thought. Those three always prowled about, as if they could not rest.

For his own part, he was exhausted and offered no complaint when the kitchen was clean and Sara took his hand, guiding him to the stairs, guiding him up to a room that looked abandoned, but which had a nice, soft bed.

He lay upon it, at Sara's urging, and she lay beside him, burying her face in his shoulder. Never had he dared dream that he would hold Sara this way, that she would seek his arms.

"Tom," she said. "I'm frightened."

He turned toward her, bringing his other arm around her. "I am, too," he admitted. "But I will die to protect you, Sara."

She lifted her head and looked at him. There was little light in the room; her face was impossible to read. But her voice told him everything he needed to know.

She spoke with sorrow, fear and yearning. "'Tis that which frightens me, Tom. I don't want to lose you."

Tess sat opposite Silver before the fire, in a deep, comfortable chair. A long day in the saddle, followed by the fullest meal she'd had in a long time, left her drowsy.

She resisted sleep, however. Of late, many of her dreams had been as disturbing as her daily life. They brought her no surcease.

And the comfort she felt in this house disturbed her also. It was odd to even think such things, but not once in the time she was able to remember had she felt so welcome or so comfortable. That alone was enough to put her akilter. Feelings like this were not part of her meager store of memories.

She glanced at Silver, who seemed to be asleep, and returned her attention to the dancing flames of the fire. They twisted sinuously, wrapping around one another to become one, then separating again and joining with others. They reminded her of something…something distant and hazy and forgotten.

She tried to open her mind to the memory, hoping that if just one thing came back to her, others might follow. Just watch the flames, let the feelings flow….

It was night, and she stood all alone in the midst of a great black plain that reflected the stars. Sorrow lay so heavy in her heart that she could not even weep. Arms outstretched, she reached for others and could find none. It was broken. It was done.

She collapsed and curled up, wanting only to die, staring up at the hard, heartless eyes of the stars.

Then a gentle voice came to her, seeming to ride on the wind. A man's voice, full of kindness. "Come with me, child," it said softly. "I will give you the power you seek, and the sorrow will be gone."

She sat up, looking around, seeing no one.

"Child," he said, "come…"

"Tess?" A hand shook her, and her eyes fluttered open to see again the fire and the cozy room around her. Silver was bent over her. "Tess, what is wrong?"

Tess shook her head, trying to free herself from the cobwebs of sleep. "I must have been dreaming."

"Weeping, you were. And I felt a cold touch come into the room." Silver's eyes narrowed, looking around; then she appeared to relax. "'Tis gone now. I do not know what came in here, but 'twas nothing good."

Tess pushed herself up straighter. "Then we must be on our way, Silver. I wish to bring no ill to your house."

"Stay, child," the old woman said. "I'm past an age to be worrying about what becomes of me. Were I so concerned about my safety, I wouldn't stay here alone to be prey to thieves and rogues. This is my home, and here I shall die, but never let it be said that Silver Haddon allowed a guest to leave in the middle of the night."

Tess couldn't help smiling at her, and realized her cheeks were stiff from tears. She quickly wiped them away.

"Silver, you don't understand. There are…evil things that pursue us."

Silver sat on the wooden stool in front of Tess and reached for the younger woman's hands. "Ah…." she murmured. "I thought it might be so."

"What might be so?"

Silver smiled at her. "You are of the Ilduin. I can feel it in your touch. My mother shared in the gift, but it skipped over me and my daughters. Who can say if it will ever appear in my line again?"

"I know nothing about it," Tess said frankly. "People keep telling me this, but I know naught about the Ilduin."

Silver nodded. "Many keep silent, even with their daughters. 'Tis not looked on as a blessing, since the First Age. Some even think it a curse."

"I may become one of them."

Silver laughed quietly. "I pray that you will not. The time comes when our world will have need of such as you, Tess. You must be strong. But wait here. I have something for you."

Tess, feeling chilled despite the nearby heat of the fire, pulled a blanket from a bench under the window and wrapped it around her legs. The room was drafty, and she supposed the wind must be building outside again.

Silver returned a short while later, carrying something wrapped in a leather pouch. Sitting on the footstool before Tess, she loosened the drawstring and poured the contents into her hands.

Tess gasped at the beautiful colors that fell from the bag, stones as clear as the most perfect glass, gently rounded in a variety of shapes, seeming to hold within their depths the purest colors she had ever seen.

"There are twelve of these," Silver said, her voice hushed. "They have passed down in my family since the First Age. My mother told me I must treasure them until I met a true Ilduin, one I could recognize as I recognized her. Then I must pass them on."

She held out the stones, and Tess extended her own hands, accepting them with trembling awe. "They are so beautiful."

"Aye," Silver agreed. "Many's the time over the years I have taken them out just to admire them."

"They are so warm!"

"They warm in your hands, Lady Tess. And in yours alone. For me they remain cold."

Tess looked at Silver, then again at the stones. "But what are they?"

"That I do not know, sadly. My mother never would tell me. But she told me this, that I must give them to the first true Ilduin I met."

"You should find another, one who knows what these are."

Silver laughed. "I have waited ninety summers. You are the first, and to you they go. When they are needed, you will know what they are."

The idea seemed preposterous to Tess, and despite their beauty, she quickly poured the stones back into their leather bag.

"Keep them around your neck," Silver said. "My mother always did."

Tess complied, though confusion and humility both filled her. When the cord was tied about her neck, she tucked the bag within her tunic. The stones lay between her breasts, right beside her heart, where they continued to feel warm against her skin.

Silver returned to her rocker, looking quite pleased. "In the first age there were twelve Ilduin. I have always thought it might be significant that there are twelve stones. But what it might mean, I was never able to puzzle out. Nor am I sure my mother knew, either. But whatever they are, I have now completed my mission." She smiled. "I had begun to wonder whether I ever would. I thought about passing them on to one of my daughters, but it seemed to me the stones were more likely to be sold somewhere, for that is how they are. Then, when they determined to travel to Lorense for the winter..." Her expression grew grave.

"Then I knew I must keep the stones, though I died with them still hidden from discovery. If they are so important to the Ilduin, then they will also be important to the mage. Take care, Tess. I hope I have not just made your life more dangerous."

21

Archer awoke in the wee hours with a headache that felt as if a blacksmith were hammering a horseshoe on his head. He staggered to his feet, feeling disoriented, his entire body cramped.

The stable. What had he done? Fallen asleep in the stable? The last thing he remembered, he and the Anari were setting up watches for the night. Ratha had chosen first watch, and Archer and Giri had been walking back toward the farmhouse and...

There his memory stopped, and the harder he tried to remember, the more his head pounded.

Fear lanced him like a boar's tusk. Ignoring the pain in his head and body, he staggered toward the door of the stable, wondering if he had been drugged somehow.

Outside, the first pale gray light was beginning to glimmer near the horizon, heralding the sunrise to come. All was quiet and still, even the wind. It was a cold dawn, his breath blowing clouds of white as he looked around.

Smoke still rose from the chimney of the farmhouse. Where were Giri and Ratha?

Still staggering, he went to the post Ratha had chosen, an old tree with branches that swept the ground, a perfect hiding place. Behind those branches, he found Ratha soundly asleep.

"Ratha!"

A moment passed; then a groan answered him.

"Ratha, 'tis dawn! Stir yourself."

Another groan. "Who hit me?"

"I do not know. Where is your brother?"

"Didn't he come?" Ratha sat up slowly, cupping his head in his hands. "I did not drink this much ale."

"None of us did. Something's wrong."

Ratha pushed himself to his feet, moving like an old man. "I feel as if someone beat me."

"I, too. Let us see if your brother is in the house."

They staggered like old men, or drunks, toward the farmhouse. In the flat gray light of predawn, the world looked more like a painting in gray than reality.

But, thought Archer as he steadied Ratha and felt the aching of his own body, this was no dream, no painting.

They were moving a little better by the time they reached the front door of the farmhouse. Archer lifted the latch and threw the door open.

Inside, all appeared peaceful. Silver slept in her rocking chair, Giri lay on the floor wrapped in his cloak. The fire still burned.

"'Tis all right," said Ratha. "Everyone is unharmed. My lord, I beg your forgiveness for sleeping on watch."

"I, too, slept, though I do not know why. In the stable. And I am not certain that everything is as it should be. Stay here and keep watch while I search the rest of the house."

"Aye, my lord." But to do so, Ratha had to slump onto a wooden bench. "I never awake feeling this bad. Am I ill?"

Archer did not answer. Instead he moved soundlessly, first through the downstairs room, then through the upper. He found Tom and Sara sleeping on a bed in one of the rooms, and for just an instant a fond smile flickered over his harsh features. But not for long, because fear and concern rode heavily on him now.

Downstairs, he roused Giri with the toe of his boot. It was no easy task. Whatever had caused them to sleep outside had evidently been stronger in here.

"What is it?" Giri mumbled.

"Tess. She's gone."

They found the footprints outside the back door, of both horses and men. Archer immediately recognized the horseshoe prints as those he had found at the site of the caravan slaughter. They headed away to the southeast, toward Lorense.

His heart slammed in his chest. Tess had been taken! And he had not doubt who had taken her, nor why. The dark mage, Glassidor, was using an Ilduin's power to maintain his hive. With another Ilduin, he could extend that power.

Tess would resist, but Lantav doubtless had some cleverer means of seduction. He had already taken one Ilduin under his power. Tess was strong of spirit, but she had no memory, and that made her vulnerable. A web of lies that she might otherwise know to be patently absurd might seem true, especially if they offered the comforting illusion of a past.

If she *did* resist successfully, then Lantav would very likely kill her. If she did not, then he would have two Ilduin in his thrall, and there would be no way to stop him save to find and assemble all the others.

It would be a hopeless hunt, he knew. Those Ilduin who remained either did not know who they were or hid their gifts for their own safety. Even in a world where magick existed, it was frowned upon except in its simplest forms, for surely it had brought about the end of the First Age.

And Tess. He feared for her safety as he would have feared for his own blood kin, had he any. He did not fully trust her, but she had come under his care, and he had failed her.

Failure was not new to him. He carried the scars of failures so old that few remembered them. But this fresh failure stung at him every bit as much as the old.

"They cast a spell on us," Giri said grimly.

"So it would appear." Archer's voice was as taut as his bowstring. His head still pounded so badly that he doubted his own ability to think clearly. "Giri, rouse the others. Ratha, make a large pot of tea. We need to clear our heads of the remnants of this spell and decide what we must do."

"'Tis clear what we must do," Giri said. "We must recover the Lady Tess."

Archer looked at him. "But to set out without plan or preparation may endanger her. 'Tis no time to rush, Giri. Now wake the others."

Tom and Sara felt as afflicted as the rest, and came downstairs looking drawn and shaky. Silver, however, had not survived the spell. They could not wake her, nor could Sara breathe life into her. With heavy hearts, they dug a grave and buried her.

"This mage," Archer said, his voice as harsh as sword against sword, "has much to account for."

* * *

Fractured images filled Tess's dreams, and she could not seem to hang on to any one of them or rouse herself from sleep.

Horses galloping, speeding through the night. Men in black robes, their faces covered. Swallowing hot soup. Arms holding her. Her feet and hands bound. Icy wind across her face.

The images came and went, flowing in brief bursts before sleep carried her back to its realm near death, in impenetrable darkness.

But even there, at the threshold of death, some kernel within her knew that something was terribly wrong.

Archer and his party galloped across the wind-ripped plain toward Lorense, no longer sparing their steeds, no longer concerned about drawing attention, ready to fight to the death any who might hinder them. Their only concession to safety was to keep Sara in the center of the group at all times.

Archer pushed forward as a man deranged, or one in thrall to anger. He allowed a pause only when necessary for their mounts, and when they paused, Sara moved among the horses, murmuring a strengthening spell she still recalled from childhood.

It seemed to work, for the horses were soon refreshed and ready for another hard gallop.

But finally not even spells could work. The horses had to be allowed to rest before they died.

They made camp in early evening, feeding the horses heartily from the grain they had brought. For their own supper they ate the leftover bread from the night before and some of Silver's dried fruit.

Archer could not sleep. He had never needed much sleep, but this night he would not allow himself even that little bit. He took the first watch and never roused the others for the later stints. The memory of the red-eyed beast that had tracked them before kept him alert.

His mind, every fiber of his being, was focused on Lorense and Tess. He sought with skills long unused, trying to sense her out there in the night. Once he thought he caught a glimmer, but it was gone before he could be certain. Her captors must have her ensorcelled still.

Squatting, he took a twig and began to draw in the dirt. The starlight was bright enough for the task. In fact, with senses long dimmed, he could almost hear the music of the starlight as it fell upon the ground. A light, airy music that filled him with longing.

He forced himself to turn that longing toward Tess and continued to draw absently in the dirt, awaiting the moment of knowledge.

It was a long wait. The plain remained undisturbed save for the incessant wind and the faint tinkling of the starlight.

He drew stars and circles of power, and arrows that pointed toward him and toward Lorense. When there was no more space in front of him, he wiped the ground smooth and began again.

He hardly felt the cold that was seeping into his bones, or the ache in legs too long unmoved. Such distractions could not be allowed. This was all about Tess. Tess…

All of a sudden the twig leapt from his hand and landed on the ground pointing south with the drawing end.

South. Due south. Tess had crossed the Adasen River and was probably now on the road between Lorense and Derda, rather than crossing the open plain.

He stood, ignoring the scream of his legs and knees as he straightened them, and looked upward. The stars of the White Lady constellation had risen over the eastern horizon.

A good omen? Perhaps.

But now he knew what he needed to do come morning.

They were being followed. Giri spied the cloud of dust behind them at their first rest break the following morning. He pointed to it, and Archer nodded.

"Lantav's minions. I suspected we would be followed," he said.

"What I don't understand," said Giri, keeping his voice low so the others wouldn't overhear, "is why those who abducted the lady didn't kill us in our sleep."

"I suspect that Silver's death was no accident, my friend. I think the spell was meant to kill us all."

"Why did it fail?"

"Because whoever sent those men did not understand who we are."

Giri cocked his head. "My lord, you forever speak in riddles about matters of this sort."

Archer smiled faintly. It was clear his heart was heavy, and even that small smile was difficult. "Come, Giri, tell me the creation story of the Anari."

"You know it as well as I."

"True. Mayhap even better. But tell me anyway."

Giri closed his eyes, thinking back to the songs he had heard while growing up. He was no teller of tales himself, being rather more rough and limited in his language, but he tried anyway.

"After the Firstborn war, when the Firstborn saw what they had done, they were filled with sorrow at their misdeeds and considered themselves flawed. They decided this flaw must be corrected and thus decided to create a new race of beings, beings who could not go to war. They called this new race the Anari and gifted them with a great power over stone so that they might glorify themselves with beauty. But the gods, when they saw this, were angered at the presumption of the Firstborn. Thus it was they took the power of creation away."

He opened his eyes, looking at Archer. "I still don't see…"

"The Firstborn created the Anari in their own image, except for one thing: though stout-hearted in defense, they had no will to aggression. But consider, Giri, that if you and yours are created in the image of the Firstborn, and the length of your lives is so long…"

Giri nodded. "The spell could not kill us. Only a severe wound, the bane poison or starvation can kill us, until the natural end of our days."

"Exactly. Apparently Glassidor does not know this about you."

Giri suddenly smiled, his teeth bright in his dark face. "It is unlikely any of my kind would have spoken of this outside our own people."

"And that is where Glassidor made his mistake." He nodded toward the cloud of dust behind them. "Apparently he has realized his error. I am guessing he has called in an outpost upon our rear."

"But what of Tom and Sara? Why did the spell not kill them, too?"

"Tom lay in the arms of an Ilduin that night. Glassidor tuned his spell so that it would not kill Ilduin, else he would have been left with Tess's corpse. Tom was protected, albeit unwittingly, by Sara's closeness."

Giri seemed satisfied. "What are we to do about them?" He indicated their pursuers.

"There is a rock outcropping about four hours' ride ahead of us. Do you recall it?"

"Aye. 'Tis said it was once called Eshkar, that once those stones were carvings of the gods, bigger by far than any man."

"The rain and wind of centuries have taken their toll, but unless I misremember, 'tis a fine place for an ambush."

Giri's eyes lit. "Aye," he said, his hand falling to his sword hilt. "I am tired of Glassidor and his minions. 'Twill be good to teach them a lesson."

22

The Eshkar rose from the plain like fingers thrusting skyward, visible for leagues around. The closer the company drew to them, the bigger they grew, until they were towering monoliths of stone set in a circle. One could almost make out the figures they had once been—some of them, at least, for much of the stone that made them up had tumbled to the ground, creating a hazardous terrain full of nooks and crannies to catch the unwary.

"Once," Archer said, making a wide sweep with his arms, "this place was sacred to the gods. 'Twas here the Ilduin came to perform the ceremonies of rebirth each spring, ceremonies of thanksgiving and blessing on all the world."

Then, as if he could see the statues as once they had been, he pointed to each in turn and chanted:

"Sarduk brings us fire and night
Elanor comes to make things right

Adis guards the lonely seas
Samal brings the lilting breeze
Makar sends the winter snow
Eremil makes the gardens grow
Metalaar rules the spring
Asenmol the summer brings
Dalenar the sun makes rise
Subik rules the starry skies
Kalekei does bring the fall
And Eshkaron does rule them all."

He lowered his arm. "'Tis a child's rhyme, a way to remember. But I pray Eshkaron is with us."

Sara dismounted, handed her reins to Tom and began to climb among the rocks, drawn as if by a physical tug. She felt a need to stand at the middle of the fingers of stone, and she had long since stopped arguing with the strong impulses that sometimes guided her.

The scramble over the fallen rocks was not easy. Soon she was breathing hard, and her hands, despite being gloved, felt bruised and sore.

More had happened here than weathering over centuries, she realized. Someone had deliberately tried to tear down these stones, but they had failed, for the most part. It had happened a long time ago; there were no sharp, fresh edges on any of the rocks, but still, it had been done, and done with purpose.

Fell purpose. The awareness began to fill here as she approached the center of the stone ring. Evil had been done here once, leaving its scar on the sacred ground. It was as if the very air had been rent and had never fully recovered.

She was gasping by the time she reached the center of the ring, less from exertion than from the pressure that seemed to fill the air here. She sat on the center stone, knowing somehow that it *was* the center, once an altar, now just a high, worn, almost level stone. She sat cross-legged, folding her hands in her lap, and closed her eyes.

"Open your heart and ears," her mother had once told her. "You will sense the underlying power of existence."

Sara had never really been able to sense it, and her mother had always laughed kindly and said, "You are still a child. When you become a woman, you will feel it."

She was a woman now, and memories of those special times with her mother filled her, the times when Sara had known she was someone special, because Mara, her mother, said so.

But Sara had never learned the many things her mother had promised. Instead, Mara had disappeared just as her daughter was entering womanhood.

Training had been forgotten, left in dusty corners of the mind as Sara had taken on the responsibilities her mother had left behind.

But the memories came back to her now, and feeling again like a small child, she tried to do what her mother had taught her lo, those many years ago.

"Do not disturb her," Archer said to the others. "She is seeking something. For now let us find our best positions from which to defend and attack."

Even within the darkness of the dream that confined her, Tess could realize that something was wrong. Some remaining sense told her that she had slept for far too long, that she needed to fight her way back to awareness.

But each time she seemed on the verge of succeeding, each time she found a hand or a foot and moved it in an attempt to awaken, something cool would be pressed against her forehead, and she would once again tumble over the precipice into the consuming darkness.

There came another dream, this one of a dark, dank corridor carved out of solid stone and lined with heavy wooden doors. Terror filled her as she looked at those doors, for she was certain something horrible hid behind them, awaiting only a chance to spring.

She knew she must traverse the corridor. There was no other way out. But all those doors...

Her feet felt glued to the floor, and taking the first step was like walking through molasses. She had to reach the far end of the hall. And quickly, quickly, for something was after her, and if one of those doors opened, some monster might leap out....

Another step. Then another. Whatever chased her was coming closer, unhampered by the molasses that slowed her down.

Desperate, she tried to run and fell. At once she rolled over to face the terror that chased her, but nothing was there.

Instead, the door nearest her popped open, and a woman looked out at her. Something about the woman was familiar, but Tess could not recall who she was.

"Theriel," the woman said, "you must remember. You *must* remember."

With an audible pop, the dream imploded and Tess was suddenly fully awake. She could feel the thongs that bound her wrists and ankles, could feel that she was riding sideways on a saddle, while some man who stank of unwashed clothes and body steadied her. She could see nothing, for a blindfold covered her eyes tightly.

But she was awake. Careful not to let on by sound or movement, careful not to tense, she waited, knowing that now her ears were her only hope of finding a way out of this mess.

If Archer and the others were still alive, they would even now be hunting for her. Of that she had no doubt. But it was not something in which she could trust. For now her own senses and abilities were all she had.

She waited for someone to speak, but no one did. They galloped on to wherever they were headed. And finally the man who held her must have guessed somehow that she was awake, for the cool thing touched her forehead again, and she was gone.

Sara was vaguely aware of the others around her, disposing themselves, talking quietly so as not to disturb her. But mostly she was aware of the rock beneath her and around her. With her eyes closed, she could still see all the rocks, as if they had ethereal bodies that were visible only in her mind. Was this what her mother had meant?

Then, faintly, she felt a gentle humming. At first she wasn't quite certain it was there, but the more she heeded it, the stronger it grew.

This place was filled with power. She could hear it, feel it. It was as if the rocks were waking after centuries of sleep, waking to the presence of an Ilduin in their midst.

An untrained Ilduin, one who knew not how to use or control such power. A shiver of fear passed through Sara. She tried to open her eyes, to break the contact with the power, but it would not let her.

Stories rolled around in her head, stories her mother had told her about how a single Ilduin's control of the powers of creation was limited, that they needed to come together as a group in some mystical way to perform great feats. That the Ilduin had foretold that someday the Weaver would come, the one who could control the warp and woof of reality by her will and hers alone, without the assistance of her sisters.

But Sara knew it was not she who was destined for such a role. Such little spells as she knew were restorative for the most part, or simple blessings. The power contained in these rocks was far beyond the summoning or control of one woman such as she.

She forced her eyes open, but the humming did not cease. She saw the four men looking at her from their positions among the higher rocks. The Anari and Archer appeared unafraid. Tom's eyes were huge, as if he could not believe what he was seeing.

She looked down at herself and saw that blue light leapt on her body; from hand to hand, from head to foot, it hummed around her and darted as though it were alive.

Fear clogged her throat, and she sat still as the stone herself, wondering what was happening, wondering what to do about it.

Protect us all, she thought, praying to whom she knew not. Please, protect us all.

Then the light winked out. The humming quieted and stopped.

The world returned to normal, but Sara knew she would never again be the same.

Archer watched the cloud grow closer. Their pursuers never let up, never paused nor rested. He began to think some power carried them along, for ordinary mortals and their ordinary steeds could not keep up such a pace so long.

"'Twill be soon now," he said to the others. "Sara, you must find a place to hide."

But Sara remained on the altar rock at the center of the circle and would not budge. When Tom tried to lift her and carry her to a safer location, it was as if she had become welded to the rock.

"Leave me," she told him, her eyes reflecting bolts of the blue light that had recently limned her body. "Leave me. This is beyond your control, Tom. Go help the others."

"Sara..."

"I will be safe. Go."

He had sworn to lay down his life for her, but she was telling him to go. Every feeling and instinct in him rebelled. "Sara, please."

The blue light in her eyes grew. "I am Ilduin," she said simply. "Go."

He went, not because he wanted to, but because he suddenly lacked the power to disobey her. Even as his mind protested, his body moved to his appointed place of concealment.

The cloud grew closer, and as it did so, what it revealed was far more frightening than mere men on horses. These horses breathed fire, and their eyes burned like red coals. The men upon them were swathed in black so that not even their eyes showed.

As they drew closer to the Eshkar, they began to slow. Clearly they spied Sara sitting at the center of the fingers of tumbled stone, and something about their sudden hesitation indicated that this was not a sight they had expected.

When they were close enough for her to pick out individual details, Sara rose to her feet.

Tom wanted to cry out to her to hide, but Archer gripped his arm and motioned him to silence.

"Hush, lad. We will have them surrounded if they approach Sara."

"But they could—"

"*Hush.*"

Tom fell silent, anger and fear warring within him. Part of him wanted to run and place himself between Sara and the approaching horsemen, but another part realized Archer was correct. With the Anari across the way, they had created a gauntlet for these men to run through if they went for Sara.

Had she purposefully made herself the bait in the trap? He knew not, but he remembered the blue lightning in her eyes. All hopes of a life with her in Whitewater had vanished in that instant. She was Ilduin. What would she want with him?

But such selfish thoughts vanished quickly in his fear for her. He wanted only one thing out of the coming battle, and that was for Sara to survive, even if it cost him his life.

Nothing else mattered.

The horsemen paused at the edge of the rocks, their fiery steeds pawing and snorting. The horses could go no farther on that rocky ground, not at any speed that would make them useful.

Ten of them there were, holding curved swords in their hands, all keeping their attention on Sara as their mounts sidled, turned and bumped into one another. Foam dripped from the horses' mouths, as red as blood.

Then one of the men lifted a crossbow from his back and aimed it at Sara. A warning rose to Tom's lips, but Archer clamped his hand over the lad's mouth. "Shh."

Sara turned as if she had just become aware of the horses and riders. She lifted her arms and spoke, her voice ringing and echoing off the Eshkar.

"Go from here at once. You defile this place."

The man with the crossbow let fly an arrow. All that kept Tom from leaping out of hiding was Archer's grip.

The arrow flew true toward Sara. Tom's heart hammered, and despair filled him.

But within a short distance from Sara, no more than the length of a man's arm, the arrow turned and struck harmlessly at a rock. Tom breathed once more.

Sara pointed at the men. "I said, be gone!"

But the men would not listen. Instead they seemed annoyed that a single woman defied them. One man dismounted; then the others followed.

As one, they began to clamber over the rocks to reach Sara.

"'Tis not very intelligent," Archer murmured. "They come in a cluster, leaving none behind to guard their advance."

Tom nodded, thinking that unintelligent opponents were to be preferred. "They may think Sara is the only one here."

"If so, they have no minds at all."

Then Archer stiffened. Tom tore his gaze away from the approaching threat and looked at him.

"The hive," Archer said. "Remember the hive?"

"Aye, the talk of one mind among them all."

"That may be what we are seeing here, Tom. The only perceived threat is Sara, so they walk blindly into a trap. Mayhap they think the rest of us are behind her."

Tom looked down at the men crawling upward across the scattered rocks. "They remind me of insects."

"Aye, and that may be exactly what they are." His teeth suddenly glinted as he smiled ferociously. "In mind, at least. At times, that may be useful. At others, it may be unsuccessful."

"This is one of those times?"

"We may hope."

The men were crawling closer, their hands so occupied with scrambling over the rocks that they had sheathed their swords. Tom thought it a pity they weren't close enough to attack.

And Sara, beautiful Sara, stood alone on her rock, facing them as if they *were* nothing but small insects crawling toward her.

Then the attackers did something strange. Without word or signal, they split into two groups and began to move toward either side of Sara, as if they intended to surround her. Tom drew a sharp breath.

"Wait, lad. Just a bit longer."

One of the men passed by, almost near enough to touch, but his head was turned toward Sara, and he failed to see Archer or Tom. The same thing appeared to be happening on the other side of the circle. Men were passing Ratha and Giri, their entire attention focused on Sara.

Then Sara lifted her arms to a peak above her head, and the blue lightning began to dance all over her. The attackers froze, clearly stunned.

"Now," said Archer, and whistled a two-note birdcall.

Tom leapt forward without waiting to see if Archer followed. His sword in hand, he ran across the jagged rocks to the nearest attacker. The attacker heard him coming, and steel rasped as he pulled his sword from its sheath.

The battle was joined.

23

Ratha and Giri leapt into the fray with rare joy in their hearts. The brothers ordinarily preferred not to fight, though they were well-skilled, thanks to Archer's tutelage. But the last days had filled them with anger, and that anger needed an outlet. What better time than when they were under attack and needed to defend Sara?

Ratha felt almost gleeful. Four against ten were easy odds, and these hive creatures repelled him. He had seen how they moved forward, showing no skill whatever, acting like drones drawn by the scent of a fertile queen bee, not caring if they died.

The hive, it seemed, had its weaknesses.

With a yell, he charged forward. Two men turned immediately to meet him, even odds as far as Ratha was concerned. It took only one lunge to slip under the guard of the first man and mortally wound him with an upward thrust to his torso.

But barely had the first man fallen than the second was on him. A better foe, this one, with a quick parry and an even quicker thrust. With one eye on the treacherous ground beneath his feet, Ratha slowed his attack and began to toy with the man, getting a feel for his style of fighting, looking for weaknesses.

Not far away, Giri was engaging three of the hive all at the same time. And holding his own quite well, Ratha noted. Then a flicker caught his eye, and he realized his opponent was being distracted by something. His movements weren't quite so sure.

Intently focused now, Ratha forgot everything except the man who faced him. Any moment now...

Again that flicker of the sword, that moment of distraction, and Ratha was able to swing his sword from the side and catch his foe in the neck. The man went down like a felled tree.

At once Ratha ran over to join his brother.

"Did you see it?" he asked Giri as they stood side by side.

"See what? Three sword blades coming at me? Aye, I *have* noticed that, brother." *Clang!* Followed by a rasp as steel slid across steel.

Ratha swung mightily, and in one movement parried two swords, one coming at him and one coming at his brother, who was occupied with the third attacker.

"Keep sharp," Ratha said, parrying yet another strike. "Something is distracting them. When it does, be ready to move."

"Aye. If it happens." Giri turned suddenly and knocked aside a blow intended for Ratha.

"Thanks, brother."

"My pleasure, brother."

"Just keep your eye sharp for hesitation."

"My eyes couldn't be any sharper. Keep *yours* on the swords."

Across the stone circle, Tom had hewn an arm off his first opponent but was now fighting for his life against a second, as Archer nearby battled the two remaining others. Blood had splashed Tom's face, sickening him, but he forced himself to ignore that.

A surprised yelp escaped him as his opponent's sword slashed his upper arm. 'Twas not deep, but it hammered painfully, and blood ran down his arm.

He wished he'd practiced harder with the sword. The hours he had spent in practice had been part of a dream he had never expected to fulfill, and consequently he hadn't kept at it as well he ought.

That was showing now, as his opponent seemed to keep getting the upper hand. Tom held him off, but holding him off was all he was doing. His arm ached not only with the effort of hefting and swinging a heavy sword, but with the jolt of each contact with his enemy's weapon.

Knowing he had not much more in him, he seized on a moment of hesitation on his foe's part and leapt forward, hoping to end it.

But the man reacted swiftly, too swiftly, and Tom saw the sword coming toward his neck even as his own plunged toward the man's belly. He doubted his would arrive first.

"Sara," he whispered, closing his eyes and thrusting with all his might.

Suddenly the world became a dazzling blue, and Sara's beloved voice seemed to ring from every rock around. "I banish thee!"

Tom kept falling forward, meeting nothing until he and his weapon met the hard rock. His sword hilt bruised his belly, then slipped, and Tom fell hard.

At once he rolled, expecting to see his foe taking advantage of his mistake…but the man wasn't there. Neither dead nor alive. He had vanished.

Tom turned his head toward Sara and saw that she now looked like a blue flame. He could barely see her features within the light.

He realized she had saved him. Somehow she had intervened and removed his opponent. Shame tasted hot as bile in his mouth.

Lurching to his feet, he plunged into the fray again, this time to help Archer. But almost as soon as he got to Archer's side, the last of the hive fell. Dead.

Tom halted and looked around. Where there had been ten men, there were now nine bloody bodies.

Sara had saved him. But *only* him.

Because he was the only one who had needed saving. Because he wasn't as strong and good as the rest.

Bile became despair in the blink of an eye. He would never be good enough for her.

The blue flame that had blossomed around Sara vanished. In that instant she collapsed to the rock beneath her. Despite his shame and despair, Tom was the first to reach her. She was breathing still, but no matter how many times he called her name, she did not awaken.

"She'll be all right, lad," Archer said, touching Tom's shoulder.

Tom looked up at him angrily, unaware that a tear rolled down his cheek. "How can you know that?" he demanded.

"Because I know Ilduin. This one called on more power than she was prepared for. She will sleep deeply now, then awake. We must let her rest."

Then he squatted beside Tom and said, "You fought valiantly and well." He squeezed Tom's shoulder, then went to join the Anari, who were examining the bodies to learn whatever they might.

In the darkness of her prison-dream, Tess felt Others. One reached out to her gently, as a sister. Another cried out in anguish for help. In her prison she could not respond, only bang at the doors from behind which came the calls.

"Tess...help me!"

"Tess, my sister..."

She sensed still more, farther away, their voices like a musical medley of wind harps. Entrancing sounds. She drifted toward them, then felt the darkness slam shut around her, closing her off once more.

"Nothing," Ratha said to Archer as he and Giri approached. "Nothing to identify them."

"They identified themselves well enough by their behavior," Archer answered. "And their hesitations revealed much."

The three men squatted to talk. Tom knelt nearby, hovering protectively over the unconscious Sara.

"What did they reveal?" Giri demanded.

"That something interrupted their attention to the fight." Archer rubbed his chin and stared up at the craggy rock formations around them. "Mayhap the Ilduin who creates the one mind for Glassidor and his assassins is not entirely on Glassidor's side."

Giri snorted. "Tell me we are not to count on that."

"Certainly not," Archer said. "But 'tis an interesting possibility. One to keep in mind." Then he fixed them with his gray gaze. "We now have a new problem."

Ratha rolled his eyes. "Aye, my lord, but we always have a new problem these days."

A rare smile flitted over Archer's face. "Aye, so it seems. But this one is critical."

"And that is?" Ratha sounded impatient.

"Glassidor now knows that we have an Ilduin with us. He is now wondering if he stole away the right woman. And he certainly wants to get his hands on our Sara, now that he has seen what she can do."

Tom suddenly spoke. "Over my dead body."

"Over *all* our dead bodies," Archer said. "But we have no time to waste. We must get to Lorense as swiftly as possible. The abductors and Tess will be entering the town by the Derda road, unless something changes their minds. It may be we can meet them before they arrive. If not, we will get to Glassidor and rescue her. But we must do *nothing* to imperil Sara."

He looked up suddenly, and all eyes followed. Above, a hawk flew in circles over their heads. "It may be," he added quietly, "that we are even now being watched."

Tom turned from Sara to look at him. "By a bird?"

"By someone using a bird for his eyes."

"So what do we do?"

Archer, who continued to watch the hawk, didn't answer directly. "Ratha? My bow."

At once Ratha rose and ran light-footedly over the tumbled rocks to the place where they had hobbled their horses. He retrieved Archer's bow and a couple of arrows.

Archer stood and selected one of the arrows. When he drew back his bowstring, he was aiming for the bird high above.

Even before he let fly his arrow, the bird called out sharply and wheeled away to the south.

The looks they exchanged said all that needed saying.

"We must go," said Archer.

Tom reached for Sara. "I'll carry her."

Giri reached out and touched his shoulder. "Not until we bind your wound, Master Tom."

Then Ratha did something Tom thought strange, although he was in no mood to question it. The Anari found a small piece of rock amidst the tumbled stone, a piece that fit easily in the palm of a hand. This he tucked into the leather pouch Sara had tied around her waist.

"'Tis powerful stone," he muttered. "'Tis her talisman, for now."

After they left the Eshkar, the world began to change. At first it was subtle, a little green growth here and there. Ratha thought that might be explained by the fact that they were slowly descending in the direction of the Enalon Sea, to the south of Lorense, and didn't pay it much mind. Winter always came later in these parts.

But gradually, the closer they drew to Lorense, the more fertile the world became, and warmer. More in keeping with the season.

They began to pass prosperous farms with crops ripening toward harvest. Fields that had not been blighted. Even off the main road as they were, they began to see people at work and children at play.

When they reached the small village of Mozar, in the delta between the Tolora River and the Adasen River, northwest of Lorense, they found a world totally untouched by all that had happened throughout most of the Adasen Basin. The markets were full, and the streets were crowded with healthy people. For the first time on their journey, they had no trouble replenishing their supplies.

Archer found that disturbing. Where were refugees like those that had crowded into Derda? Why had none of them filled this village? Did Lantav Glassidor have the power to make thousands of people go where he wished? Or had he somehow driven them with his black-clad minions?

But they had no time to pause and question people. Overhead, the hawk still soared as it had soared over them since the Eshkar.

They had to keep moving, even if they were moving directly into a trap.

Archer paid for them to board the ferry that would carry them across the Adasen River to the Derda Road. His hope that they would find Tess before she fell into Glassidor's hands was slim, but he was ready to take on Glassidor and every one of his minions at whatever cost. This was one mage who could not be allowed to live.

Sara had begun waking for short periods, but she seemed disoriented still. Archer wondered if Tess had perhaps had to do something along the lines of what Sara had done and it had cost her memory. It would certainly explain why she alone had escaped the attack on the caravan.

Giri, having helped Ratha tether the horses to the ferry rail, came to stand beside Archer as the ferry began to cross the Adasen River. Here the river was wider, but also slower, a big difference from the rapid rush north of Whitewater, where it was born in the mountains.

"'Tis passing strange," Giri remarked.

Archer nodded, his thoughts on Tess and Sara, on the unexpected appearance of not one but two very powerful Ilduin. On the way they had somehow come together in Whitewater, then joined a journey that would lead them to Glassidor.

The gods worked in mysterious ways, but he was beginning to feel their hands here. Strange, for they had abandoned this world centuries ago.

Giri spoke again. "I fear for Lady Tess."

"I, too." More than he wanted to admit, even to himself. He regarded her with so much distrust, largely because she alone had survived the attack on the caravan and had what might be consid-

ered a convenient memory loss. But as the time lengthened since
her abduction, he found he was worrying terribly about her.

But there was another worm in his brain that wouldn't leave
him alone. What if she had been involved in arranging her own
abduction?

It was a thought he would never voice aloud, and it reminded
him painfully of a time when he had trusted more easily. A time
of greater innocence.

He didn't at all like the man he'd become.

24

The stones in the pouch under her tunic were growing warmer between her breasts. Warmer than skin temperature, but not quite warm enough to be uncomfortable.

The sensation drew Tess's attention from the prison of darkness in which she had resided, bringing her fitfully back to the real world. Her entire body felt cramped from lack of movement, and the thongs around her wrists had begun to rub her raw. Her boots protected her ankles, but her legs ached and threatened to cramp at any moment.

She tried to hold as still as she could each time she roused, for fear that cool thing would once again touch her forehead and send her back to the darkness.

But it did not.

Little by little she returned to herself for longer periods, until she realized she was lying on something soft, like a bed. Then she smelled stone and dampness, and a kind of incense that at once soothed her and made her nose twinge.

There was no sound save the dripping of water. She waited, battling off the darkness, listening for any sense of where she was and who might be there. A sigh. A rustle of cloth. Any sound that might betray she was not alone.

But there were no sounds, however faint, except for the dripping water, the increasing beat of her own heart, and those strange noises in the ears when all is deathly silent.

Slowly, carefully, she allowed one eye to open to a slit. She was in a room of some kind, small. It hinted at better appointments in the gold filigree that adorned some of the walls, but there was nothing in it that she could see other than the bed on which she lay.

Growing braver, she opened both eyes and lifted her head to look around. Stone floor, walls that looked like some kind of plaster over stone. In the far corner a small fountain.

At the sight of it she realized she was parched. But how to reach it?

She stirred on the bed, making a small amount of noise, and waited. No one came. Nothing else stirred. The stones between her breasts grew a little warmer, seeming to clear her mind and draw her further from the sickening darkness that hovered at the edge of her mind.

Drawing on yet more courage, she tried to sit up and realized her feet had been unbound. That must mean she had reached her final destination.

Lantav Glassidor. The name of the mysterious mage floated into her mind. He must have taken her. He must have some use for her. A small sob of laughter nearly escaped her when she thought of how disappointed the man would be. Ilduin? Yes, she might be. Everyone seemed to think so. But of what possible use could she be to anyone when she knew nothing of her powers or how to use them? Glassidor was bound for disappointment.

And she was bound for what?

At least her hands were tied in front. She was able to rise and stagger toward the fountain in the corner, where she bent her head and drank thirstily. How long since she had been taken? How many days had she slept away? She was thirsty enough to feel as if there wasn't enough water in the world to slake her need.

But eventually she could swallow no more.

Turning, she surveyed the room in which she was held. Bare except for the bed and one heavy wooden chair she hadn't noticed before. The window was a deep, narrow slit, too small to crawl through, that offered only a view of blue sky. The door was heavy wood, banded with iron, and the lock appeared heavy and strong.

Returning to the bed, she sat on its edge and studied the ropes around her wrists. Her cloak was gone, but she still wore her own garments, which meant that the stones she carried most likely remained undiscovered.

However, since she had no notion what purpose they were meant to serve, they did her no good, either.

Except in some way, with each passing moment, she felt more refreshed. That might be the water. Or it might be the stones, which had awakened her in the first place with their heat.

The knot that bound the rope around her wrists was one she did not recognize. Studying it, she could see no way to undo it without risking making it tighter. A very canny, skillful knot. But if someone could tie it, then it must be possible to untie it.

It wasn't as if she had anything else to do right now.

All of a sudden she heard a clank and a rasp at the door. She looked around wildly, wondering if she should pretend to be asleep

still, then realized the chances were good that she had been observed somehow.

The door swung open, revealing a tall, jolly looking man in a
black robe with some odd kind of flat hat on his head. Behind him
stood two armed men, swathed all in black, even their faces.

"My dear," said the jolly man, "how good to see you awake. You
must be hungry."

He snapped his fingers and stepped to one side. The guards, too,
parted, and two men in black tunics entered, carrying a table laden
with food, which they placed directly in front of her, effectively
making it impossible for her to rise from the bed without knock-
ing the table over.

"I take care of my guests," said the jolly man. He waved away
the servants and set the guards at the door. Then he closed the
door, leaving the two of them alone.

"But," he continued as he sat in the heavy chair facing her,
"'twould be much easier for you to dine if your hands weren't
bound."

He snapped his fingers, and the rope fell from her wrists. "Better?" he asked.

Tess stubbornly resisted the urge to rub her wrists, or to look
at the rope, which had fallen to the floor. She would give her cap-
tor no enjoyment of any kind. "Who are you?

"Ahh, I am your host for the indefinite future. Lantav Glassidor.
You may have heard of me?"

She nodded slowly.

"Now eat, my dear. Get your strength back. Then we shall discuss how we can save the world."

Her head jerked a little in astonishment. "Save the world?"

"Aye. Surely you don't think I have any other purpose?"

* * *

Lorense wasn't a much bigger city than Derda, but the differences were nonetheless remarkable. Here everyone and everything thrived. A room at the inn meant sumptuous accommodations for the entire party, followed immediately by a large, delicious meal in their private parlor. From the window they could see that the streets remained busy until well after dark.

As for the location of Lantav Glassidor...well, everyone was eager to tell them about the wonderful mage who had saved them from the blight that had struck the north and west. But strangely, no one seemed to know exactly where he could be found.

"So," said Ratha, "am I to feel confused or seriously misled?"

"Misled," said Archer grimly. "A wise eagle does not soil its own nest."

"Aye," agreed Giri. "A wise general also surrounds himself with allies. There are none in this city who would help us to find Glassidor."

"Then we will find him by other means," Archer said firmly.

Tom spoke. "We couldn't be wrong about him?"

Sara, who had been lying on the settle, drowsing on and off, spoke. "No. Can't you feel it? However blessed this place may appear, it *feels* cursed."

Archer nodded. "Aye, Sara, that it does. This place is no less wrong than every other place we have passed through."

Sitting on a bench before the fire, he let his chin settle on his chest. "Give me time to think on this. And keep your guard high. We are strangers here, and even if we have not been identified by the hive, being strangers makes us a threat. They will seek us out."

Sara pushed herself up into a sitting position. "Tom, I need something to drink, if you will be so kind."

He leapt up at once to bring her a mug and the water skin. He filled her mug repeatedly until she set it aside.

Finally, feeling shame and even a touch of fear, he murmured, "Thank you for saving me."

She blinked. "When?"

"At the Eshkar."

Slowly she shook her head. "I do not remember that very clearly. It was as if something from the stones filled me and guided me."

"You burned like a blue flame."

Her eyes widened; then a soft smile came to her face. "If I was an instrument for helping you, then I am grateful, Tom." She cupped his cheek in her hand. "But I was merely an instrument."

He turned his head and dared to kiss her palm. He might never be good enough for her, but he still adored her with his entire being.

"Now eat, please," said Lantav Glassidor to Tess. "You need your strength, and I promise it is nothing but healthy food. No surprises."

She wasn't sure she believed him, but as she looked at the food, she could sense nothing wrong with it. Wrongness was all around, she realized suddenly. This room, this man, all of it was wrong somehow. But not the food.

Giving in to her body's needs and the suspicion that she would need every bit of her physical strength, she at last began to eat. Roast chicken, fresh greens, bread still piping hot from the oven. The wine she ignored, drinking more water instead.

Each mouthful seemed to increase her sense of self, her mental acuity, and...her awareness that everything around her was wrong, as if time and space had been warped.

While she ate, she said nothing. Let the man talk uninterrupted, she thought. Let him think I believe his every word. In fact, he would have been easy to believe, if he had not abducted her.

"I am certain you noticed the destruction of the lands to the north and west," he said to her. "You traveled here from White-water, I believe."

She gave a nod, pretending to be unable to speak because her mouth was full.

"Terrible, terrible blight," he said, as if it pained him beyond description. "So many lives lost. So many farms destroyed. I know that some say it was my doing, but my dear Lady Tess, had I the power to do that, I would also have the power to have made all those farms prosper, to have held off the winter until its usual time."

She looked at him then, meeting his gaze directly. She noted that his eyes were so dark that it was impossible to tell where the pupil began. It was not that she had never seen eyes like his before, at least in color. It was the feeling she got that someone other than Lantav Glassidor was also looking out of them.

A chill suffused her, and she quickly returned her attention to her food.

"How many of the old tales do you know?" he asked. It seemed like a change of subject, but Tess was certain it was not.

"Few," she answered briefly, then popped a piece of bread into her mouth to excuse herself from saying more.

"'Tis a pity how they have been forgotten." He sighed. "There are lessons to be learned from the distant past."

Tess nodded and continued to chew the bread as if her life depended on it.

"You have heard of the two brothers who warred and brought an end to the First Age?"

Again she nodded.

"Annuvil and Ardred, they were called. Annuvil disappeared. He is said to have been killed in the war. But Ardred survived, an immortal. The gods carried him away to their plain of existence."

That was too much for Tess. "How do you know that?"

Glassidor frowned. "Because he has returned, my lady. It is he who is called Lord of Chaos. With powers beyond imagining, he blights the land and moves the seasons out of their course. None can withstand him."

"Then how can you fight him?"

"With Ilduin, my lady. With Ilduin. Only they can confine and restrain him. That is why I must beg your pardon for abducting you. I could not wait for your party to reach Lorense. You traveled too slowly. My city is now at the front of his next attack. I need all the help I can get to battle him, to save my people. I have one Ilduin aiding me now. I need you, as well."

"How do you know I am Ilduin?" Tess demanded, forgetting her decision not to confront the man. "Even I do not know that."

"I know," said Lantav Glassidor, "because I summoned you."

Tess felt shock ripple through her, and she stopped pretending to eat. She sat there, waiting for the feelings to run their course, feeling the stones warming yet again against her breast, as if to comfort her. *Her sisters...*

Lantav smiled. "But rest, my lady. This has all been a shock to you." He rose and took a step toward the door. Then, as if remembering something, he faced her again.

"But, unless I am mistaken," he said slowly, "you were not the only Ilduin traveling with your party."

"I don't know what you're talking about."

"Of course not," he said pleasantly. "But fear not, my lady. I'll find your sister."

After the door closed and locked behind him, making her aware anew that she was not simply a guest, she had one thought and one thought only, and it screamed out of her mind as if it would fly instantly to the right ear.

Run, Sara! Run swiftly. Run now!

Sara suddenly sat bolt upright, her eyes staring into the distance. "Tess!"

Everyone turned immediately to her. "What about Tess?" Archer demanded.

"She just told me to run. Now. Swiftly."

Tom gaped at her, but the others didn't seem surprised.

"Good advice, I'm sure," Archer said. "But I will not leave this town without Tess, and I will not let you go off alone. You would be too much at risk."

"I'll take her," offered Tom, knowing full well he wasn't enough protection, but wanting to do anything he could to save Sara.

Sara shook her head. "I'll not leave this town without Tess, either."

Archer's mouth twisted into a frown. "By this I would guess that she has just learned that Glassidor knows about you, Sara. We must keep you hidden from him somehow."

"Aye," said Ratha. "Well hidden. And well guarded until we find Glassidor."

Giri spoke from the floor, where he had spread out his bedroll and was lazing. "By this I read that Tess is still alive and once again in possession of herself. For this we should give thanks."

"Chaos," said Sara, her voice hushed. "Who is the Lord of Chaos?"

For a long time no one spoke. The fire crackled, and a gentle rain began to beat against the windows. It was Tom, finally, who cleared his throat and answered.

"Don't you remember, Sara?" he asked. "Chaos is he who will bring the great war."

"The end of this age," said Giri, his voice rough. "Why did you think of him, lass?"

"I don't know. Tess, maybe."

Archer rose from the bench and strode to the window. "Glassidor cannot be Chaos. The Lord of Chaos, once unleashed, will be able to do far more evil."

"Aye," agreed Ratha. "Only the Ilduin will be able to stand against him."

"Or the Weaver," said Tom.

"The Weaver." Archer repeated the name as if it brought him unbearable sorrow. "Aye, the Weaver. If she returns."

Suddenly he turned and faced them all. "If Glassidor gains the assistance of enough Ilduin, the balance of power may be tipped enough to summon Chaos. Perhaps that is his purpose."

Into the silence came Giri's hushed voice. "May the gods protect us all."

Long after the others had fallen asleep, Archer stood at the windows, keeping watch over the street and rooftops. His thoughts were deep and brooding, edging into places he had not remembered for many years, places he would have been content to lock firmly away forever. But that, it seemed, was not to be his lot.

Turning, he reached for his scabbard where it leaned against the wall and drew his sword quietly from it. Thin moonlight occasionally showed through the gently weeping clouds, and when it did, the steel gleamed so whitely it almost hurt the eyes.

Holding it like an offering, blade on one hand, hilt on the other, he felt a door creak open in his mind. He remembered the day his father had placed this very sword in his hands. He remembered the gravity of his father's gaze and the equal gravity of his words: *My son, use this only to defend the innocent and to bring peace.*

He had failed. He had failed most grievously, and since that time, the sword had ceased to sing in his hand.

But holding it now, he felt it vibrate. He caught his breath and steadied his hands, certain he must have caused the movement himself.

The moonlight struck the blade again, and this time a prism of color sprang from it, though the blade remained icy white. Then it hummed almost inaudibly.

Astonishment fixed him for long moments, for he had thought this would never happen again.

But it was happening now, and he tightened his grip on the sword, drawing the vibration into his own being. Then he closed his eyes and faced the truth.

The conjunction was near. Chaos was trying to return.

"Tess." He whispered her name, fearing that she was a key that could be turned either way.

Time was running out.

* * *

Tess slept not at all, whether from nerves or from having been forced to sleep for at least several days, she did not know, nor did she care. In the darkness of night, without even a candle to reveal anything she might do to any unseen watchers, she reached within her tunic and drew forth the bag of crystals Silver had given her.

One at a time, she removed each stone and held it in her palm. They all glowed faintly and felt warm, but three glowed much more brightly: a clear one, a blue one and a red one.

Did this mean other Ilduin were near? Of course it must. One would be Sara. The other would be the Ilduin who was working with Lantav Glassidor. And the third...

Even as she thought of it, the clear stone grew hot in her hand and began to gleam more brightly. At once she folded her fingers over it, to hide it from any watchers, and felt it vibrate in her hand.

This one must be *her* stone, she realized. Responding to her closeness. But what did that mean? What could it do? Anything?

Quickly she tucked it into the pouch and studied the other two. The blue one was clear throughout, like a summer sky, deep enough to fall into. To her touch it felt comforting. Sara. She could almost feel Sara through it.

That one she dropped back into the pouch for later. Her greatest concern was the other stone, the red one, the one that must represent the Ilduin who was aiding Glassidor. As she stared into it, she thought she saw something dark at its heart, a deep flaw.

Fear pierced her, and she closed her hand around it, afraid to look deeper into that flaw.

Then she heard the cry in her head. "Tess...help me...please...."
Something about the voice was familiar, and yet Tess could not

place it. She held the stone again, closed her eyes, took a deep breath and let her mind go away inside itself, hoping that some memory would push itself to the surface. But nothing did. The same voice called out for help, almost sobbing as it did so, and Tess imagined her arms wrapping around the woman, holding her.

"So long," the voice said. "So very, very long."

Tess could feel the woman shuddering against her as she sobbed, long, plaintive cries emerging with a pain that clutched at Tess's heart and left her almost gasping to breathe.

Then she felt a warmth rising within her, enveloping the woman. The cries slowly subsided into lingering pleas that fell upon the core of Tess's soul like moonlight on a diamond.

"Save me," the voice said, quietly now. The panic was gone, and now Tess heard only an earnest longing. "Please. Save me."

"I will," Tess said. "You will be free before the next sunset. I promise you."

"Thank you," the voice said. "Thank you."

She didn't know how much time had passed when she realized her hands were clenched between her breasts, holding the red stone tight to her skin. She only knew the connection had been broken, as if a piece of her soul had been pulled away. With a long, sad sigh, she put the red stone back into the pouch and closed her eyes.

For a long time she sat in the dark, the pouch in her hands, afraid of what she was learning. She had no background from which to deal with this, simply a huge void that had left her as ignorant of this world as a newborn babe.

But as her initial shock eased, she realized that she couldn't hide. She had already been identified as Ilduin, and she suspected that put her in a dangerous position. Her only hope was to learn as much as she could as swiftly as she could. Especially since it now seemed as if Sara was at risk, too. In just the short time she had known the young woman, she had come to love her as a sister.

She needed to combat both her own fear and the void of her memory. To protect Sara, to protect Archer and the Anari and young Tom, all of whom were probably even now searching for her.

For a few seconds she allowed warmth to fill her as she thought of her new friends and her absolute faith that they wouldn't abandon her. Had she ever felt that way with anyone before? She didn't know. Nor did she really need to know.

All that mattered was what she knew and believed and felt now. Even about Archer, who sometimes treated her as if she might at any moment turn into a poisonous snake. They would not abandon her. Therefore she owed it to them to find the powers they believed she had.

Opening the pouch once again, she took the clear crystal out, concealing it within her palm. The bag she closed and slipped once again beneath her tunic to hide its precious burden.

Then she cupped her hands around the clear crystal and waited for whatever would come.

In the morning, Archer ordered everyone to pack up. "We will spend the day seeking Glassidor, and I doubt it will be safe to return here tonight. For all its outward charm, I do not think this city offers any true welcome."

No one disagreed. They consumed a quick breakfast from their own provisions, then descended the stairs to leave the inn.

In the hallway they encountered a well-dressed woman and her husband, also on their way out. They all stepped back to allow the pair to pass.

The woman sniffed as she passed the Anari and said to her husband, "Whatever is the world coming to?"

Tom stiffened visibly. Sara's jaw set in a tight line. The Anari simply nodded and waited for the couple to leave. As they made their way out into the bustling street, Tom noticed more sidelong glances. On two occasions, passers by crossed the narrow street.

"Are we that frightening?" Tom asked, looking at his companions.

Their weapons were well-hidden, and they'd all had time to bathe at the inn. Their clothes looked road-worn, to be sure, but not scandalously so. Sara was as beautiful as was humanly possible, and Archer's black-green cloak almost shimmered in the autumn light.

"It's Ratha and me," Giri said.

Tom wanted to disagree. His upbringing had not prepared him for this. Whitewater was a trading village, and foreigners of all descriptions were the norm, not the exception. He realized that in many ways he'd had the best of both worlds: a small town where ties were close, and a cosmopolitan home where outsiders were welcomed. Those who might raise their noses to a stranger received a quiet but firm talking to from Bandylegs or Tom's father.

As he looked around at the people of Lorense, Tom saw a very different attitude. On the surface, they were met with smiles and welcomes. But those smiles never quite reached the eyes, and the welcomes seemed to carry a silent wish that Tom and his companions would quickly be on their way elsewhere.

This was especially true when the Anari were with them. The silent glances were increasing almost by the moment, especially when Archer and the Anari chatted freely together. When Ratha reached out to take Sara's shoulder, holding her back as a carriage clattered down the street, a woman beside them gasped.

Their morning's investigations had netted no new information, and Tom suggested over lunch that they might cover more ground by splitting up. Archer shook his head.

"You don't know this city, lad. You and young Sara might easily get lost or, worse, found."

Tom nodded. "You're right, of course. It just seems like we're wasting time. No one is going to talk to us. Not about Glassidor."

"No one will talk to you while we're with you," Giri said. His dark eyes showed neither anger nor resentment, but his voice carried both. "The closer we get to Anari lands, the more I feel it."

"You may be right," Archer said. "But remember what happened when we split up in Derda. Somehow, I don't think you're any less likely to encounter trouble here. More so, in fact."

"It's ignorant," Sara said, quiet fury in her eyes. "Ignorant and stupid."

"Yes, lass," Ratha said. "But it is the way of the world. My brother and I have lived with this for all of our days. I expect we'll live with it for the rest of our days, as well."

"Perhaps not," Tom said. "An ill-tamed horse that rears defiant in the corral is a mockery to its owner. That same horse, running free on the plains, is a balm to the tired spirit."

Archer's eyes seemed to peer into Tom's soul. "You surprise me more each day, lad."

"What?" Tom asked. "It's true."

"Of course it's true," Sara said quietly, nodding to Archer. "That's the point, dear Tom."

"I don't understand," Tom said. "I just meant..."

"What you meant and what you said are two different things," Giri said, smiling. "You speak simple truths, but simple truths speak the greater through you."

Tom shook his head, looking down at the small meal he had barely touched. He picked at some steamed greens and finally raised his eyes, hoping the conversation and their attention would have drifted elsewhere. But that was not to be.

"You have a gift, lad," Archer said. "You don't yet realize it, and maybe that is for the best, at your age. But I see it, and I think your fair Sara sees it, also. A wisdom that looks at a tree and sees the forest is a rare and precious talent."

"I'm no mage," Tom said. "I hear you talk with Sara, and before with Tess, and you feel things I do not. I have no gift of magick. And if I see the forest in a tree, it is nothing that anyone else would not see."

"Perhaps not," Sara said. "Perhaps you are simply a country lad who talks before he thinks, unworthy to breathe the same air as the more noble beings with whom he walks. And if that be so, then I am a fool. For when I look at you, I do not see a dumb country lad. And neither, I dare say, do our friends. So we are all fools."

"I didn't say that," Tom said, feeling his cheeks flush with the memory of Sara saving him at the Eshkar. "I'm just…not special. Not like the rest of you. Everyone knows Master Archer. And you, Ratha and Giri, have strength beyond all knowing in your bodies and in your souls. Sara and Tess are Ilduin blood. I am none of that. I can barely handle a sword."

"Look at me," Sara said, her eyes suddenly intense. "Look at me, Tom."

He met her eyes, and for a moment it seemed as if all the air had been sucked out of the world, leaving only utter, dead silence. Then he saw a dim image, the back of a man, sitting at a desk with an oil lamp beside him and a heavy book before him, dipping a quill, taking a long, slow breath, then writing on the fresh parchment. Farther off to the side, a woman sat in a chair, rocking a baby.

The image drew in upon itself, then winked away.

"What…what happened?" Tom asked. "What was that?"

Sara's hands shook as she raised a goblet of water to her lips. She took a sip, and a moment to steady herself, before she spoke. "Only you can know that. Only you can see. And that is your gift, my dear Tom."

Archer's eyes darkened. "It is folly to perform such in public, young lady."

Sara met his gaze. "Then folly it be. Glassidor knows we are here. We can find him, or he can find us. One way or the other, we must all be ready to meet him. And we will need whatever gifts we have."

Tom had never heard her speak like that before, and certainly never to a man of Master Archer's stature. Her voice bespoke an iron will that would not yield.

Archer, too, seemed to sense it. For a moment he appeared to consider a further rebuke. Then he nodded. "It may be, lass. Forgive my outburst."

A moment of awkward silence passed, and Tom reached out to squeeze Sara's hand. As he did, a thought grew in his mind.

"The wise wolf hunts by the stream," he said. "For then the quarry will come to him."

20

Lantav Glassidor watched as what remained of the woman seemed to drift into a peaceful dream. He regretted what had become of her, and yet he knew there was no other way. Perhaps the new Ilduin could renew her strength. If not, he would simply have to use the new one. And the other, the young one who had slain him at the Eshkar. The memory of the searing flame still angered him. But more than that, it excited him. The power he had felt as he died! The prophecies were coming to pass.

He shook off the dark feelings of death, as he had done many times before. At first it had surprised him. Somehow he had expected the connection to break in the moment before passing. When it hadn't, he had recoiled in horror, almost ripping the poor woman apart. Only her scream had brought him back from that precipice, reminded him that it was not he who had fallen into darkness. For the next few months, he had avoided both her and the others. The darkness was too black to look into ever again.

But with the passage of time, he realized that he would have to face death, and experience it, again and again. That was the price of prophecy. He learned to bear it, first with disgust and later with disinterest. Only in the past few months had he begun to look at it with a macabre curiosity. Each final heartbeat was another chance to reach beyond this plain into the very land of the gods themselves. Someday, with the help of these new Ilduin, he would be ready to step through that doorway and free the Chained One. And death itself would die.

The woman stirred, breaking his reverie. He watched as her sightless eyes opened and reached out beyond seeing, until a smile broke on her face.

"Breath of my womb!" she said.

Then, knowing that he stood beside her, knowing that their minds were as one, she threw up a wall, leaving only the image of a girl with long, flowing hair, helping her mother in the kitchen.

It was clever, but an instant too late. He had seen, and as he smiled, he heard her gasp a silent plea. For an instant the plea tugged at his heart, for in sharing her he shared all of her, and the flicker of her goodness lay within his breast. But he knew he was called to a higher purpose, in which there was no room for regret.

He flickered through his subjects until he saw one near the market and settled there. The market was busy today, and it took a moment to find the table where the girl and her friends were sitting. He found a shady spot in an alley across the courtyard and leaned against the wall, watching them.

Then he began to dance through the rest of his subjects, one by one, approaching the market, each from a different direction. This would be a noose from which they could not escape.

＊ ＊ ＊

"In the shadows," Giri said, quietly. "Across the way. The alley."

Ratha nodded. "I see him."

"I, too," Archer said. "It seems we have found the right stream, young Tom. The question is whether we are the hunted—or the hunters."

"They will take us where we want to go," Tom said. "Glassidor has too much support here in town for us to fight our way out, re-gardless. The bear who seeks honey follows the bees back to the hive."

Archer nodded. "Yes, and the bees are gathering. Two at the far end of the market. Another stands there by the smith's wares."

"Shall we draw out their stings?" Giri asked.

"Yes," Archer said. "Tom, once we rise, you stay behind fair Sara. We will keep her in our midst. If Lantav wants to meet us, he shall meet us all."

Breakfast had come and gone a long while ago, but Tess had not seen Glassidor since last night. Apparently, at least for now, he had matters of greater concern to occupy him.

Throughout the night, she had felt the pull of the unknown woman who pled for help. By the hour the call seemed to grow weaker and rarer, as if the woman's strength was being siphoned for some other purpose.

Troubled, Tess paced the confines of her cell and tried, with her nascent powers, to get some sense of what was going on around her. There was no longer a guard outside her door, she realized. Not that that made a great deal of difference, considering that she was well locked in.

Impatient with the feeling that she was trying to see through a dense murk with inner eyes that did not yet know how to understand what they saw, she reached within the pouch and took out her own crystal.

Maybe if she stared into the small stone that warmed her palm...

The next thing she knew, she was being propelled toward the door, as if her feet had a mind of their own. Her hand reached out and touched the lock. To her amazement, she heard the rattle and rasp of the tumblers turning.

All of a sudden she was shaking from head to foot. She backed away from the door, trying to conceal the crystal quickly, fearful of whatever might be coming through that door. For all that he appeared genial, eventually Lantav would want to use her for something, and she feared his purpose as she might have feared her own demise.

But no one came through the door. She waited with pounding heart, her breath coming in quick gasps, until eventually she understood that no one would come through.

Slowly she looked down at the crystal in her hand. Had some magical power unlocked it for her?

A burst of courage filled her. Or perhaps it was a flash of anger. *He* had summoned her? He had torn her from her own life and stripped away her memory, and, for reasons beyond all understanding, left her in the horror of that caravan, to bring her here and make her his puppet?

No. That was not going to happen.

She walked to the door and opened it a crack. No sound, no motion. She opened it wider and stuck her head out. There was no one in the corridor as far as she could see.

Quickly she stepped into the hallway and closed the door. Then she touched the lock with her hand and willed it to seal. A rasp greeted her attempt, and when she tried the door, it refused to yield.

She looked once more at the crystal in her hand and wondered what other powers it might hold. If it held any at all. She was so confused, with people telling her she was Ilduin, which meant she had great powers. But were the powers hers, or was she merely a channel for them? Perhaps the stone held the power. Regardless of whence the magick sprang, it would be nice if she could use more of it.

For example, she thought irritably, right now she would prefer to be invisible. Instead, full size and in full view of any who had eyes to see, she was forced to tiptoe down the hallway toward another corridor. Thank the gods for the softness of the white boots Bandylegs and Sara had given her, for they made no sound.

Now all she had to do was find a way out of this warren. The stone that had helped her unlock the door had become once again cold in her hand.

Perhaps that was best, she thought, tucking it back in the pouch and concealing all the stones once more. The use of power around here might well give her away. She would need to rely on her own wits to escape. So be it.

The corridors were strangely empty, and the rooms with open doors revealed more cells like the one in which she had been kept. After she peeked into a few of them, she began to think that she was in a barracks of some kind.

A barracks shouldn't be completely empty at any time of day, should it? Unless something serious were happening.

Her heart slammed, and she slipped into an alcove with a small window. Empty barracks. Her friends…were they being hunted, or had they been caught? She could not tell, not even when she reached out to Sara.

All right, she told herself. *Think!*

Where would a man who needed protection house his soldiers?

At the base of his dwelling. Where, even abed, they could instantly become a first line of defense. Where, whenever needed, they would be easy to summon. And a man with Lantav Glassidor's megalomania—save the world indeed!—would probably prefer to be well up above the world, surveying it from a safe distance and comfortable grandeur.

If she could find a door that led outside, she would escape. But what if her friends were already here? What if Lantav had captured them and even now held them? She couldn't simply walk away.

Then she heard footsteps. Looking wildly around the alcove, she spied a small door. Quickly she opened it. It concealed a small space barely large enough for her to fit into. She couldn't imagine its purpose, but that didn't concern her.

Footsteps passed by the alcove. She waited, but just when she was about ready to risk emerging, she heard more steps.

A lot more steps. Something was happening, and she didn't dare leave her hiding place.

The party remained at the table, watching the gathering of black-clad men grow.

"They look like a gathering of crows," Giri snorted.

"Aye," said Archer. "Remember, we do as they say."

"I'm not giving up my sword," Ratha said.

"Aye," said Archer sternly. "You are, if need be. If I can give up mine, you can surrender yours."

Ratha looked ashamed. "As you will," he said finally.

"Besides," said Archer more kindly, "I know that when you need a sword, you will be able to take one from any of these men."

Ratha brightened. "'Tis true."

Giri slapped him on the back. "Of course 'tis true, brother. You've taken mine any number of times."

The two of them laughed at some apparently private joke, but Archer returned his attention to the hive. Ordinary citizens were swiftly leaving, apparently having remembered they were needed elsewhere. Soon it would be the five of them against approximately thirty of the hive.

Apparently Glassidor felt he needed better odds than at the Eshkar.

When the square was clear of all save the hive, three of the black-clad men approached them. One spoke.

"We have come to take you to see Lantav Glassidor."

Archer nodded once, almost regally. "'Twas such a meeting we sought. We will come."

"First you will give us your weapons."

Three more men came forward in response to a summons none of the party heard or saw.

Sara and Tom promptly rose and passed over the swords they had concealed in their backpacks. Ratha and Giri were more sluggish, muttering under their breaths as they handed over their weapons.

Then Archer rose. What he was about to do, he had never done before, not once in his life. He had always sworn that his sword would never leave his hand until he died.

Turning it over felt like a betrayal. It felt as if his heart were being torn and his soul rent. All that made him do it was the thought of Tess in Lantav's hands and being used for some terrible evil.

Feeling as if he were being skinned alive, Archer passed his sword to one of the hive. "See that no ill befalls it," he said softly. "For ill will befall him who harms it."

He doubted his warning made any impression on these mindless drones. Whoever heard his words, it was not the man before him.

Then they gathered up their bags and allowed themselves to be surrounded and guided west toward Lantav's lair.

Lantav rubbed his hands with pleasure. Now he had a third Ilduin, as well. He almost laughed as the man in the black cloak spoke his warning words to Lantav's minion. "Ill will befall him indeed." He nearly laughed. "These fools are too confident for their own well-being."

Lantav had no doubt that now that he had three Ilduin at his disposal, these troublesome travelers would soon be under his control and part of his hive.

He thoroughly enjoyed the knowledge that his summoning of one Ilduin had brought him two, instead. The fates were most definitely on his side.

As they should be, considering his great mission.

But he was not about to risk his own neck in even the smallest way. It was not that he was a coward…oh, no! But he was the linchpin of the plan, and thus he must preserve himself.

Hence his body remained with the shell of the woman who had brought him this far, while his consciousness stepped into his most senior lieutenant in the great hall. With the prospect of three Ilduin to do his bidding, even a senior lieutenant became disposable. In the lieutenant's body, he mounted his chair at the head of the room and waited. Soon. Very soon.

"The blessings of Lorense be upon you," the man said as they entered the hall.

Archer studied Glassidor and decided the man looked about as

Archer had expected. Tall, lean, with sharp features and intense eyes. He sat on a throne, as if he truly ruled the world. And in his mind, he probably did. That would end soon, however.

"And in your service," Archer said, completing the ritual greeting. "I am Archer Blackcloak, and these are my companions, Sara Deepwell, Tom Downey, and the brothers Ratha and Giri Molabi, Anari freemen and my friends. We come to discuss issues of trade and to seek assistance for those who live upriver."

Glassidor's eyes narrowed. "Issues of trade, you say?"

"Aye," Archer replied. "An ill and bitter winter has befallen the northern lands, and the people want for food. I come as their representative."

"And who appointed you their...representative?"

Archer turned to his friends. "My companions and I were chosen by Master Bandylegs Deepwell, innkeeper and sheriff of Whitewater. We set out from there. As for the others whose plea I offer, I have accepted that duty for myself, having been sorely moved by the great suffering I witnessed. I am on a mission of mercy, Lord Glassidor. I come in peace."

Glassidor nodded to the pile of weapons the guards had placed on a table against the wall. "You come in peace, yet armed for war."

"Sorrow and suffering have befallen the Adasen Basin," Archer said. "In such times, people often mistake friend and foe. We felt it appropriate to be prepared."

"The wisdom of a serpent," Glassidor said. "It comes in peace, but its fangs bear deadly poison."

Archer struggled to contain his anger. Doubtless Glassidor knew who they were and why they were there. The verbal dance was tedious, yet honor compelled him to observe the rules of court.

"Surely Lord Glassidor does not liken us to serpents," Archer said, his voice tight but firm. "We did not slither into this fair city, nor conceal ourselves within it, nor resist your summons."

"Of course," Glassidor said. His eyes fixed on Sara. "You come in honor, and yet you conceal your most potent weapon."

Tom moved closer to Sara, while Archer merely turned to face Glassidor directly. The situation was about to get ugly. He could only hope that his blade would know when that time came.

"We conceal nothing," Archer said. "She is of Ilduin blood, as is one of our companions who has gone missing, taken in the night by bandits. We thought you might know of this woman and help us to find her."

He paused and fixed his eyes on Glassidor. "Unless it is you who is acting in deceit."

"You insult my court," Glassidor said. "Why would I bargain with such a man?"

Archer's face flickered in a smile, though his eyes remained as sharp and cutting as diamonds. "Because, Lord Glassidor, this might be your last chance to save your life."

27

They were here!

Tess had emerged from concealment to follow the sound of footsteps and had heard the faint echoes of Archer's voice. But something was very wrong. The words of the other man were the words of Lantav, but the voice was not. Lantav was elsewhere and acting through his hive.

As footfalls sounded behind her, she darted into yet another alcove, straining to hear what Archer was saying to the fake Glassidor.

At the mention of Sara's name, Tess felt a sudden surge of heat from the pouch between her breasts. She paused and opened it, and saw the red stone gleaming. As she took it in her hands and let herself feel the woman's presence, her heart slammed in her chest.

Lantav had Sara's mother.

And Sara's mother lay dying, her life force being sucked dry by Lantav's constant use of her Ilduin power.

A cold fury grew within Tess as she remembered the tears

young Sara had shed when talking of her mother, as she remembered the sad face of Bandylegs as he had handed over the white gown Tess now wore. Their lives and their hearts had been ripped apart. And the man responsible for their grief was here, in this palace.

She remembered the terrible suffering at Derda, the frozen corpses stacked like cordwood after the ice storm. She remembered the blighted fields through which they had passed.

She cast back to her earliest memory, of a young girl whose family lay butchered around her, the girl slowly dying in Tess's arms.

Every memory Tess possessed bore the black and ugly shadow of Lantav Glassidor.

She opened the pouch again and saw a faint glimmer in the white and blue stones. The blue one must be Sara. The red, Sara's mother. The white, her own. She clutched the three stones in her hand.

"If the Ilduin blood has power," she prayed, "let that power arise now."

From the white stone, a pinpoint beam of light shot forth toward a door across the alcove. With a certainty she had never known and the white heat of fury coursing through her veins, she strode toward the door.

I'm coming, she thought. *I'm coming now.*

Mara Deepwell opened her eyes and, for the first time in her memory, felt light enter them. The awful man stood beside her, his eyes closed in concentration, a bitter and evil smile on his face as he prepared for battle.

Mara knew she had little strength left. He had bled her white. But she had spent the last months learning to shield part of her mind from the hive. She had seen—she had done!—such horrific things in these past years, and she had no doubt the gods would burn her soul. The memory of every slaying, every drop of bane poison melded into daggers or spread across crops, every anguished plea that had fallen on cold, unfeeling hearts, welled within her. The gods would curse her soul. Of that she had no doubt. But she would fight with what she had left.

As she watched Archer turn to look at the weapons on the table, her jaw tightened. The hive will was strong, but she had Ilduin will. However weak her strength, her will was now emboldened.

Do it, she thought, looking at Archer. *Do it now.*

"Do it," Sara whispered, not knowing why, nor what she was urging. The words seemed to have come from somewhere outside herself. "Do it now."

She watched as Archer's sword began to glow. In the twinkling of an eye, it flew into Archer's hand. As if sensing his tension or hearing her words, Ratha and Giri sprang into action.

Tom stepped forward as if to join the fray, but she grabbed his arm. "No, Tom. Come with me. I need you."

Tess found herself at the base of a stairwell. Certain it would lead her directly to Lantav, she began the climb, the stones warm in her hands. She was not needed where Archer and the others spoke with Lantav's minions, for she knew her companions and knew they would be able to deal with that threat.

Instead she sought Sara's mother, the Ilduin who was in thrall to Lantav and who seemed to be growing weaker by the moment.

Separating the red stone from the others, she clutched it tight.

I am coming, sister. Be strong.

Filled with white heat, she had no room left for fear.

* * *

Sara tugged Tom out of the great hall as the battle was joined. They slipped away unnoticed.

"Where do we go?" Tom asked. His every instinct and sense of loyalty demanded that he return to the hall and aid his friends.

"We must find the Ilduin," Sara told him, her voice low and urgent. "We must find the source of Glassidor's power before it is too late."

Sara had not brought her sword. Apparently, with her emerging powers, she no longer felt need of it. Tom, on the other hand, was glad he had seized his. Sara, for all she was Ilduin, might need a defender as she led him through a warren of hallways and stairways that he grew certain had been designed to confuse.

But Sara seemed to know where she was headed, so Tom followed, because he could no more have abandoned Sara than he could have grown wings.

The battle was well joined in the great hall. Three against thirty.

"Not bad odds." Ratha grinned at his brother.

"Nay, not bad at all," Giri agreed.

The advantage, of course, was that thirty men could not fight the three of them all at once, especially since they had chosen to stand back-to-back-to-back, becoming a triangle of invincible steel. Only fatigue or a momentary lapse of caution could fell them.

From the instant the sword had flown to Archer's hand, he had been in an altered state. He felt the lightness of it, as if it hefted its own weight to spare his arm. He saw it gleam as if with its own internal light. And he heard it sing, a low humming of power.

Too long had it been since his sword had been anything but dead steel. Too long... For a wild moment he wondered if it meant the gods had forgiven him his terrible sin. His thoughts sought to reach back to the last time the sword had sung in his hand, but he could not let them. He must keep his attention on the here and now, lest they all die.

But the sword's power filled him with wild joy and even more strength, and he was no longer the wanderer Archer Blackcloak but the man he had once been.

A fierce grin lit his face, and he swung yet again, the sword slicing through an attacker as if he were merely a phantom, not made of flesh and blood.

Before long the three were surrounded by a mound of bodies and the floor was slick with blood. The rest of the attackers mindlessly tried to climb over the heap, only to meet their doom without a chance of using their own weapons.

A cry of rage issued from Glassidor on his throne. The three ignored it. Once they were done here, he would be next.

The cry of rage also issued from Lantav as he stood next to the Ilduin he had used these many years. Somehow she was defying him, he was certain.

Angered, he turned and struck her. "Call the others," he demanded. "Now. Or I'll see your daughter dead."

It was the threat he had been making for years, and it worked, as it always had, for now her daughter was here, within this building, in more danger than ever before in her life.

For years Mara had suffered this man's abuse and misuse because she had known that a coin or two in the right palm would ensure Sara's death, that Lantav would not need *her* to accomplish the murder of a single child.

And with time he had managed to use her own powers against

her, binding her ever more tightly to his control through spells and potions that weakened her own will. For a long time now, she had barely been able to remember who she had once been.

But now she remembered. And now she knew the dangers. Summoning what little of her strength remained, she sent out the call for the rest of the hive.

"Good," said Lantav. "Good."

But behind the wall she had built in her mind, she knew things that Lantav did not. Things she would never let him know. Such as the fact that the Ilduin he thought safely locked away had escaped her cell and even now was seeking him, an Ilduin with so much power that it resonated within Mara and strengthened her will just enough.

Just enough to defy her master and maintain the wall behind which she did it.

Tom was certain that they were nearing the top of Lantav's tower, that with each step they were walking closer to his lair. Finally he pulled Sara into an empty room and closed the door behind them.

"What are you going to do?" he asked her. "When we find this man, how are you going to handle him?"

"I don't know."

His jaw dropped. "Then don't you think 'twould be best to await the others?"

"I cannot wait."

"Why not? The man apparently has powers of his own, and an Ilduin to magnify them. Are you ready to face that, Sara? Are you?"

To his horror, a tear appeared and trembled on her lower lash.

"Sara?" Unworthy though he was, he could not help himself. He at once stepped forward and drew her into his embrace, tucking her head into his shoulder.

"Sweet Sara," he murmured. "Sweet, sweet Sara. It does no one any good if you hare off without a plan. This is a dangerous man we face."

"I know, Tom. I know." More tears rolled down her cheeks. "But don't you see? The Ilduin he uses is my *mother*."

Horror rooted his feet to the floor and for a time locked the words in his throat. "How...how do you know?"

"I can feel it now that we are close." She lifted her damp face from his shoulder and looked up at him. "He uses her against her will. I must save her!"

There was no argument to make against that, nor did he even wish to.

"Then we will save her," he agreed stoutly. "But, Sara, we must think first. If the two of us burst in on this man, who knows what the outcome may be? What if he is surrounded by protectors? What if your mother is so in his thrall she turns against us?"

Sara bowed her head and for a dozen heartbeats said nothing. Then she raised her wet face once again. "My mother will not harm me. No matter what he commands of her."

"You are sure?"

She nodded.

"Then perhaps we should seek Tess. The two of you together..."

He trailed off as Sara's gaze grew almost opaque. Then she said, "Tess is on her way, too. I can feel her climbing through a narrow staircase toward him."

"Then let us go. But carefully, Sara. We must not engage him before Tess arrives. 'Twill be safer with the two of you, not just for us, but for your mother, as well."

At last Sara nodded agreement. Satisfied, Tom carefully opened the door of the chamber and peered out into the corridor. No one was there.

"Let's go."

Archer turned from the charnel heap and strode toward Glassidor. His voice was cold and his eyes colder. "Where is your power now, mage?"

Glassidor laughed. "There are hundreds more where those came from, and they're on their way here now. Can three men defeat an army? I think not. Surrender and I may be merciful in your deaths. I may even spare your lives, if you could be of service to me."

"The sun will turn to black ash before I surrender to you," Archer said.

At this, Glassidor cocked his head and regarded Archer with a knowing smile. "Do you really think the gods will allow you to do that a second time?"

Archer froze in his tracks.

"Oh, yes, I know who you are, Archer Blackcloak. And I have waited a long time to see you die. A very long time."

Tess suddenly felt the grip of a terror deeper than any she had ever known. A shudder passed through her, so powerful that she nearly dropped the stones from her palm. This was a new presence, a darker presence even than Lantav Glassidor and his evil hive. It seemed to spring forth from beyond the darkest recesses of her buried memories. Leaning her forehead against the cool stone wall, she gathered herself. She could not let herself consider the larger battle she now joined.

Keep it in the here and now, she thought, though the phrase seemed awkward in the language she had learned over the past weeks. This was about a young girl who had died in her arms, about hungry men, women and children who had frozen in the ice at Derda, and a woman whose husband and daughter had grieved for far too long. This was personal. For only in the personal could she find strength.

As she reached the top of the stairs, a door opened. Tess froze in her tracks and prepared to do battle empty-handed if need be. No one would get in her way. Not now. Not ever again.

"Lady Tess!" Sara whispered, emerging from the door. "I felt your approach."

Then she looked into Tess's eyes. What she saw both frightened her and renewed her confidence. This was not the frightened, confused Tess she'd seen over the past few weeks. The woman who stood before her now was ready to kill—or die.

"Let's go," Tess said, not even nodding in greeting to Sara or to Tom, who stepped out behind her. "We haven't much time."

"What are we going to do?" Tom asked. "I was talking to Sara. We need a plan."

"We're going to kill a man," Tess said.

"Yes, but…"

"Tom," Sara said, touching his shoulder, "I think this is a time to trust Lady Tess."

He nodded, although she could see the hurt in his eyes. He wanted to be brave, strong, powerful, in control. He wanted to be all the things he saw in Archer. And in time, perhaps, he might be. This was not that time, nor had she moments to spare to comfort his ego. She trusted Tess and the Ilduin power. He must do likewise.

Tess was already moving, striding purposefully, and Sara hurried to keep up. Tom, chastened, sidestepped behind them, watching lest someone spring upon them from the rear.

28

The door of the small tower room slammed open. Lantav jumped, temporarily losing his connection with the woman and, through her, his connection with the hive. Turning, he faced two women and a youth. The youth he discounted. The younger woman was clearly Mara's daughter, the one he would kill if necessary.

But the other woman... Lantav stared in dumbstruck awe. The woman he had captured, Tess, had somehow escaped her cell. But more, she had somehow escaped the uncertainty and reticence he had seen in her during their previous meeting.

This woman felt no such weakness. Her eyes blazed with fire, white fire, and she faced him as if he were nothing but a worm to be stepped on.

"Sara," said Tess.

"Aye?"

"Take this to your mother." She pressed something into the younger woman's hand. Lantav thought he glimpsed something red.

"No!" He stepped forward and pulled forth the sword that had dangled useless at his side these many years. "I will kill her if she approaches."

"Really?" Tess smiled, but it was not an expression that Lantav found reassuring. "How do you propose to do that, you misbegotten son of a drunk and a streetwalker? Your powers are puny, and most are not your own."

Lantav, for the first time since he had begun his pursuit of magehood, felt that his *own* life might be at risk. Sweat began to pour down his spine.

But the greater darkness within him, his ally, his mentor, his master, would tolerate no such weakness. Unwillingly, Lantav stepped forth and placed himself between Mara and her daughter.

"Touch me," he said, his voice surprisingly deep and steady, "and you will engage the wrath of one who is stronger than me by far. One who would like nothing more than to end the blight of the Ilduin. He is the Ilduin Bane."

At his words, the room seemed to dim, as if a black cloud were filling it. An oily, chilly black cloud.

They all stood frozen before it.

Images began to fill Tess's mind, as if the darkness wished to display its power. The images felt both as if they were pieces of her past and as if they belonged to someone else.

She glimpsed a city full of beauty, built of white, sun-washed stone, with gardens everywhere. Fountains trickled in courtyards, filling the world with watery music. The people she saw were all garbed in flowing robes, and their faces reflected a beautiful serenity.

But then that image vanished, to be replaced by one of two

brothers, one fair and beautiful, the other dark and chiseled like stone. They laughed with one another....

Then the fire rained down, and the fairer brother's face filled with unholy anger. Screams replaced the sounds of beauty and music, and terror filled every face.

Then, before her eyes, in a single moment of horror, an entire city vanished in an explosion of fire and smoke.

Faster and faster the images came, all of them carrying the same message: See what *I* can do?

Somehow she had to stop this mental assault. But how?

Archer faced Glassidor, who still lolled upon his throne as if he had nothing to fear. The Anari stood back, guarding Archer, uncertain what he would have them do now. It was clear that Archer's stance had made them uncertain.

"Aye," said the man on the throne, "I watched you creep around this world all these many years, a wanderer with no place to lay his head. Archer Blackcloak indeed. The time for your atonement has come."

The man on the throne rose. "I have waited for this moment." His face filled with evil delight. "You are but a paltry shadow of yourself now. And the time has come for me to take my revenge."

Within Archer, emotions battled. He had known this moment would come eventually. Part of him felt that whatever was dealt to him, he deserved. But the rest of him knew the danger of unleashing this man's power into the world unopposed, and how many would suffer for it.

He had wandered these many years waiting for this moment. That was the only way he could atone. Without the hope of this moment, he would have ended his life long ago.

With one swift movement, he hurled his sword. The blade spun through the air almost faster than the eye could see. Then, for one terrible moment, it hovered in the air as if caught in a giant grip. The other man laughed as if relishing his power, as if relishing the fact that now Archer was defenseless.

But in that moment of laughter, something happened. Archer willed the sword to complete its task. It trembled in the air, then swooped toward the man, piercing him through.

He fell, grasping at the sword, a cry of pain escaping him.

Then, as he lay there, his eyes open, black as the pits of hell, he looked straight at Archer. "We are not done yet."

A moment later, he died.

"What in the names of all the gods was that?" Ratha demanded. His face reflected confusion.

But Archer did not answer him. He lifted his hand, and his sword returned to him, as pristine as the moment it had left his hand.

"By the gods," said Giri, his voice hushed.

"Aye," said Archer. "By the gods. Now we must find the others."

But before they even left the chamber, shouting from outside drew them to a window. They could see, beyond the gate, a growing army trying to break in.

Archer looked from the army back across the room to their dead leader, his confusion apparent.

"What's happening?" Ratha asked. "If he's dead, how can the hive still function?"

Then an icy certainty crept through Archer's mind. "That," he said, pointing at the dead figure in the chair, "was not Lantav Glassidor. He was merely speaking through another of his minions. We have wasted time, and now we are the poorer for it."

He turned toward the stairwell, but Giri grabbed his arm. Giri pointed at the mob. "We must stop them, Lord, or none of us will have a chance."

Archer nodded.

Instead of heading upward to seek the rest of their party, they headed downward to defend the gate.

Archer felt torn by conflicting responsibilities, but he realized their only hope now was to hold off the hive. He would have to trust that the two fledgling Ilduin would be more than Lantav and his ally could handle.

If not, all was lost.

Sara halted in confusion, poised between Tess and Lantav. Each time she tried to approach her mother, Lantav moved, blocking her way. Worse, Tess seemed to be engaged in some terrible struggle she could not escape.

Sara's gaze drifted reluctantly to her mother. Once she had been such a beautiful woman, but these years under Lantav's control had turned her into a dried husk of what she had once been, hardly able to sit up in the chair that held her. The sorrow that filled Sara was deep, as deep as it had been when her mother disappeared.

Now she was found but perhaps lost in the same moment. Sara's heart railed against gods that could allow such a thing to happen. That could allow her mother to have been used this way. Grief pierced her with an ache that almost overwhelmed her.

Suddenly Tom was at her side, murmuring, "Give me the thing she wanted you to give to your mother. I am of no consequence here, and he cannot guard against all of us."

Without a word, taking care that Lantav didn't see, Sara relinquished the red stone to Tom.

He stepped back from her, seeming to move away. Lantav spared him barely a glance, for he was involved in his dual contests with Tess and Sara.

Tom reached the edge of the room and little by little began to work his way around to a position that would put him behind Lantav and Mara.

Sara squeezed her eyes shut for a few seconds, steeling herself against the pain in her heart and her fear for Tom. Then she looked at Tess, wondering how she could help.

But at that instant Tess said something to Lantav that shocked Sara to her very toes.

"Had I known how powerful you would become, I would have chosen *you*."

Archer and the Anari ran down the stairs and through the door that led to the courtyard. By the time they arrived there, a dozen or more of the hive had surmounted the walls and were inside, attempting to unbar the heavy wooden gate.

Archer, Ratha and Giri at once waded in, tight abreast, swinging their swords in broad arcs, a blood-letting deadly whirl of steel and will. The hive army was ill-trained to fight such tactics. Each hive soldier focused on the man directly in front of him, not adapting to the killing blows that fell from the sides. For Archer and the Anari, it was a nauseatingly mismatched struggle. Their long experience and silent cooperation more than made up for the hive's greater numbers.

Or it had thus far. Even as they fought those who were already inside, more were climbing the walls. The danger of being overrun was increasing by the minute.

* * *

Lantav had never dreamt that the Chained One would take him
over this way, using his body the way Lantav had used the bodies
of the hive and the Ilduin. He had never imagined that after all these
years of tireless service he would be treated like a puppet to be
played with. From the corner of his mind that was still his own,
he began to rage. He deserved better than this!

But the Chained One merely bound Lantav tighter and laughed
within his head. *Puny man-thing,* the Chained One said. *You are
nothing without me. You would* be *nothing without me.*

Betrayal pierced Lantav like a lance, but he knew better. The
Chained One would have accomplished nothing at all without Lantav, for Lantav was his only channel to this world.

Not for long, the mocking voice answered. *You see how the White
Lady chooses me.*

Lantav railed. *She's not Theriel, you fool. She's some farmgirl I picked
up out of the horse muck and brought here because the other is dying.*

And finally, finally, the bonds about Lantav began to loosen. He
had given the Chained One some food for thought.

Tom was still easing around the edge of the room toward a position from which to dart forward to give the red stone to Mara.

Now Tess reached out and pressed a blue stone into Sara's hand.

"Mother?" said Sara.

The woman's eyes opened, and something like a smile split the
husk of her sunken face. "My child."

"Stay back!" Lantav warned.

Tess returned her attention to him. Somehow he had pushed
back the dark presence, though it still remained. Perhaps her
words, born of the images the Chained One had given her, had

helped. It was rather unsettling, however, to realize she was being mistaken for a woman who had died many hundreds of years ago. There must be some way she could take advantage of that.

In her mind's eye, she realized that she saw Lantav as a black hole in the golden cloth of reality, a place where the fiber had been singed and burned, where the surrounding fibers had warped and melted. He needed to be killed before that black evil spread any farther.

But she had no weapon, nothing but a white stone in her hand.

At that instant Tom darted forward and placed the red stone in one of Mara's hands. Lantav turned, swinging his sword, but Tom darted away in the nick of time.

Mara cupped the stone tightly to her breasts. "Aid me now, sisters," she breathed. "Aid me now."

And from her hands a red light began to fill the room.

Archer, Ratha and Giri knew they were looking death in the eye. The more hive soldiers they dispatched, the more there seemed to be. Their tightly choreographed tactics of constant motion were exhausting, and each took stock of his diminishing strength.

"We must find a choke point," Archer said, the words rasping on ragged breath. "A place in which we cannot be outflanked, and where two can do the fighting while the other gathers his breath."

"Aye, m'lord," Ratha said. "If we stay here, in the open, we will die this day and for naught."

The palace doorway was suitable, though a bit wider than Archer would have liked. The two in the doorway would have to swing their swords in a broader, flatter arc, and that would exhaust them even faster. Still, exhaustion was better than the risk of being flanked.

"To the doorway," Archer said.

Slowly, deliberately and in unison, they stepped back, their blades never still. Blood and bits of flesh flew this way and that as the hive soldiers pressed their futile attacks in wave after wave. In this test of skill versus numbers, Archer realized that defending the doorway was the only sane option. He cursed himself for wading out into the courtyard at all but knew that was merely another regret to add to an age-old stockpile.

They reached the doorway, a carpet of carnage strewn in front of them.

"Ratha, fall back and take your rest first. When you feel ready, relieve Giri. Giri will relieve me."

"Aye, m'lord," Ratha said, and dropped out of the formation, leaving Archer and Giri in the doorway.

"Rest quickly, brother," Giri said. "This is no time for a snack or a nap."

"You will be the one napping," Ratha replied from behind them. "Archer and I will have to finish them off alone."

"At least your tongues are not tired," Archer said, hewing off a head and part of an arm with a mighty swing. "Perhaps, if you rested them, your bodies would refresh more quickly?"

"'Tis the Anari way of battle," Ratha said. "Else we might regret what we are doing."

"Regret," Archer said, "is what we *ought* to feel."

29

Sara felt a wave of warmth flow through her, unlike anything she had ever known before. The blue stone gleamed in her hands, but more than that, she felt the warmth of her mother's love for the first time in so many years.

"Yes, mother," Sara said, her voice a quiet sigh. A soft melody began to flow. "Sisters, we. Darkness, flee."

The words seemed to come from the gods themselves, for she had never heard them before. But at those words, Lantav's face went pale.

"The Ilduin song," the dark voice whispered from within him. "So long has it been since I have heard it. So light in its words, yet so black in its outcomes."

Sara felt the memories flood in, even as the rest of the song began to form on her lips.

"Sisters, we. Darkness flee.
Death, the dying by our light.

This we sing, life we bring,
End of sorrow, end of night."

Sara saw the image as clearly as if it were happening before her. Eleven women singing, their voices raised up to the gods, and a dazzling, blinding light seeming to rise up above them. But high in the air it turned to fire and sped away, leaving a trail of scorched air in its wake.

"Dancing fire, death's own pyre,
Warms the heart and hearth and bed.
Living flame, give thy name,
To the lost, the tired, the dead."

Then Sara saw something that would have terrified her, had she not been held sway in the song and in memories that were not her own. Far away, the fire approached on the horizon. Brave men, and women who had borne great pain and sorrow, looked up with trembling hearts. In a tower, high above, dark eyes tethered to a darker heart saw the flame, and the mage made for the stairway and the only hope of escape.

"Crackling fair, doom beware,
Gilded dreams that rise to life.
Breath of love, from above,
End of suff'ring, end of strife."

The fire crashed down from the sky, an all-consuming white heat that instantly turned flesh and bone and wood and thatch to ash. Even stone melted before the flame, and Sara saw the city atop the mountain hewn low as if by the vengeance of an angry god, leaving in its wake naught but a sea of glass.

"Living justice, living heart,
Heals the wounded, hails the Twelve.
Doves of Eshkaron descend,
Into man's own heart to delve."

Sara fought against the overwhelming weight of guilt that the images had wrought. With Ilduin blood came Ilduin stain, and yet she could not let that deter her from the path ahead. She heard Tess's voice joining hers, and the voice of her mother, the voice that had sung her to sleep as a baby. The voice of the purest heart ever born, now twisted in upon itself, begging to be free of the chains that had bound it for so long.

"Sisters, we. Darkness, flee.
Given touch to salve the soul.
Banish night, glowing light,
Give our blood that all be whole."

Sara felt the stone pierce her flesh and the spreading wetness in her palm. She reached out to Tess and saw that her hand was stained with blood, as well. Their hands clasped, the blood suddenly turning to cold fire. In Mara's hand, fire now grew, as well, and for a moment her visage was of the young woman Sara had so adored. A smile spread across her face, and Sara knew the moment was ripe.

Archer stepped back as Giri tapped his shoulder, and with the fury of battle now borne by the Anari, he gasped for breath and let his weary arm hang at peace. The muscles screamed with white hot pain, worn down by the pace of constant combat.

As his pulse thudded within him and he drew great gulps of air into his lungs, he felt in his heart a song he had thought long dead. Memories rushed at him in unrelenting waves that were little different from the waves of hive soldiers he had just faced. Betrayal, death, horror.

And the pain of knowing he had caused it all.

Though his body still screamed with exhaustion, he could rest no longer, for his rest was more draining than the fury of battle. He stepped up and tapped Ratha's shoulder, then joined in the fray as Ratha withdrew.

"There are fewer now," Giri said, streams of sweat pouring down his iridescent ebony face. "But still too many remain."

"It is as if he is bringing more into the hive as we fight," Archer said. "That, or the power of his Ilduin is far greater than we imagined."

As one, a band of hive soldiers charged forward, now armed with pitchforks and scythes. These were farmers, not warriors, fed into battle only because their minds had been usurped by a terrible presence. Archer saw only emptiness in their eyes, and woe filled his heart as he and Girl resumed the grim business of maiming and death.

Back and forth they went, Ratha stepping into Giri's place, then Giri into Ratha's, for Archer refused to yield his place in the doorway. The ground before them was a mass of writhing bodies, severed limbs, screams, blood, tears and soulless eyes. Fewer than twenty of the hive soldiers remained, and for a moment they hesitated, as if looking for the best way to wade through the remains of their comrades.

Archer waited for the final attack, fighting away the memories that tried to resurface, taking strength from the cold fire in the Anari eyes beside him.

"Let them come," Giri said. "Let them come, and we will rend them all from this wretched place."

There was a bleak anger in Giri's voice that Archer had not heard for years, since the day Archer had taken the brothers from the slave block. It was the anger of one who had gone beyond his own boundaries, beheld what he had become, weighed himself in the balance and found himself wanting. There was no hint of the playful joy that had softened Archer's heart so often through these years. There was only a stone-cold killer, waiting for the opportunity to ply his trade once again.

Archer glanced back at Ratha, thinking that perhaps he could relieve Giri before his spirit broke, but Ratha's eyes bore the same distant, unfeeling fury.

Seeing that, Archer had no doubt that his own face bore the same expression.

"Let them come," Archer said, accepting the reality of the moment. "Let us finish this."

Lantav watched as the fire began to swirl in the hands of the Ilduin around him. The dark presence, the power that he now realized had carried him to this point, turned and fled into the warp and woof of time itself. He was alone, as the armies and supporters of the Chained One had been left alone. Left alone to die.

Behind him, the broken woman rose to her feet. Before him, two Ilduin stood with fire in their hands and ice in their hearts. Between him and the door, the lad with his sword. There was no escape.

But he could take one with him.

And he knew which one to take.

Tom watched in horror as Lantav reached into the folds of his cloak and withdrew a dagger so black that it shone in the light of Ilduin fire. Seemingly in an instant, before Tom could react, Lantav whirled and slashed the dagger across Mara's throat.

Sara screamed in horror, and Tom charged forward to avenge her agony and grief. Every tear she had shed in the little inn in Whitewater flowed through his thoughts. The nights she had sat in the courtyard, eyes staring with vain hope across the commons, waiting for the return of a mother torn away.

Torn away, and now torn and bleeding at the hands of the man who stood before him.

Rage and love and cold purpose pushed away terror, and Tom lifted his sword to strike the man whose life had been spent stealing the lives of others.

"It is time to die," Tom said, muscles pulling with all his might as he brought the sword down at his target.

"No!" Tess commanded.

She flicked her hand at Tom's sword, drops of her blood spattering it, and with the sound of an axe chopping into wood, it froze in midair. Tom looked at her, but she merely shook her head and turned to Sara.

"Cleanse this place," Tess said.

On they came, the last band of Lantav's hive, their eyes burning with desperate purpose. Giri watched with a grim smile, then hefted his sword and went to work. For the souls of Anari who had died in chains. For the cries of mothers whose babies had been taken away. For the backs that had borne the scars of the scourge. For the children he had buried at Derda. For the life of his people, for the lives of those slain, and for the life of the man who had saved his and now stood beside him, Giri set himself to the grim task.

A part of him raged against the joy he felt when his sword opened a man from crotch to sternum. He both sought and rebelled against the tingling clarity of death faced and death dealt. His soul stood on a sword's edge, poised between light and darkness. For the moment, he chose the darkness. Savored it. Lived in it. Killed in it.

He swung again, lopping off a man's leg at the knee, watching as the blood shot forth over Giri's body, hearing the man's screams. *Aye,* he thought. *Scream. Scream and die for your dark master.*

The moment dissolved into a dizzying blur of steel and flesh and blood and fury. The moment consumed him, and fatigue gave way to a light-headed, childish glow in his body. Wading forth, feeling Ratha and Archer step up beside him, he slashed his way through the confused and broken band before them.

And now for the wounded, he thought, looking around for more bodies to maim. *Let death take them all.*

Sara watched her mother slump to the floor, her hands clasped to her neck, the stone glowing, and none of it sufficient to staunch the geyser of her life spraying forth in streams of flame. She saw the light of the stone dim, until it was but dull rock. She felt the presence of her mother leave her.

And she looked at the man who had done this. Not a man, for no man could be so savage. An animal, consumed by its own lust for power. A rabid dog and nothing more.

With a moan, she stepped toward him, holding her bleeding

hand over him. "Ilduin blood cleanses," she said, as if her mother spoke through her. "It cleanses the heart that can be saved. It cleanses the world of what cannot be saved. It is the judge."

"No!" Lantav said, and tried to turn away. But it was as if his fear rooted him.

"You have spilled Ilduin blood. Let Ilduin blood judge you now!"

Again and again she cast her blood upon him, watching it ignite, oblivious to his screams, which echoed in the room like the howls of a trapped wolf. He fell to the floor, curled into a ball to shield himself from the fire, but Sara gave him no mercy.

Stepping forward, she dragged her wrist across Tom's still frozen sword, opening her veins. Then she stood over Lantav, watching as fire poured onto his face.

"Burn for all," she said, sobbing. "Ilduin flame heals. And cleanses. I cleanse you from this earth, Lantav Glassidor. For the soul of my mother, and all the rest you have slain, I cleanse you."

The last of his screams died as her blood dripped onto his lips and the fire seared them closed. For one last moment his eyes stared at her.

And then they went blank.

Archer watched as Giri prepared to cleave a man whose arm lay white and cold beside him.

"Giri, no!" Archer said, leaping forward to grasp Giri's wrist.

"Let us finish them," Giri said, looking into his lord's eyes. "Let us wipe them from this place like the spoor of a bane-bear."

"No," Archer said, his grip still firm on Giri's wrist. "This battle is won. There is nothing to be gained by spilling more blood, and our souls to be lost."

"I have no soul," Giri said. "Not anymore."

Archer nodded. "No, but you will. And soon. Lay down your sword, my brother. This is finished."

Archer watched as Giri stared at the wounded man, then at the nightmare vision that lay around them, and finally into Archer's eyes. The tension in Giri's arm lessened. Finally he dropped his sword. His eyes welled with tears.

"What have I become?" he asked, turning to Ratha.

"We became what we must," Ratha said, embracing him.

Archer's arms slipped over their shoulders, and for a long moment they stood there, gasping for breath.

"We became what we must," Archer echoed, sorrow in his eyes. "And we survived."

Tess gripped Sara's wrist and pulled her away from the flaming man at their feet. She closed her eyes, willing the severed vessels to seal themselves. There would not be two Ilduin slain on this day.

"It is finished," Tom said, his sword now hanging limp at his side.

"No," Tess said, watching as Sara knelt to embrace her mother's body. "It has only begun."

Outside in the courtyard, Archer said, "We must do what we can to save these poor wretches. They were not responsible for what they did."

Ratha and Giri, still embracing, looked at him, leaden realization coming over them. They looked around again at what they had wrought and knew they would never forget this day.

But then Tess stepped through the door they had been guarding with their lives against so many. As if unaware of them, she began to walk among the bodies. When she found a man still alive, she turned her hand over and let a drop of her blood fall on him.

Soon Sara joined her, doing the same thing. Together they sang quietly, words inaudible to the others.

For centuries to come, Lorense would remember the day the evil wizard burned to dust, the day the wounded and near-dead rose and walked again as whole men.

 **Epilogue**

They buried Sara's mother that very afternoon, in a dell sprinkled with starflowers. No one mourned with them. No one in Lorense had ever met Mara Deepwell.

But Sara mourned, tears flowing steadily down her cheeks, while Tom held her tight and murmured endearments.

Both Ilduin were exhausted, Archer noted, as if, in giving healing, they had given of their own strength. As soon as he could, he pried them from the grave site and guided them back to the inn, where they were to stay a few days.

Tom took Sara at once to her room, no doubt to hold her until she fell asleep, and long after.

Tess remained awake, sitting near the fire as if she were chilled to the bone, though the day was pleasant.

The expression on her face gave Archer no comfort, for it was clear she had been irrevocably changed. The innocence that had once covered her like a cloak was gone. And innocence could never be regained.

He waited patiently for her to speak, knowing that eventually she must unburden her heart.

And he was sorely troubled, for not since the days of his youth had he seen Ilduin heal as these two had. Not since then had he seen the effects of Ilduin fire.

"Archer?" Her voice startled him out of his gloomy reflections.

"Aye, my lady?" The respectful title fell naturally from his tongue.

"The Ilduin blood cleanses."

"Yes."

"And heals."

"Yes. Those who are pure of heart. Or of pure enough heart." She nodded. "It judges."

"Aye."

"Then why did the eleven Ilduin send the rain of fire?"

He caught his breath, not certain what answer to give her.

"'Twas not," she said, "over a disputed marriage."

"No."

She nodded, and looked at the palm of her hand. "Then why?"

Still uncertain, he said, "'Twas to end a war. To kill the evil that had killed one of the Ilduin. In those days, an Ilduin could be harmed only on pain of death. One of their sisters had been killed."

"I felt that. But then why do I feel as if my blood is stained?"

"The stain of those days remains in us all, I fear."

"Apparently so. Glassidor was trying to start it again."

"And you stopped him."

She gave him a faint smile. "But only him. There was an evil behind him, one that I fear will not stop because of a single battle."

A grim fist gripped Archer's heart, for he knew it was true.

She rose and held out her hand to him. He rose and accepted it. "We must fight together, for however long it takes."

He nodded. "That we must."

She moved to him then, coming into his arms, holding him close. Long reinforced walls nearly fell before the feeling of warmth her closeness gave him.

But then she stepped away and turned to look into the fire. "I am changed. I must learn to accept it."

"We all must. Today we looked into ourselves in ways we never have before."

"Sadly true."

Just then the door burst open and the Anari brothers rushed in.

"We're leaving," Giri said. "Now."

"But why?" Archer asked. "What happened?"

"We have had news from home. The Bozandari Army slaughtered an entire village of our people, supposedly hunting for rebels. If there weren't any rebels before, there certainly will be now."

Archer nodded. "I will go with you."

"And I," said Tess, turning from the fire.

"My lady," Giri started to object.

She shook her head. "There is evil to be fought, and there will be people who need healing. I will go."

The three looked at her, and for a moment their eyes deceived them and seemed to garb her in white light. One blink and she was back to normal.

"Thank you, my lady," Ratha said.

She waved a hand. "Just call me Tess. I'm still the same woman without a memory who you've had to cart across half the empire."

At that, the brothers laughed.

"We'll leave in the morning," Archer announced. "I want to be sure Sara is well enough to return to Whitewater with Tom before we leave them."

A voice spoke from behind them. "I'm quite well," Sara said, coming into the room. Her face had lost some of its youth, but her stance was tall and her step firm. Tom came behind her.

"And what's more," Sara said, "Tom and I shall go with you. This was only the first battle."

Archer nodded. "I fear you are right, Sara."

"I know I am right." She looked at Tess, who nodded. "We felt the power behind Glassidor. I don't know if these are the prophesied times or not, but I *do* know that that evil will not quit so easily."

Tess spoke. "Most definitely he will not." She held out her hands, and they all joined together in a circle, hand to hand.

"We are bound," she said. "Bound in spirit and heart. We will face the evil one whenever he comes."

A chorus of *Ayes* answered her. And bit by bit spirits lifted after the horrors of the day. The memories of what they had done would never fade. But knowing why they were fighting made the sorrow easier to bear.

The myths of old had claimed their fates. Prophecies spoken. Destinies set. They could only hope they were fit for the burden.

GUARDIAN OF HONOR

Robin D. Owens

With their magic boundaries falling and terrible
monsters invading, the Marshalls of Lladrana
must follow ancient tradition and Summon
a savior from the Exotique land....

For Alexa Fitzwalter, the Marshall's call pulled
the savvy lawyer into a realm where she barely
understood the language, let alone the
intricacies of politics and power.

Torn between her affinity for this new realm
and Earth, will she return home if given the chance?
Or dare she risk everything for a land not her own?

LUNA™

LUNA™

A sweeping fantasy set in an ancient Greco-Roman civilization. A goddess has been born—the daughter of Epona's beloved Incarnate Priestess and the centaur High Shaman. Elphame is unique. Her story of self-discovery is an epic adventure that will lead to her destiny and an unexpected love.

Visit your local bookseller.

www.LUNA-Books.com   LPCC213TRR

Bestselling fantasy author Mercedes Lackey turns traditional fairy tales on their heads in the land of the Five Hundred Kingdoms.

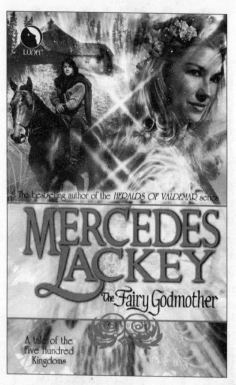

Elena, a Cinderella in the making, gets an unexpected chance to be a Fairy Godmother. But being a Fairy Godmother is hard work and she gets into trouble by changing a prince who is destined to save the kingdom, into a donkey—but he really deserved it!

Can she get things right and save the kingdom? Or will her stubborn desire to teach this ass of a prince a lesson get in the way?

Visit your local bookseller.

LUNA™

www.LUNA-Books.com

LML245TRR

In *Wildcard, USA TODAY* bestselling author Rachel Lee
shows us that when the deck has been stacked against you,
working outside the law is the only card left to play.

RACHEL LEE

Following a victorious evening, shots ring out, and the Democratic presidential
front-runner is left near death. As the official investigation begins, FBI special
agent Tom Lawton is sidelined and given work intended to keep him out of the
way. Determined to find out why, he launches an investigation of his own—and
uncovers a web of deceit constructed by his own superiors.

Soon he has uncovered far too much and working alone is no longer an option.
Tom's only hope is Agent Renate Bächle, a woman with secrets of her own. On
the run for his life, he must determine whether he can trust her to guide him
through the corridors of a conspiracy that threatens a nation, or whether she is
simply another spider in the web....

WILDCARD

"...attention-grabbing...this well-rounded story is sure to be
one of Lee's top-selling titles."
—*Publishers Weekly* on *Something Deadly*

*Available the first week of February 2005,
wherever paperbacks are sold!*

MIRA®

www.MIRABooks.com

MRL2129TR

ATHENA FORCE

The Athena Academy adventure continues....

Three secret sisters

Three super talents

One unthinkable legacy...

The ties that bind may be the ties that kill as these extraordinary women race against time to beat the genetic time bomb that is their birthright....

Don't miss the latest three stories in the Athena Force continuity

DECEIVED by Carla Cassidy, January 2005

CONTACT by Evelyn Vaughn, February 2005

PAYBACK by Harper Allen, March 2005

And coming in April–June 2005, the final showdown for Athena Academy's best and brightest!

Available at your favorite retail outlet.

Silhouette®

BOMBSHELL™

COMING IN FEBRUARY 2005
FROM SILHOUETTE BOMBSHELL

WENDY ROSNAU

presents the first book in her
THRILLING new Spy Games series:

THE SPY
WORE *Red*

Savvy and unstoppable, Quest agent Nadja Stefn had accepted a top secret mission to infiltrate Austria, kill an international assassin and seize his future kill files. But this femme fatale secret agent also had a dangerous agenda of her own, and time was running out....

SPY GAMES:
High stakes...killer moves

Available at your favorite retail outlet.

www.SilhouetteBombshell.com   SBTSWRTR

Rachel Lee wrote her first play in the third grade for a school assembly, and by the age of twelve she was hooked on writing. She's lived all over the United States, on both the east and west coasts, and now resides in Florida.

Having held jobs as a security officer, real estate agent and optician, she uses these, as well as her natural flair for creativity, to write stories that are undeniably romantic. "After all, life is the biggest romantic adventure of all— and if you're open and aware, the most marvelous things are just waiting to be discovered," she says.

LUNA™
www.LUNA-Books.com

LRLBIOO5TR

THE TEARS OF LUNA

A shimmering crown grows and dims and is always reborn. Luna has the power and gift to brighten dark nights and lend mystery to the shadows. She will sometimes show up on the brightest of days, but her most powerful moments are when she fills the heaven with her light. Just as the moon comes each night to caress sleeping mortals, Luna takes a special interest in lovers. Her belief in the power of romance is so strong that it is said she cries gem-like tears which linger when her light moves on. Those lucky enough to find the Tears of Luna will be blessed with passion enduring, love fulfilled and the strength to find and fight for what is theirs.

A WORLD YOU CAN ONLY IMAGINE ™

LUNA™

www.LUNA-Books.com

THE TEARS OF LUNA MYTH COMES ALIVE IN

A WORLD AN ARTIST CAN IMAGINE ™

Over the next year LUNA Books and Duirwaigh Gallery are proud to present the work of five magical artists.

This month, the art featured on our inside back cover has been created by:
IAN DANIELS

If you would like to order a print of Ian's work, or learn more about him please visit Duirwaigh Gallery at www.DuirwaighGallery.com.

DUIRWAIGH Gallery

Please stay tuned next month for details on how to enter for a chance to win this great prize:

• A print of Ian's art

• Prints from the four other artists that will be featured in LUNA novels

• A library of LUNA novels

No purchase necessary.
To receive official rules and an entry form, write to:
LUNA Books Sweepstakes Requests
225 Duncan Mill Rd., Don Mills, Ontario, M3B 3K9
or visit www.LUNA-Books.com

Sweepstakes ends December 31, 2005.
Open to U.S. and Canadian residents who are 18 or older. Void where prohibited.

LBDG1104TR